FORBIDDEN KISSES

THE STERLING BROTHERS
BOOK 2

LAYLA HAGEN

CHAPTER ONE

Duncan

"Dad, Dad, I had an awesome day." My son, Jeremy, was beaming with excitement the second I came through the front door.

I smiled at him. His enthusiasm was contagious. "What did you do?" I asked.

"We went on a roller coaster."

I stopped in my tracks, looking from him to Maggie, his nanny. She was in her late sixties, and I wouldn't have pegged her as someone who wanted to go on a roller coaster.

"He insisted," she said, "and I couldn't say no. And it's appropriate for his age."

"It was awesome. She turned green and threw up." My son was at that age where he found the strangest things exciting.

"I'm sorry, Maggie," I said. "I'll have a little something extra in your paycheck for your efforts."

She, of course, told me it wasn't necessary, but the poor woman puked! That was over and above the call of duty.

Once that was settled, I turned my attention to Jeremy and asked, "What else did you do?" Catching up with him after work was my favorite part of the day. Hell, if I could, I'd spend the entire afternoon with him, but that wasn't always possible.

"I ate popcorn. And ice cream. But Maggie said she needs to talk to you tonight, so I'm going to my room."

"You do that, buddy," I said.

Jeremy was ten going on eighteen. Sometimes I couldn't believe he was so grown-up. But then he did something like mention poor Maggie's throwing up to her face, and I remembered once again that he was a kid after all.

Once Jeremy was out of earshot, I asked Maggie, "What's wrong? Are you still feeling sick? Want me to call a doctor?" One of the perks of living in a condominium was that I had 24/7 access to a concierge who could get me anything I needed—including a doctor. It had been a lifesaver when Jeremy was younger.

"No, don't you worry. It wasn't that bad. Although I won't get on a roller coaster again any time soon."

We both smiled at that. Couldn't say I was a fan of carnival rides either.

"So, what do you want to talk to me about?"

She smiled sadly. Fuck, this wasn't good news. In my extensive experience as co-CEO of Sterling Investments, I'd learned a few things. One of them was that when someone gave an apologetic smile, they were about to drop a bombshell.

"Well, remember when I told you that my mom had surgery last week?"

"Yes, and you said she woke up feeling just fine."

"It turns out that she severely underestimated how much time it'll take her to recover and how brutal these first weeks will be. But then again, no one tells you that, or probably no one would ever have a hip replacement."

My chest constricted. My first instinct was to tell Maggie that I would gladly pay for her mom to have round-the-clock care before I agreed for her to leave us. But I stopped myself in time.

She frowned. "Duncan, I've been with you and Jeremy for years. I really wouldn't be doing this if my mom didn't need me."

I ran a hand through my hair. I hadn't expected this. "When do you need to go?"

"As soon as possible. I'd like to go tomorrow, if that's okay with you. A few neighbors are pitching in, but you can't ask strangers for help all day, every day. She can barely make it to the bathroom with her walker. She's exhausted her insurance that had covered her home health care, so now she'd have to pay out of pocket with money she doesn't have."

"I can pay for anything she needs."

She smiled weakly. "Thank you. That is very generous, but I'd rather take care of her myself."

Clearly, this was an emergency, and I could see Maggie's mind was set. I had no choice. "Just let me know when you'll be back."

"I think she's going to need me for the next three months. She insisted that one month would be good, but I spoke to her doctor, and given her medical history, it's going to be a slow recovery rather than fast. I don't want to leave her before she's ready."

"Take all the time you need." My mind was already spinning. Jeremy came home from school every day at two o'clock, and Maggie watched him until I arrived at six.

"I'd like to tell Jeremy myself, if that's okay with you. I didn't bring it up today because I wanted you to know first."

"Sure. Thank you."

"I think your mom and dad would be more than happy to watch him now and then until I can return."

"Yes, I'll think about that," I said with a nod.

Maggie went to Jeremy's room to say goodbye while I stood there thinking about what the heck I was going to do.

She had a point. My parents were both retired. But recently, my brother Chase had bought back the retail store they'd owned when we were kids and gifted it back to them. Long story, but they'd sold it when they divorced all those years ago, and now they were running it together once again.

My parents had a complicated history. They'd been at odds for years after their divorce, but after Jeremy was born, they spent more time together and had grown much closer. They could probably watch Jeremy a few afternoons a week. But they had their hands full now, transforming the store into a place for pottery classes that Mom would teach and for selling fishing supplies, respectively. Strange combination for sure, but it was none of my business.

I couldn't ask them to put that on hold, and I didn't want Jeremy to just hang around there as they tried to get their stores put together. He would be bored and get in their way. He needed someone who'd oversee his homework and play games with him and stimulated him intellectually. His mother lived in Ireland, so there was no way for her to be able to jump in, unfortunately. I'd have to search for an interim nanny.

Maggie came out with Jeremy. He didn't look as sad as I'd expected him to.

"Everything all right, buddy?" I checked.

"Yes. Maggie said she's going on an adventure for three months and that she'll be back."

It was one of the things I liked most about Maggie: she knew how to put a positive spin on things.

"All right, then. I'll leave you two," she said.

I wished her all the best before she left, and then it was just Jeremy and me.

"Buddy, want to help me make dinner?" I asked him.

"Yes. Pizza!" he shouted and proudly pushed his chest forward.

Three times a week, I came home at five and we prepared a quick dinner. The rest of the evenings, we ordered in or went to a restaurant.

"Sounds good. Let's prepare a salad first, okay, bud? You start with the vegetables." This kid would eat pizza 24/7 if I allowed it.

Jeremy ran to the kitchen and put the small stool near the counter, stepping on it. He was tall enough, but he still couldn't reach it comfortably without help. He was in charge of washing the vegetables, and I chopped them. I did most of the cooking, obviously, but he was happy to be involved. He always talked my ear off about his day while we made our meals.

"How was school?" I asked.

He shrugged. "Fine, I guess. It's no fun. I like my afternoons more. They're giving us too much homework. I told Mr. Mason that we're kids. Kids should have free time."

I barely bit back a laugh. If there was ever any doubt that he was a Sterling, this would settle the matter.

"I like being outdoors." That was no surprise. This was San Diego. Everyone liked to be outdoors.

"Buddy," I said in a calm, constructive voice, "talking back to the teacher isn't polite."

"But they need to know."

"They went to school, too, son. They know what's best for kids. If you don't agree with it, you can phrase it differently so they don't get upset. You could ask if it's possible to have more free time."

He frowned at me. "But you never ask people nicely if they don't agree with you."

"What?" I asked.

"I heard you on the phone a few times. You just tell people what you want them to do."

Fuck. I couldn't argue with that. It was true. I wasn't an easygoing CEO. Some might say I was too strict, but I liked things done a certain way, and on my timeline. But parenting didn't come with a handbook, though I often wished it did.

"You don't have to do everything your old man does, okay?"

"When am I going to get a new nanny?"

"I haven't looked for one yet. You're probably going to spend a few days with Grandma and Grandpa at the store."

"Yes! I love that," he said.

"If you want, you can always come to the office."

He jerked his head back, nearly falling off his little stool. "No, that's boring. Though if Uncles Finn and Knox are there, I might come."

I started laughing. I had five brothers, and Jeremy made it no secret that Knox and Finn were his favorites. Hell, they probably ranked above *me* on his list of favorite people, but I didn't mind. I appreciated that my son had a tight relationship with my brothers.

"We can work something out," I told him. "Now come on. Let's do this."

"Dad?" he asked, as if he was about to whisper a secret.

I looked at him. "What? You didn't get into *more* trouble at school, did you?"

"No. Can I pour the tomato sauce?"

"Sure."

We were making pizza today, and this was a big milestone for him. Two months ago, he'd spilled an entire can of tomato sauce on the floor, and ever since, he'd been afraid to even touch it. I was happy that he had the courage to work with it again.

"But can you watch me?" he whispered in an even lower voice.

"Right here, Jeremy." I put my hand over his small shoulder, and he seemed to instantly relax.

He frowned as he cupped the rather large jar with both hands and turned it upside down. He dipped his tongue to one side, moving his head circularly as he spread the sauce around. Then he took the spatula I handed to him and, with very precise movements, spread it all around the dough.

"That's great," I said.

"I did it!" he cheered. "This is going to be delicious."

I loved seeing him grow into a confident young man. I liked

to think I was doing my best, but sometimes I still wondered if it was enough. I chopped mushrooms and pepperoni and arranged them in two bowls. The third contained cheese. Jeremy helped me pile on the toppings until we were both satisfied.

"All right, while it's in the oven, let's call Grandma and Grandpa and see what they think about you spending time at the store."

"Yes," he said with a grin. "But I already know they'll be happy. They love having me there."

I kissed his forehead before he got down from the stool. After sliding the pizza into the oven, I pulled my phone out of my back pocket, pressed Mom's number, and put her on speakerphone.

"Duncan, darling, how are the two of you?" she answered.

"We're good, Grandma. We have a question," Jeremy responded.

"Maggie needs to take some time off to help her mother," I said without further ado. "I'm going to search for a new nanny, of course, but would you mind watching Jeremy this week in the afternoons?"

"Of course not. We'd love to have him."

"Thanks," I said as Jeremy squealed his delight.

"I made pizza, Grandma. I'm not afraid of ketchup anymore." He meant tomato sauce, of course, but I didn't want to overshadow my son's excitement with a small detail.

"Good for you, darling. I'm proud of you!" she exclaimed, then hesitated. "Jeremy dear, I'd like to speak to your dad for a bit, okay?"

"Sure, Grandma," Jeremy said as I took the call off speakerphone, bringing it to my ear.

"Everything okay?" I immediately slipped into problem-solving mode.

"Yes. I was going to ask if you need any help looking for a nanny. Several friends in my reading club have nieces and nephews, and maybe someone has time."

"Sure. Why not? But I'll also contact some agencies and put out a job posting myself."

"Just so you know, those agencies usually take weeks and possibly months to find someone."

Fucking great. "I'll figure something out," I said, then changed the subject. "Is everything good with the store?"

They had their hands full with some renovations. Right after Chase bought it for them, they insisted that they only wanted to do some small changes, like sanding floors and repainting. But recently they'd discovered that the building's foundation needed reinforcing.

"Yes. Your dad is in charge of the crew, and he's doing it brilliantly."

It still felt weird to hear Mom praise Dad. Growing up, they'd fought constantly. It was why they divorced. I was used to barely being able to be in the same room with them because they would snap at each other all the time. But they'd grown closer during the past two years.

My brother Griffin said he'd caught them flirting once, but I refused to believe it until I heard it myself. He was probably embellishing the story, although that wasn't like him.

"All right. I'll keep you posted about my search, but I'm grateful for any contacts," I said.

We said our goodbyes, and I set the phone down on the counter.

This wasn't how I liked to do things. I liked to be prepared and took time with important decisions, giving them careful consideration. Finding a nanny for my son on a few days' notice meant I'd have to cut corners. But I had enough people in my circle that I could find someone soon enough, complete with a background check.

"Dad, we're going to burn the pizza," Jeremy said, sounding frantic.

Apparently I'd been woolgathering longer than I'd thought. Moving quickly to the oven, I immediately opened it.

"I think we've got it just in time." There was a very fine line between burned and crispy. We'd landed just on the right side of crunchy.

I took it out and sliced it, spreading out the pieces and letting the temperature cool a bit. Jeremy knew the drill and already had the plates and salad bowls on the table. He was waiting in his chair.

I brought the pizza over and served us each a slice, then dished out the salad with a touch of dressing.

"You're the best dad in the world," Jeremy exclaimed, his mouth full of pizza.

I'd never tire of hearing him say that.

CHAPTER TWO

Riley

I loved living in Chula Vista. Well, I liked living in San Diego, period. The weather was amazing, the food even more so. I loved the eternal summer, and I loved my best friends. I was lucky to be able to room with Julia and Christine during our last year of law school. Julia had inherited the home from her grandmother, and we rented out the two spare bedrooms from her.

She peeked her head through the open door. "Hey, girl, dinner is ready. Want to join us?"

I sighed. "Yeah. Just a minute."

"What's wrong? Another one bite the dust?" She grimaced.

It was a running joke between us. All of us had sent applications en masse to start working as junior associates at nearby law firms, but the market was competitive.

"No, I actually got good news. Jackman & Sons made me an offer."

"Girl, that's amazing. So why do you look like someone pissed in your food?" she asked.

"Because the position starts in four months. What am I going to do during that time? I need to work and make money."

"Crap."

"Yeah, exactly," I said. "It's also conditional on my passing the bar exam."

I'd expected that, of course; I'd just hoped that they'd take me on right away, even if it was doing something mundane. I'd worked as a waitress and a bartender during most of my college days in law school, and I was ready to kick-start my career and pay off some of these student loans. I'd taken the bar exam in February, and we'd just had our graduation ceremony last week. It was May already, and I still didn't have those damn results!

"You know what? Let's look on the bright side. At least you've got an offer," Julia said. "So, let's have some dinner. I made gorditas."

Julia was fantastic in the kitchen, and over the years, I'd picked up valuable cooking skills from her. I loved these little corn cake things. She knew just how to make them with the right amount of meat, cheese, and all the good stuff.

We went into our small kitchen that also doubled as the living room, and all three of us gathered at the kitchen island, where we usually stood and ate.

I groaned. "Why are the results taking so long? I can't believe they're torturing us like this."

Christine shrugged. "Hey, I'm just happy we survived law school."

"I'm going to have to get some other jobs until I start this one," I muttered.

Julia grimaced. "You don't have enough to cover rent?"

I shook my head. I never liked to discuss financial stuff because they were my friends, but Julia was also my landlord, and I didn't want to put her in a bad position.

"I can cover this month," I said quickly. "And I can always go back to The Shack and ask if they need another waitress." But my soul was dying a bit at that prospect. I wasn't what one would call an extrovert. I liked being surrounded by friends, but waiting tables was draining. I didn't have whatever it took to get those extra tips that some of the staff was able to muster.

Still, a girl had to do what a girl had to do. And if that was what it took, I'd gladly wait tables. Honestly, I'd take any job I could find at this point.

"All right, let's dig in," Julia said.

The gorditas were delicious. I was only half paying attention to what the girls were talking about, mulling over my next steps. I was going to browse Craigslist tonight and keep my fingers crossed for some cleaning jobs. They were right up my alley. Cleaning was something you did by yourself, so points for my introvert self.

After dinner, I went into my room and noticed a missed call from my sister, Paula. I'd call her later. She was probably going to try and console me, but that wasn't what I needed right now. My hopes were to begin the job next month so I could splurge with my first paycheck and take her out for a fancy dinner. She deserved it. Paula was in school, studying business and working two jobs on the side. I couldn't wait for a decent paycheck so I could help her out.

I opened my laptop and searched Craigslist, checking out the job listings. There was a legal website I used to apply for my professional job, but for little side jobs like this, Craigslist was king.

I fell down the rabbit hole for what felt like hours; fortunately, I did have a lot of leads for cleaning and pet-sitting jobs. I was about to close my browser when one listing for a nanny job really caught my attention.

I smiled as I read it. I loved, loved, *loved* kids. Growing up, I wanted to be a kindergarten teacher, but my mom always gently tried to steer me toward careers that would pay better. One thing led to another, and I ended up in law school, but my heart was still with teaching little kids. I'd always loved that there was a six-year difference between me and my younger sister.

I read the listing carefully. It was for three months, from two o'clock until six o'clock Monday through Friday. The residence was in Camel Valley, and the boy was ten years old. That sounded super tempting.

I scrolled down to see what they were paying, and my eyes about popped from their sockets. Okay, that was a very generous amount for four hours a day. It was definitely more than I made at The Shack, including tips.

Don't get your hopes up. You don't have any nanny experience.

But that didn't keep me from applying. It was one of my mantras in life: I never held myself back.

After I'd applied, I noticed that the employer had uploaded a questionnaire. That was a first with Craigslist; usually, people simply used the questions from the website. I downloaded the document and opened it, expecting to see a few general questions. Then my jaw dropped. There were sixty questions, though some I'd expected, like **Are you a smoker? Do you have experience with children?**

Oh, what the hell. The questions I'd had to answer when applying for legal positions had been much worse. I could knock this out in no time.

As a got farther into the list, I became really excited about the opportunity. It also said that overnight stays might be required but would be announced well in advance. Honestly, the thought of being in some fancy residence in Camel Valley sounded amazing. I was certain it was going to be more peaceful than living with Julia and Christine. I loved them both, but they liked to party—a lot. Even if I didn't go out with them, whenever they came back from a night out, they were typically very inebriated, loud, and did I say loud?

I poured myself a glass of white wine to help me finish the questionnaire. I had a great feeling about this.

CHAPTER THREE

Duncan

"Duncan, are you sure you don't want me to take this over?" Magda, my HR manager, asked. She was managing the background checks on everyone I was interviewing today.

"No, this person will look after my son. I want to get a good feel for them."

"All right, just wanted to make things easier for you."

"And I appreciate that, but some things I can't delegate."

I got up from my chair, taking my laptop with me. Magda had sent me everything electronically. I'd scheduled the interviews in a coffee shop a block from the office. I had five today, and I was determined for one of them to work. I'd met candidates on two other days this week, and they were abysmal. That's why I'd asked my HR manager to sort through all of the other résumés and only schedule the top five. Magda had more experience with hiring than me, though it was usually for financial experts, not nannies—but experience was experience.

Sterling Investments was one of the biggest financial service companies in the country. Our offices were on several floors of a building on the corner of Market Street and 4th Avenue. I was proud of what I'd built from the ground up with my brothers, but now some of them were focusing on other ventures. We all met at least once a week for a strategy session, discussing all of the businesses, but Chase and I were the two who focused mostly on Sterling Investments.

Speak of the devil. Chase caught up with me just as I was leaving.

"Done already for today?" he asked.

I nodded. "Yeah. I'm going to interview some candidates to be Jeremy's nanny."

Chase nodded. "I wouldn't want to be in your shoes. I can hire someone for Sterling Investments in a heartbeat, but a nanny? That's more complex." He was absolutely right. "Let me know if I can help with anything."

"Will do."

I knew he meant it. I was closest to Chase, and even though we didn't always see eye to eye on things, I'd never doubted that he had my back—all of my brothers did.

I walked at a brisk pace to the coffee shop while reading through the résumés again on my phone. Magda had attached notes about the background check for each one, but I didn't really care about them. If she'd vetted them, it meant everything was good. She'd alert me if anything was amiss.

Three candidates were in their sixties—retired kindergarten teachers. They sounded perfect. The fourth was a fifty-year-old teacher who retired early because of health problems, which already made me wonder if she could keep up with Jeremy.

It was the last candidate who I was least optimistic about: a twenty-four-year-old graduate from law school with zero experience in babysitting. At first glance, she wasn't at all qualified. I should have asked Magda why she kept her résumé.

Entering the coffee shop, I sat down at one of the tables by the window. I had to wrap this up today. My parents were doing a great job, but they had their hands full with the store. This was really not a good time for them to watch Jeremy.

And no matter how much I shifted things around at the office, I couldn't take off every day at two o'clock. He had school for another month, and then he was starting summer school, which was also only until two o'clock. The last thing I wanted was to have my son at work with me. That was the worst of both worlds—I couldn't focus enough on work, and I definitely couldn't focus on him. I didn't want him to feel ignored.

Four interviews later, my optimism completely faded. How was it possible that not one of the candidates was good enough?

The first one flat-out admitted she was happy she was retired because she never really liked kids. Hello? This was a nannying job! Why would she even apply? The second one told me she didn't understand why youngsters these days were so obsessed with not letting kids watch TV, considering back in her time, the TV had basically been their nanny and they turned out fine. Obviously, she went into the *no* pile. Jeremy's screen time was minimal no matter if it was the iPad or TV.

The third one said she could only do mornings, which infuriated me because the job posting specifically asked for nannying in the afternoon. The fourth one... well, it turned out my fears were not unfounded. She'd admitted that since her knee surgery, she couldn't move around a lot. She was hoping that she and Jeremy could mostly stay at home. That was definitely not okay.

After she left, I nearly threw in the towel, but I had one interview left, so what the hell? It couldn't be any worse than the ones before.

I went to the counter to order a coffee, surveying the place. The café was surprisingly empty. Some customers were wearing headphones, speaking in low voices, probably working. Otherwise, the place was pretty nondescript and depressing. Or maybe that was just me because I hadn't found a nanny for Jeremy.

Once it was my turn, I asked for a black drip coffee. The

barista rang it up with a smile and turned to start making my drink.

The second I grabbed it from the counter, a bombshell beauty walked through the front door. She had dark brown hair that she'd pulled into a ponytail. Her eyes were green, her lips were perfectly shaped, she had high cheekbones—and I couldn't stop watching her. She scanned the crowd as she came in, so I checked the rest of her out. Her yellow dress was snug around her waist. Damn it, I couldn't look away from her.

When I headed to my table, the realization hit me. She was still looking around, as if she was *searching* for someone. Changing my path, I walked over to her, mentally whipping myself into shape.

"Riley?" I asked.

She blinked, looking at me with a smile. "Yes. Are you Duncan Sterling?"

"Yes. Do you want something to drink?" I asked her.

"Oh no, no, I can't drink anything caffeinated now or I won't be able to sleep. Sorry, I'm rambling," she said. "I'm a bit nervous."

"There's no reason to be," I told her. *Don't check her out, Duncan, for fuck's sake.* Once she sat down, I lowered myself into the chair opposite her. "So, you took the bar recently?"

"Not exactly. In February."

"Then why are you interviewing for a nannying job? Sorry, I don't mean to be rude," I asked.

She shook her head. "No, it's a valid question. I do have a job offer that starts in August, hence why I'm happy this position is only for three months. The company wants to wait for the bar results, which I don't have yet."

"That makes sense. It takes time to get the results, I'm sure," I said. "All right, so thank you for making time to meet me today. Let's start with a simple question. Why do you want the job?"

She smiled sheepishly. "I love kids. I was looking for a job like cleaning or waitressing, although I do prefer cleaning because I can do that on my own."

She didn't like to spend time with people? Jeremy was a handful. "So, you don't like to socialize?"

"Oh no, I do like kids. I don't like grown-ups as much," she said very confidently. I cocked a brow at that. "Yeah, I know I'm going to be a lawyer. The jury's still out if I'm going to be a good one, though."

I liked Riley's energy. I was certain Jeremy would like her too.

She looked around. "Is your son here?" she asked.

"No, I've had four interviews before this. He's got too much energy to sit for that long."

She pressed her lips together. "I'm your fifth choice, huh?"

I decided to be completely honest with her. "Actually, Riley, you're the last candidate standing. Everyone before you flunked their interviews, so to speak."

She genuinely grinned. I liked that. She was the first out of them all who sincerely wanted the job. "So, I have no competition? Damn, I'm good at winning that game."

I laughed. Her excitement was palpable. "My concern is that you don't have any experience nannying."

"No, I don't. But does it count that I've always wanted to be a sitter and to work with children? I also have a younger sister, and I helped raise her. We're six years apart, and now that we're older, she's become my bestie."

Damn, she was cute. Which worried me.

"Besides," she went on, "your son is ten. I would have probably had a bit more trouble with someone much younger, but I think he and I can get along well."

The more she spoke, the more attractive she seemed.

Damn it, stop this, Duncan. She's younger than you and potentially your only chance at finding a decent nanny.

"It's all there in the questionnaire," she added.

"I haven't looked at that," I admitted. "My HR person did." Clearing my throat, I said, "Tell me more about you."

"Honestly, I'd always thought I'd have kids by twenty-five." She pressed her lips together. "Sorry, that's probably too much information."

I was shocked by her admission, as she was right, it was deeply personal.

"Anyway, law school and generally a law career aren't compatible with having a child, or a marriage for that matter, so I want to get my fix and be your son's nanny."

I liked her easygoing nature. And the look on her face right now that made me want to kiss her.

No, Duncan! Just no!

Riley continued, "But first, I'd like to know why your previous nanny quit."

"She didn't quit," I said. "She's taking a few months' break because her mother had surgery and required her help."

"Poor thing. Is she okay?" Her entire face transformed. A deep frown marred her forehead, and her cheeks sank in. How could she be concerned about a stranger?

"Yeah, it's all good. Her mom just needs more help around the house than she previously thought."

"So then it's a sure thing that she's going to be back in three months?"

"Yes."

"Great. I won't leave you in the lurch when my job starts."

She was responsible. That earned her a lot of points in my book.

"When would you like me to start?"

I liked her confidence too. Riley was the type of woman I'd love to date. But I couldn't date right now—especially not her. She was Jeremy's new nanny.

"Tomorrow, if possible," I said, half joking, but she nodded.

"Sure, I can do that."

I stared at her. "Are you serious?"

"Yes."

"All right, then you're hired."

She gasped. "Really?"

"Yeah. I think Jeremy, my son, will like you."

"I thought maybe you'd want to vet me or something."

"My HR person already took care of it. She contacted the employers you listed as references, and apparently they all gave glowing reviews."

"You move fast," she said with a laugh.

"I need to. Usually, I'd take more time and interview more candidates, but my parents have their hands full right now, and they're the ones watching my son."

"All right, then. Can you tell me a bit about Jeremy? What he likes to do, what his favorite toys are, stuff like that? It would help me bond with him."

I felt it in my bones that it was a great decision to hire her. She didn't seem to ask just to make conversation but rather because she really cared about my son's well-being.

"He's going through a Spider-Man phase," I said.

She laughed.

"And he likes being outdoors, a lot."

"Well, that's easy," she replied. "San Diego has a lot of options."

"Exactly. Which brings up an important point. Do you own a car?"

Her face fell. "No. Is that a deal-breaker?"

"Not at all, just wanted to know. I can arrange for you to have a company car."

Her mouth formed an O, but then she pressed her lips together. "That sounds great. So, that means I'll take him on trips around the city?"

"Yes. Maybe even outside the city. But we'll discuss everything in advance."

"Of course."

"And he likes to go to the movies. I try to limit screen time, but it's not always possible."

"That's fine. I'm good at bribing kids with alternatives," she said with a grin. "Do you have any parks nearby?"

"Yes, there's one, but there's also a pool in the condo complex. It's got two slides. Jeremy absolutely loves it, so I think you're going to spend some time at the pool. Is that a problem?"

She grinned. "That I'm being paid to play with a kid in the pool? No, Mr. Sterling, it's absolutely no problem, I assure you. Does Jeremy have any food restrictions I should be aware of?"

"Please call me Duncan. And I don't expect you to cook," I said as she leaned back in her chair, running her hands through her hair, a lock of it falling over her left breast.

I took in a deep breath. She was twenty-four, and I was thirty-three. She was going to be my boy's nanny. What the hell had gotten into me?

"Still, it doesn't hurt to know."

"No allergies. I cook a few times a week, and then the rest of it, we just order food."

She tipped her head to the side. "Listen, I'm no slouch in the kitchen. I can totally prep some early dinner so you'll have it when you're home."

"That would be amazing," I said. "His previous nanny said she couldn't watch him and cook at the same time, but I'd pay you extra if you had time to do it."

"No, no extra payment needed, I really enjoy cooking." She narrowed her eyes. "His mom isn't in the picture?"

"No, we aren't together, haven't been for years. She lives in Ireland."

My tone was final. I didn't want to discuss the matter of his mother further.

"All right. Do you have a picture of him?" She sounded shy all of a sudden.

"Sure, I've got a million." I took out my phone and slid it to her. "And my screensaver."

She clicked the screen, "Oh, this is such a cute picture."

"I took him to Disneyland a while ago. He climbed on that

boulder because he insisted that he wanted to be the same height as me in the picture."

He was still much shorter, but he'd been happy anyway.

"He looks a bit like you."

"Yeah, he does," I said. "All right, Riley, my HR person will be in touch."

"Okay."

"We won't be able to finalize everything in time for you to start tomorrow, but how about the day after?"

"Sure, that sounds great. I can't wait. It was great meeting you, Duncan. I think this will work out just fine."

"So do I," I said, then shook her hand. Her skin was incredibly soft. I held on, rubbing the back of her hand with my thumb. I barely tamped down the impulse of getting closer to her. "Have a great day," I said.

"You too."

CHAPTER FOUR

Riley

Thursday morning, I texted Mom, letting her know I was starting my first day. My sister and I texted her regularly, updating her on our lives.

I arrived at the condo complex at 2:30 in the afternoon and wondered if Duncan would be the one to meet me. A guard let me inside the gated community, and I found the unit quickly enough. It was beside the most luxurious pool I'd ever seen. It looked like something straight out of a movie, with stones all around it, mimicking a riverbed.

I was beyond excited that I'd gotten the job. I hadn't expected to start so quickly.

And I also had to say that I didn't expect Duncan to be that attractive.

When I'd walked into the coffee shop, I'd noticed him before he even introduced himself. The man was a work of art. But he was my boss, and I'd never mess with that, especially when there was a kid involved.

Duncan lived on the top floor, and from what I could tell, the view had to be scrumptious.

I knocked at the door, listening intently. A woman was speaking softly, and then she opened the door. "Hi, you must be Riley," she said. "I'm Duncan's mom, Susan."

"Nice to meet you." I said, stepping inside. She shook my hand with Jeremy right next to her. "And you must be Jeremy." I smiled at him.

"Wow! You're young. And so pretty."

I started laughing. "Nice to meet you too."

"Oh, Jeremy," Susan chastised.

"What? You said I couldn't tell people if I thought they were ugly, but I think she's pretty. That's why I told her that."

The innocence of kids. I loved it.

"I appreciate the compliment," I assured him.

Susan shook her head but smiled. "His previous nanny was in her sixties, so that's why he's so excited. Duncan is at work. I picked up Jeremy from school, but you'll have to do it from now on."

"That's no problem." I took my tote off my shoulder and put it down on the gorgeous console that was clearly custom-made because it fit in the entryway perfectly. I also took off my shoes.

"I'll show you around," Susan said. Jeremy walked right next to us.

The loft was decorated in shades of blue, black, and gray, but it didn't look dark in the slightest. Metallic lamps hung from the walls and the ceiling. The enormous couch was made of leather, and I could see myself relaxing there with Jeremy when he got tired. We could make popcorn, and I could even make some peanut-butter-and-jelly snacks. I wouldn't have to worry about him getting the couch dirty because the leather would be easy to clean.

My soul was happy that this job had popped up, and not just because I didn't have to wait tables. I was getting paid a handsome amount, so I wouldn't have to worry about additional employment to get by. No, I was genuinely happy to be here. The place had a great vibe.

"This is the master bedroom." She pointed to a door, but we didn't go inside. Fair enough, I didn't have to see it. "This is the home gym." She pointed to another open door. There was a treadmill, a bike, and a rowing machine, as well as a weights section. "Next to it is Duncan's office."

"And this is my playroom," Jeremy said.

I poked my head inside. The room had floor-to-ceiling shelves full of toys: cars, puzzles, Legos.

"We'll have so much fun here. And this is my bedroom." He took my hand, leading me into the room next door.

I glanced at Susan for permission, and she nodded, smiling. Clearly she was at ease that he seemed to accept me so quickly.

Duncan wasn't kidding when he said Jeremy was going through a Spider-Man phase. His whole room was a mix of blue and red, and he had a human-sized Spider-Man figure hanging from the ceiling. It creeped me out a bit, but Jeremy looked at me with pride.

"What do you think about Spider-Man? Isn't he awesome? He's my favorite Marvel hero."

"He's definitely great." I had zero knowledge about the other Marvel heroes, but I was going to catch up so we could discuss it at length.

The living room and the entryway were clearly professionally decorated, but the playroom and bedroom were quite obviously designed by Jeremy himself. I liked that Duncan didn't mind letting his son do his own thing, that he wasn't insisting on using a color scheme for his bedroom or something.

I turned to Susan. "If you need to leave, we'll be just fine."

"Are you sure?" she asked, looking from me to Jeremy.

He nodded. "Yes, Grandma. I can show Riley all of my cars."

"Good luck," Susan said.

"And all of my video games."

"When do you usually play games?" I asked.

Jeremy sighed. "Only on Saturday morning. Dad allows me an hour. Sometimes, if I'm really good, then also Sunday mornings."

This was good. It was nice to set a specific time, and mornings were better than evenings when it came to screen time.

"I know you have Duncan's number, but I can also give you mine just in case you need anything, okay?" Susan suggested.

"Sure, I'll put it in my phone."

"Great. I still have to show you the kitchen."

She rattled off her phone number as we walked back past all the other rooms. The kitchen was adjacent to the living room, and it opened up onto a terrace.

If I'd thought this place was divine before, now I was convinced of it. The kitchen was dark gray mixed with black accents. With the light filtering in through the huge windows, it was exquisite. I'd never imagined a black kitchen could look so good.

"Duncan said you might cook a bit," Susan said.

"Yeah, I don't mind. I actually quite like it. And in a kitchen like this one, it will be a privilege to cook." At home, I had to fight Julia and Christine for space.

"All right, then. You've got my number, and you've seen the condo. The condo keys are on the counter, and Duncan mentioned that you'd have a car to use within the next few days, but he probably told you that. He's going to be home around five thirty or six."

I nodded. "Good to know."

"Then I'll leave you to it."

"Sure. Thank you, Susan. It was great to meet you."

After our goodbyes, Jeremy asked, "Can we go back to my room?"

I laughed, ruffling his hair. "Of course."

He took my hand again, leading me through the condo.

God, I loved kids so much. They had an innocence that I simply adored. Their hearts were open to giving and receiving warmth and love. I had to pinch myself to believe I'd gotten so lucky.

CHAPTER FIVE

Riley

We went straight to his playroom, and I sat down on the floor with him.

His eyes widened. "Oh, you can sit on that chair. Ms. Williams always sits there. She says her hips are too bad."

I couldn't help but laugh. Then I snorted and put my hand over my mouth.

"Sorry, that was very unladylike. I'm good on the floor," I said.

Poor woman. I couldn't really imagine keeping up with Jeremy in my sixties, but some people were young at heart even if their hips weren't on the same page.

For the next hour, he told me more information than I thought one could possibly know about a toy car. He tried to get me to learn the names of the cars. I remembered Fiat and Mercedes because they had real car names, but I couldn't remember the made-up ones. Still, I'd trained to be a lawyer, so if I heard them a few times more, I was sure that I would commit them to memory.

"What do you want to do now?" I asked him after he put his cars back.

He turned around. "Can I play a video game?"

Hmm, mental note: I should just give him options, not a blank slate. "You said your father only allowed you to do that during the weekend."

"But you're not Dad," he said quickly.

Game on, Jeremy. "How about going outside?" Then I got an idea. "Or maybe you have something we can prepare for dinner?"

He shrugged. "No, Dad and I always go to eat in the city on Thursday. I'm in the mood for tacos."

"I can make you some if you want."

His jaw dropped. "I didn't know nannies could cook."

"Well, not all of them can. But I do."

"And you know how to make tacos?" His eyes widened. "You're magic. I thought only old people knew things."

I chuckled. "Nah, we just know more and more things as we get older. I'll look at what you have in the fridge, and then we can go shopping for anything else we might need."

There really wasn't much in the fridge, just some prepackaged salad, ham, and cheese. Certainly nothing for tacos. I looked in the pantry next. They had tortillas, at least, so that was good. "What are your favorite kinds?"

"Fried chicken," he said. "And Dad loves pulled pork."

Ah, pulled pork was a bit hard to do in a pinch, although they did have a slow cooker, and there were about two hours until Duncan would be home.

"Would you like to go on a little shopping trip?" I asked.

"Yes, please."

"Do you have a Costco around here?"

"What's that?"

I bit back a laugh. It had to be wonderful to grow up in a world where you didn't even know what Costco was.

Once I explained, he told me, "There's a grocery shop inside the community."

That was so cool. One day, after I paid off my student debt, this was definitely the type of place I'd like to live in, where everything was inclusive—a pool and a grocery store and who knew what else.

"That's neat," I said. "Come on, let's go."

I hadn't discussed with Duncan how we would handle any money I'd pay out of pocket, but I assumed I would have to show him the receipts and he would reimburse me.

Jeremy led me to the grocery store. At first, I was excited because the place looked exquisite and seemed to have fruits and veggies and grass-fed meat. Then I looked at the prices and nearly had a panic attack. That couldn't be right. I didn't even have enough cash on me to pay for all of this. I'd left my cards in my wallet at home because I stupidly didn't realize I might need it. But even so, the total sum would be so much that I wouldn't dare pay it, fearing Duncan think I was a total idiot for shopping here, let alone if he didn't pay me back. He didn't strike me as the type to do that, but who knew. I'd been stiffed so many times back when I waitressed that I didn't want to risk it. I took out my phone, looking at other supermarkets in the area. There was an Albertsons a few blocks away. We could definitely walk that distance.

I turned to Jeremy. "Hey, what do you think about going to another supermarket? I found one nearby."

"Okay," he said. "I love seeing new places."

"So, tell me about school, Jeremy," I said as we followed the route on Google Maps. Even though it was straightforward, I had zero sense of direction and didn't want to risk going the opposite way.

"It's okay, I guess."

"You don't sound very excited."

He frowned. "Are you supposed to be excited about school?"

"Hmm." I considered this. "I don't remember if I ever was."

"So, you're going to be my nanny only until Ms. Williams returns, right?"

"Yes. Why?"

He sighed dramatically. "I like you."

God, he totally had my heart. "I'll tell you a secret, Jeremy. I like you too."

We arrived at Albertsons a few minutes later. I often shopped here, so I knew the layout of the stores by heart. In less than twenty minutes, we had everything we needed for tacos with fried chicken and pulled pork, as well as ingredients for avocado salad and pico de gallo. However, our trip had cost us half an hour, so now I didn't have that much time to make the pulled pork. I decided to simply fry it instead.

Once we were back in the loft, I brought the groceries to the kitchen.

"Dad always lets me take stuff out of the bag. Can I do it?" Jeremy asked me.

"Sure."

I watched him in awe as he brought a little stool from a corner and put it next to me, then climbed onto it and expertly removed the items, separating them by meat and veggies.

"Do you often cook with your dad?"

He nodded. "Yes, always."

My heart did a little flip. I could just imagine that hunk of a man—

Damn it, Riley. Take out the hunk part. He's Jeremy's dad, that's it. That's all he's going to be.

I chopped everything professionally and made sure Jeremy was far enough from the stove so oil didn't accidentally land on him while I fried the meat.

I'd given him the task of assembling the tacos. He was surprisingly good at it for a ten-year-old. I kept an eye on him and gently nudged him when he filled them too much.

"They could burst while you eat them if they're too full," I said.

"Okay," he said quickly. He finished filling the last taco while I started prepping the pico de gallo.

"What's going on?" Duncan's voice boomed through the condo.

I straightened up, heat coursing through me. I'd been so involved with the food that I hadn't heard him come in.

"We made dinner!" Jeremy exclaimed. "I told Riley that we sometimes go for tacos on Thursday. Then she asked what our favorites were, and then she *cooked* them! She's magic! She knows stuff, and she's so young, and she can sit on the floor with me." He said all of this without even taking a breath.

I smiled before focusing on my pico de gallo and finished slicing the last few tomatoes. After I put them in the bowl, Duncan came up to me.

"Hey."

"Hi!" My voice sounded a bit strange. He was far closer than he'd been at the coffee shop. His presence was even more over-powering now.

"Riley, it's your first day. You didn't have to cook."

"I know, but Jeremy and I had some time, so we decided to cook dinner. I like making tacos. They're my favorite. And he's an excellent chef."

Jeremy beamed. "Did you hear that, Dad? She called me a chef!"

Duncan looked at me with warm eyes.

"All right," I said, "everything's ready. Unless there's anything else, I'm going to leave the two of you to enjoy your dinner."

"Why don't you have dinner with us?" Duncan asked, rolling his shoulders slightly backward.

"What? No, I couldn't."

"You did say tacos are your favorite."

I smiled sheepishly. "I wasn't trying to get you to invite me."

"I know. But it would be good for us to catch up about your day. Then we'll finalize a few more things. I've got the keys to the car. I had it brought to the garage. It was ready earlier than I anticipated. I can show it to you after dinner. Unless, of course, you have other plans."

I shook my head. "I have zero plans."

"Then you're our guest tonight."

"Okay, um... I'll set the table, then."

"No, your work is officially over," he said, tapping his watch.

I'd never seen anyone wear an actual watch before. It wasn't a brand I recognized, but I was certain it was expensive. It looked exquisite. I could even see the mechanism with all the little gears inside.

"Ready, buddy?" Duncan asked Jeremy.

"Yes, Dad," Jeremy said in a serious voice.

Duncan took the plate with tacos from the kitchen island and brought it to the dining table. Jeremy put place mats on the table along with forks, and Duncan brought the knives and plates and tall glasses of water.

"All right, dinner is served," Jeremy said in a serious voice.

I looked at Duncan, who smiled at me brilliantly. When had he undone his top button? His shirt had been perfectly buttoned up just a few seconds ago.

I sat next to Jeremy at the wooden table, and Duncan was sitting opposite me. It was good that we were on opposite sides because I couldn't be around him and not lose my wits. I wasn't entirely sure why he had that effect on me. We'd only just met, after all—and he was my boss.

"So, how was your afternoon?" Duncan asked Jeremy.

"I showed her all my cars, and then we went to the store here, but then we went to Albertsons."

Duncan frowned but didn't say anything. I was certain he'd circle back to that later. I shimmied nervously in my chair, putting one taco with chicken and one with pork on my plate. I didn't have much to contribute to their conversation, but Jeremy seemed more than happy to fill him in.

"I was thinking we could go to the pool tomorrow," I said once Jeremy finished giving Duncan the rundown of the day.

He nodded feverishly. "Yes, yes, yes! I love the pool, but I wanted to show you my cars first."

"The tacos are delicious," Duncan said.

I dipped my head. "Thank you."

While we ate dinner, Jeremy was asking me the names of his cars. I tricked him into saying them out loud before I repeated them, though I wasn't sure how long it would last before he caught on to my tactic.

"Buddy, why don't you get started on your evening routine?" Duncan interrupted after Jeremy finished eating.

When he pouted, my heartstrings pulled. This kid was so cute.

"Come on, it's seven o'clock. You can start by brushing your teeth."

"Okay."

"Say goodbye to Riley."

How long could brushing teeth take?

Jeremy turned to me. "Bye, Riley. I can't wait to see you tomorrow. Thank you for wanting to be my nanny." To my surprise, he hugged me. And I hugged him right back, loving the feel of his little body in my arms.

The moment he left, I turned to Duncan. "How long does it take him to brush his teeth?"

"A very long time. He first looks at his cars, then goes to choose one toothbrush from the five depicting his favorite Marvel characters. It's a whole routine, but it's the only way I could get him to agree to brush every evening. So, if it works, I'm happy. I like to start him early on his nightly routine because that gives him time to wind down."

"He also told me that he's only allowed to play video games on Saturday morning, and sometimes on Sunday."

"Yeah, I made the mistake of letting him play in the evening a few times, and then he crawled into my bed at night because he was afraid. There are no monsters or anything in his games, but who knows what triggers him?"

Oh, be still my beating heart. I liked that he had his priorities straight. He didn't mind comforting his son when he was upset.

"You're a fantastic dad," I said.

He shrugged. "I'm trying to do my best."

"Jeremy's such a good kid. I thoroughly enjoyed today."

"I'm glad you say that, that you're not just viewing him as a paycheck." He smiled, and I shimmied in my seat.

"I'll let you in on a secret. I've honestly thought long and hard about being a teacher because I've always loved kids. Sometimes, I think I have two personalities: one who wants to be a lawyer and get rich, and the other one who simply wants to enjoy life and have time for the little things."

———

Duncan

Riley was the most refreshingly honest person I'd met lately. "Not many people would admit that."

She shrugged, as if she wasn't worried in the least. "I don't mind. I'm an open book. I think it's a bit sad that we have to decide to be one thing or another so early in life. I still don't really know what I want."

The more she spoke, the more striking the age difference between us became. I might only be nine years older, but it felt more like twenty. She was still searching for her direction in life, and I was deeply seated in mine. There was rarely time to be impulsive. I scheduled everything to the tiniest detail. Most of that was because when Jeremy was a baby, he did best by following the exact same routine. But I preferred to have a rigid schedule too.

"Dinner was amazing," she said after a few moments.

"Of course it was. You cooked it."

She smiled. "I mean, I liked the company too."

I leaned in over the table. "I'll let you in on a secret—so did I. Quite a lot."

She swallowed hard, biting her lower lip. Christ, I couldn't pretend; I was attracted to her, but I had to get it under control. I hadn't brought any woman to meet Jeremy ever, and I wasn't going to start now. And I was *definitely* not going to start with his nanny. That would just confuse the hell out of him.

"Should I pick him up from school tomorrow?" she asked.

"Yes. I've already given the school all the information on you. You're cleared for pickup, so there shouldn't be any issue, but just in case they give you grief, tell them to call me. I'll email you all the details so you know exactly where to go."

She nodded. "Great."

I took a car key out of my pocket. "The company car is in the parking lot. Spot 17."

"Great. I'll get situated with it tomorrow before I pick up Jeremy."

"You can use it as your personal car as well."

She shook her head. "No, no, I'm fine without a car."

"Are you sure?"

"I promise."

"Then I'll walk you to the door," I said.

"I can clean up."

"No. You already went above and beyond, cooking *and* shopping. That reminds me, I'll get you a credit card to use when you're with Jeremy. Why did you go to Albertsons?"

She bit her lower lip. "The grocery store in the community is extremely expensive."

That didn't even cross my mind. "What do I owe you?"

"You really don't need to pay me back, though I left the receipts on the counter by the canisters."

No way was she covering the bill. I'd add it to her next paycheck and then some.

"Okay, and feel free to shop at the local store next time. Charge it all to the credit card." I didn't want her to leave. How crazy was that? She was Jeremy's nanny, for God's sake. "Oh, and thanks for making our favorite fillings."

"No problem. I have to say, I loved cooking with Jeremy. He's so good in the kitchen. He told me about the two of you and how you cook together. You must have rubbed off on him, as he certainly knows his way around."

Every time she spoke about him, an inexplicable warmth coiled through my chest. Ms. Williams, although very competent, had always spoken about him almost as if he was her subject. This was new and uncharted territory for me. I liked it that Riley cared.

I opened the door and immediately pressed the button for the elevator. She stepped sideways as the doors opened, and I accidentally brushed her back with my knuckles. She sucked in a deep breath, and so did I. Damn it, I had to get a hold of myself. Then again, it was only our first day working together. I was certain that things would change.

"Good night, Duncan, and give Jeremy a hug for me," she said before stepping into the elevator.

I nodded as the doors closed and tried to push Riley to the back of my mind... to no avail.

Yeah, things might change... but not for the better.

CHAPTER SIX

Duncan

On Monday morning, I met with my brothers for our general meeting. It was the only time when all of us were at Sterling Investments. After the staff finished their weekly report, they filtered out. My brothers and I stayed behind. Usually, we used this time to brainstorm ideas about each other's current businesses and potential new ones.

My second-oldest brother, Chase, was sitting between Griffin and Wyatt. Knox and Finn, the youngest ones, stayed together as usual.

"All right, who's got anything to bring to the table?" Griffin asked.

Chase went first. He usually had the most ideas. He mentioned the articles he'd read about the wine business. This was something we'd discussed in passing before. A winery in Napa Valley wouldn't be bad, but it might be a lot to look after.

"I agree," I said. "I'll look into it."

"Honestly, I'd be in, but only if we did it as a family venture," Knox said.

"Why?" I asked. We each had separate businesses. Although, owning a business together had its perks, especially with the logistics of this venture being more complex.

We were a powerhouse together. We fed off each other's strengths when setting up Sterling Investments. Knox and Finn had still been in college, but their coding skills were unparalleled. They rest of us were thankful when they'd joined us too.

"I just feel like that would be a cool family business. Then we could all fly out to Napa Valley together. Though, on second thought, I guess we can do that even if only one of us owns it," Knox said.

Wyatt smiled slyly. "Anyone want to fly out to Napa this weekend... for research?"

That was surprising coming from Wyatt. He usually wasn't impulsive—that was more like Griffin.

Griffin shook his head. "I'm out of this one. I promised Mom and Dad I'd stop by the store and help them with renovations."

Wyatt straightened. "What? You didn't tell me that."

"I went back and forth with them," Griffin said, "and they finally agreed."

"What do you mean?" I asked. I'd been out of the loop about this. "Last I knew, they were redoing the foundation."

Griffin looked at all of us. "They're doing more than that. The place needs refreshing, and Mom has very specific ideas about what she wants."

"Why didn't she tell us? Why didn't she tell me?" I asked. I'd seen her a few times last week, after all. "Why aren't they hiring someone?"

"They did. And then decided not to use them." Griffin turned to me. "Maybe she figured you'd have enough on your plate with Jeremy."

"But now things are getting back on track. I've hired a new nanny for him."

"Really? Mom didn't mention anything," Wyatt said as Chase glanced at me suspiciously.

"Another sixty-year-old who tells Jeremy how young men should behave," Knox teased. "No wonder we're his favorites."

He looked far too full of himself. It was time to put my smartass brother in his place.

"First, fuck off. Ms. Williams does her job well. Second of all, no. Riley is young—she's twenty-four. I think she's amazing. She bonded with him instantly, and as a perk, she's a great cook."

Chase looked at me intently but didn't say anything. Wyatt narrowed his eyes. Griffin glanced at Wyatt and then at Knox and Finn, who looked stunned.

Yeah, I smelled victory. I'd put them in their place.

"You're attracted to her," Knox stated matter-of-factly.

What?

Fuck.

My.

Life.

That was *not* what I thought he would say.

I cleared my throat. "Sorry, what?"

"Yeah," Finn said. "That whole speech you just gave about her? Holy shit, man."

"What are you talking about? I just told you why she's a good fit." Yeah, she was gorgeous, but I was over that. I was in control.

"For Jeremy or for you?" Chase asked.

"Really? What made you even think that?" I asked him.

"I don't know what to say. The way you talked about her took me by surprise too. I just couldn't put it into words until Knox did."

"Thank you. Always nice to get credit for things," Knox replied.

"All of you are out of your minds," I said.

"So, you're not attracted to her?" Wyatt asked. He was usually the most cerebral of all of us, weighing pros and cons, and never jumped to conclusions.

I took a deep breath.

"He's hesitating," Wyatt said.

I looked around the table, and the fight went out of me.

Why would I want to keep this from my siblings? They'd hound me about it until the sun went down. Besides, it wasn't as if I was going to act on anything. But I could admit to them that she was attractive.

"I'm not indifferent to her," I hedged.

"Ha," Knox said, victorious.

"But I am behaving perfectly professionally," I added.

"Good, as you should," Griffin said, "because she's your son's nanny."

Wyatt looked at him. "Since when are you the fun police? Chase usually does that."

Chase jerked his head back. "That is in no way true. However, I don't think it would be the best idea—"

"Look, no one at the table thinks it would be a good idea, okay?" I concluded. "Let's forget about it and move on. We've agreed that we'll look into the Napa Valley idea. Anyone else want to contribute ideas?"

I liked that we scheduled these meeting Monday mornings. It set the tone for the entire week, and I always walked out of here full of energy and ready to take on the world.

"Yes," Chase said. That was to be expected. He was a genius and always had great concepts. "Ever since that whole debacle with Hannah's inn, I've taken an interest in the hotel business."

Debacle was putting it mildly. His fiancée had needed funds to invest in it but refused to take money from him, so he tried to pose as an investor.

"You saw an investment opportunity?" Wyatt asked, straightening up.

"Yeah, it's a chain that made Hannah an offer recently. She turned it down because they don't actually focus on B&Bs but rather luxury hotels. But it got me thinking that we could invest in the chain itself. I'm going to work on a proposal this week if you all agree to it. I don't want to waste my time otherwise."

There was a murmur of agreement around the room.

"I, for one, thought the hotel business was a good deal ever since we tried to fake-invest in Hannah's inn," Finn said with a grin.

Chase groaned.

"No, we're never going to let you live that down," I said.

Hannah had had financial troubles when she took over her grandmother's inn, and my brother had this idea to set up a shell company to pose as an investor in order to buy shares in her company. I told him I wasn't going to be part of it. I was low-key still annoyed at the rest of my brothers for not taking my side in wanting to talk him out of it. Of course, Hannah found out eventually, but she ultimately forgave him.

"All right, we have two very clear directions," Griffin said. "It makes no sense to continue brainstorming. Let's look into both these things and regroup next week. And if we really want to pursue them, we'll hit the ground running."

"I agree," I said. "But in the meantime, we could also make a plan to help our parents. I can even drop by with Jeremy. He likes when I show him construction things."

"Here's a thought: why don't you drop by with Riley too?" Knox asked.

"Why would I do that?"

He shrugged. "Is she attractive? If one of us asks her out, you'll resist temptation more easily."

"Now, you listen to me. Riley is completely off-limits to every single one of you bozos."

Chase was fighting laughter.

"What?" I asked him.

"Take it from a guy who was sitting where you were only a few months ago—being completely professional won't pan out."

"You have no idea what you're talking about," I replied.

"I actually do. You were pissed at me for creating that shell company to help out Hannah. But when you're crazy about a woman, you do crazy things. I suspect that you're about to find that out for yourself."

I scoffed at the idea. I knew I was stronger than that—and was determined to prove them all wrong.

CHAPTER SEVEN

Riley

I barely resisted the urge to pinch myself. I couldn't believe this was my life. Jeremy and I were spending another afternoon at the pool, which was hands down my favorite place in the whole city. There were only few other residents here, either sitting on lounge chairs or swimming in the water.

I couldn't understand why this place wasn't chock-full of people. If I lived in this complex, I'd probably never leave the pool. I'd even bring my laptop here and a pair of headphones and do all my meetings from my lounge chair. I felt like I was on a vacation while the slides kept Jeremy very entertained.

He was old enough that he didn't need me to go down with him. I'd asked him in the beginning if he wanted me to, and he vehemently said no. I was waiting for him in the pool in case he needed help. The last thing I wanted was to embarrass him. He slid right down and dunked under the water. He resurfaced seconds later, giggling and spitting water everywhere.

"What did I tell you? You need to keep your mouth closed."

"I know, but I thought I could keep my head afloat. Maybe next time. Can I go again?" he asked me eagerly.

"Let's take a short break." He'd been going at it for almost two hours, and I learned that when he got tired, he was more careless. I didn't want him to hurt himself.

"Can we eat the snack you made?"

"Sure we can."

I was wearing a black bikini, which I wasn't entirely sure was appropriate for a nanny job. It wasn't what I'd call super sexy, but a one-piece would probably have been better. But right now, I wasn't in a position to splurge on a bathing suit that I was only going to use for a few months, so this one would have to do.

Jeremy and I got out of the pool and sat on two lounge chairs I'd carefully set up under the shade of one of the palm trees. I preferred natural shade to umbrellas, if possible.

I'd made brownies with him earlier, and he grinned as I took the lid off the Tupperware. He reached for one and shoved it into his mouth.

"Don't swallow it whole."

"So good," he said while chewing on it. His little face was too adorable. I snapped a picture of him with my phone. Then I ate one, too, closing my eyes and savoring it.

It was truly delicious.

We each took another one, and then I opened the bottle I'd filled with a mix of apple juice and ginger ale and poured it into glasses for each of us.

He gulped it down and then said, "I'm feeling much better after the break. Can I go back on the slide?"

I laughed. "Let's wait twenty minutes, okay? You just ate. I don't want you to hurt your tummy."

He pouted. "Okay."

"What did you and your dad do over the weekend?" I asked him.

"We were at the pool. He taught me how to swim butterfly. Do you want to see?" He straightened up again.

"Twenty minutes, remember?"

He went back to pouting.

"Do you want to tell me another one of Spider-Man's adventures while we wait?" I asked.

"Yes!"

His eyes lit up as he began to rattle on about Mary Jane and Spider-Man. I used this trick a lot because he always lost himself in stories about Spider-Man and didn't notice time passing.

Jeremy was retelling me how Peter Parker got bitten by a radioactive spider when he suddenly jumped up from the lounge chair.

"Dad," he exclaimed.

My breath caught. I turned around and saw Duncan walking toward us from the building.

I instantly felt self-conscious. It was only four o'clock. He never came home this early. I wanted to throw something over my bikini, but I couldn't put on my dress because I was still wet. *Crap.*

"Hi, Duncan," I said. My voice was ridiculously high-pitched. "Did you text me that you were coming home earlier? I didn't check my phone."

"No, it was a spontaneous decision. I have another call later on, but I can do that from my office upstairs. What were you two up to?"

"Riley is an amazing listener," Jeremy cut in. "She already knows all about Spider-Man."

Duncan looked at me sympathetically.

"I don't mind," I assured him.

"Dad, you want to come in the pool with us? You can show me the butterfly stroke again."

"I'd like to, bud, but I've got another call in forty minutes."

"That's a long time."

Duncan looked around. "All right, I suppose I could bring my phone and then do the call from here," he said. "I'll go change. I'll be back in ten minutes."

I bit the inside of my cheek. I felt awkward, and not just because the man was impossibly hot. I wasn't sure what to do.

Should I stay? Should I go? I felt like I was interrupting their father-son time.

"Want me to leave earlier?" I asked.

He shook his head. "No. I don't know how long the call will take, and I'd like you to keep an eye on Jeremy."

"Okay."

"Is that fresh juice?" He pointed to Jeremy's cup.

"Yes."

He stepped closer, bending at the waist and picking up the cup. He was dressed to the nines. I got a glimpse of his neck as he gulped down the drink. Even that was sexy. Goose bumps covered my skin just from watching him before he headed upstairs with a wave. How on earth was I going to react when I saw him wearing swim trunks?

He came back down ten minutes later, as promised, and I got my answer. Jeremy and I were in the pool again. I noticed Duncan approaching us before Jeremy did. The man looked absolutely incredible. He had a twelve-pack or something—it was definitely a hell of a lot more than just a six-pack. His chest was mouthwatering with a light smattering of hair. I imagined how those muscles would feel under my fingers or my lips. I'd map them with great care, moving up his shoulders and down his arms. I couldn't get enough of them. And his legs were just as toned as his arms.

He put his phone on the table between my cup and Jeremy's, then walked toward the edge of the pool. I heard a few giggles and looked over my shoulder. Two women were ogling him with their heads together, whispering. I felt an insane jealousy coursing through me.

Oh, wow. That was new and uncalled for. I didn't remember ever being jealous before. Lucky me that it would happen now, with the father of the boy I was nannying. I was clearly losing my mind.

Duncan raised his arms and dove into the pool. Then he swam right next to me.

"Dad, you're here," Jeremy called. He'd reached the top of the slide. "Watch me."

"I wouldn't miss it," he said.

I concentrated on Jeremy as well. Once again, I felt self-conscious about my bikini. It was a bit more revealing than what everyone else was wearing.

Duncan came even closer, and our arms brushed. That brief contact was enough to send my senses into a tailspin.

I drew in a deep breath, and even through the pungent smell of disinfectant around the pool, I still could smell Duncan's aftershave. I peeked at him out of the corner of my eye, but his gaze was fixed on Jeremy.

Jeremy slid down the next second, landing in the water perfectly with his feet forward. He managed to keep his head afloat this time.

"See, I did it, Riley!" he exclaimed, then walked toward Duncan.

The pool wasn't deep on this side; the water reached to Jeremy's chin, which was perfect. Still, I understood Duncan's request to watch him at all times because the other side of the pool was over his head. Even so, all types of accidents could happen in and around pools that had nothing to do with the depth of the water.

"Well done," Duncan said.

"Can you show me the butterfly stroke again? I wanted to show it to Riley earlier, but I forgot the steps."

"Sure, buddy." Duncan looked around once. His eyes seemed to gloss over me completely. That was a relief. I'd been afraid that he would be annoyed by my swimwear, but he didn't even seem to notice it.

My stomach rolled in disappointment. Crap, I had no business being upset that my employer wasn't considering me attractive. It was a good thing.

I walked over to the edge of the pool, watching Duncan and Jeremy. Jeremy was staring at his dad with utmost attention. My mouth watered at the sight before me because somehow Duncan seemed a million times sexier when doing the butterfly stroke. Clearly, he swam often, moving with grace through the water. He dunked his head every time, and when he came back up, he didn't gasp for air; he took an elegant intake of breath before dunking again. I could watch him for hours.

Apparently, so could Jeremy, who'd moved closer to me. "Isn't Dad amazing? I don't know how he does it."

"Does he swim often?" I asked.

"Oh yeah, every day."

"Well, then, he's had a lot of practice."

Afterward, Duncan straightened up and walked over to us. I nearly swallowed my tongue. His muscles seemed more pumped and defined from the effort. I was not going to survive the next few months working for this man. He was far too sexy.

"Your turn," he told Jeremy. "I'm going to walk next to you in the water and watch."

He took Jeremy's hand, and they went to the middle of the pool. I relaxed, figuring that with his back to me, I wouldn't be so on edge.

Oh no, that was a mistake. His back was just as sexy as his front. I couldn't explain what was happening to me, except that I'd never been around such a hot man. The guys I'd dated were fit, but Duncan wasn't just fit. He was a work of art.

He patiently explained every move to Jeremy, correcting him firmly but gently, melting my heart. If I had a kid, I would raise him in the exact same way.

The unexpected effect of the butterfly stroke, though, was that Jeremy was completely spent five minutes later. He was red in the face as he walked toward me and said, "I need a break. Riley."

"Want another brownie?" I suggested.

"Yes, please."

"Now I've got a new strategy," I whispered to Duncan, who joined me as Jeremy got out of the water. "Whenever he's got too much energy, I'm going to ask him to swim."

"It knocks him right out, but don't get your hopes up. He's going to be fit as a fiddle in twenty minutes."

It turned out that Duncan was wrong. Jeremy wanted to go on the slide only ten minutes later.

CHAPTER EIGHT

Duncan

"Dad, I want us all to get on the slide."

"Buddy, you said you were old enough to do it yourself."

"I know, but I've seen other parents do it."

"I'll go with you," Riley said, then turned to me. "Come on, Duncan. It's going to be fun."

I focused on the brownie I was about to eat, shoving it into my mouth and chewing slowly. Today, I thought I'd surprise Jeremy, but I'd been the one surprised by how sexy Riley was in that bikini. I was also shocked by my visceral reaction to her. I actively avoided looking at her, though I was starting to accept that I didn't have as much control over my body as I thought. At least not where Riley was concerned.

"Come on, Duncan," she repeated when I didn't budge. "It's good to let your inner child come out to play from time to time."

I swallowed the brownie, then looked her straight in the face. As long I maintained eye contact and didn't look at her body, I was safe.

"You don't know how to do that?" she teased.

"I honestly don't."

"Pools are for fun."

I rose to my feet. "I relax by swimming."

"Ha, but see, that's the difference. I wasn't talking about relaxing but about having fun. And going down the slide, well... the thrill is not knowing if you're going to face-plant or dive in feet first."

"And that's fun for you?"

She grinned. "Obviously. I like the unknown."

Her enthusiasm was catchy. "Okay, fine. Let's go."

Jeremy screeched with joy.

Damn it, I was an ass. When he'd told me two years ago that he wanted to do it alone, I'd assumed that he really meant it. But maybe he'd simply noticed that I didn't enjoy the slide and wanted to please me.

Jeremy went first up the ladder, and Riley climbed in front of me. I nearly walked face-first into her perfect, round ass. I'll never know how I managed to bite back a groan.

I looked sideways as I went, trying to think more about the upcoming call I needed to make, then numbers and more numbers. I needed to distract myself. Her bikini was simple, but her body made it breathtaking. I was so attracted to her that I could barely get my thoughts together.

"Okay, Dad, you first," Jeremy said once we were all at the top. "Then you can catch me."

"All right." The sooner I got off this platform, the better. There wasn't enough space for us all, and I was far too close to Riley. I lowered myself and went down the slide.

"Oh, Jeremy, pity we don't have a camera," Riley said loudly.

I looked over my shoulder as I flew down the slide. "What do you mean?"

I hit the water as gracefully as a whale and swallowed a mouthful of water. When I got up, I saw that Riley and Jeremy had succumbed to a fit of laughter.

My entire body instantly relaxed. I hadn't seen my boy laugh like this with anyone besides my youngest brothers. It was great that he and Riley hit it off so well, but I couldn't see any way of persuading her to continue being his nanny once her new job started. I knew lawyers worked crazy hours, so it definitely wouldn't work.

Then Jeremy pointed to the slide, and Riley hurtled downward. I reacted far too late. She slid down so quickly that she slammed right into me. I instantly gripped her arms, pulling her up. She burst out laughing, spewing water straight into my face.

"Oh my God, I'm so sorry."

"Are you hurt?" I asked.

She opened her eyes. "Wait, let me rub my eyes. I got some water in them." Closing them, she wiped the backs of her knuckles across them before opening them once more. "No, I'm not hurt. Are you? I slammed into you, didn't I?"

"Yeah, you did."

"Oops, I'm sorry. Rule number one, always get away from the slide once you land." She waved me forward. "Come on, let's move."

I chuckled. "Really? Now you're all about rules?"

She smiled sheepishly.

"Why did you distract me when I was deciding on the best way to go down the slide?"

"Oh, Duncan. You don't see anything wrong in that sentence? 'Deciding on the best way to go down the slide'? It's meant to be fun!"

"Okay, that does sound wrong," I admitted. When did I become such a stick-in-the-mud? I'd always thought I was the cool brother—responsible, yes, but cool. Now I was worried about myself.

"Yes, but we'll loosen you up yet," she teased.

Jeremy didn't come down the slide right away, and I realized that he was talking to a neighbor friend of his, Andreas.

"Those two are going to chat for a while, probably exchanging stories about Spider-Man," I said. "Let's you and I move away from the slide and give them space."

She nodded.

We headed to the edge of the pool. Instead of taking the stairs, Riley pushed herself up on the edge... or at least tried to. She gasped and then dropped back into the water. She was holding her hands weirdly around the left strap of her bra.

"What's wrong? Did you hurt yourself?"

"No, my swim top came undone," she said.

Numbers. Think numbers, Duncan.

It wasn't working.

"I think I can tie it back," she mumbled.

She was red in the cheeks as she straightened up. She clumsily tried to tie it behind her neck, then let out a frustrated groan.

"I can do it," I said.

"Oh, thank you. I don't want to accidentally flash anyone."

Her words were like gasoline poured on fire. The idea of seeing her without a bra was intoxicating.

"Turn around," I commanded.

I sucked in a deep breath as she twirled, pulling her hair to one side. It had come undone from her bun when she came down the slide.

I pulled at the elastic strings, knotting them. Her skin was smooth beneath my fingertips. I was trying my best not to touch it, but it was impossible. While I did a second knot—to make sure this didn't happen again—the backs of my fingers brushed her. There was no mistaking her reaction. She shuddered as her skin turned to goose bumps, then sucked in a breath.

Fuck, she felt the tension between us too. I wasn't imagining it.

"Is it okay if I turn around?" she whispered.

"Yes."

I was so deep under her spell that I didn't realize until it was too late that the gentlemanly thing would be to take a step back and put some distance between us.

Slowly, she turned to face me. My mouth almost brushed hers, and she gasped again.

I looked at her mouth for a split second. *What would happen if I kissed her right here, right now? Pinned her against the edge of the pool and devoured her the way I want to?*

She took a step back and cast her gaze downward. Her breathing was labored. Then she turned to the slide, looking at Jeremy.

"He's not coming down any time soon, is he?"

Her voice snapped me out of my thoughts. I looked at the top of the slide. He and his friend were sitting down cross-legged. Jeremy was gesticulating with his hands.

"No, he's probably telling him things about Spider-Man."

Riley laughed. "Yeah, that's the one thing that gets him so animated."

That impulse to kiss her intensified. How did she know my boy so well already?

"I used to be just like that when I was telling my sister my favorite stories growing up. She was much younger than me, so obviously we couldn't read them at the same time. I'd sit on the family couch in our trailer and do my best to reenact it. She loved it so much."

She grew up in a trailer? That sounded hard. "Was it just you and your sister, or do you have more siblings?"

"No, just that one sister. I think my parents wanted more kids, but they couldn't really afford it. We were cramped in the trailer as it was."

"Where did you grow up?" I asked.

"Florida."

"Do your parents still live there?"

She shook her head. "No. My dad took off when we were

kids. Mom lives in Montana now, still in a trailer. One thing that's on my wish list once I've made it as a lawyer is to buy her her own place. She'd love that."

That was an ambitious goal, and I liked her even more for it. "You're a good person, Riley."

She shrugged. "Mom sacrificed a lot so my sister and I could go to the best schools. And let me tell you, that's a hurdle when you live in a trailer and are barely making ends meet."

I'd somehow moved close to her again. She half turned, glancing up at me. I couldn't look away from her mouth. *What has gotten into me?*

When she licked her lips, I couldn't stifle a groan. She didn't miss it, her blush intensifying. She turned around, but I could still see the goose bumps on her arms when she raised them, waving. "Jeremy, come on. We're waiting."

He grinned and slid right down to us, landing in the water perfectly and then swimming toward me and Riley.

She's Jeremy's nanny. She's much younger than you. She's completely off-limits. Get that through your thick skull.

Riley avoided my gaze as I got out of the pool for my phone call.

Fucking hell, I don't want her to be uncomfortable. I need to get my shit together.

———

After she left later that afternoon, it was too late to cook, so Jeremy and I ordered pizza for dinner. While we waited for the delivery, we called his mother. He usually spoke to Shona either before or after dinner. I appreciated that she was flexible and never missed a call.

"Hi, Jeremy," she said. "Hey, Duncan."

"Mom, we were at the pool."

She chuckled. "I can see that. You have wet hair. Did you have fun?"

"Yeah, we did."

"He's very proficient at the butterfly, although he was mostly on the slide today."

"I'm so proud of you, Jeremy," Shona said.

"I'll leave the two of you to chat." I liked hanging around when they were on the phone, but I knew they were more at ease talking if I wasn't actively part of the conversation.

As I cleaned the table, I heard her saying, "I can't wait for you to come to Dublin."

Jeremy stayed with her for two weeks every summer.

"Me too. Is Jamie going to come with us on our adventures?"

Jamie was Shona's boyfriend.

"Oh no, baby. I'm sorry. Jamie and I... well, we aren't friends anymore."

I looked at Jeremy immediately. His smile fell. "But why?"

"Sometimes relationships between adults don't work out. But I have a new friend. I can't wait to introduce you to him."

My brothers didn't understand why I didn't introduce anyone to Jeremy, and this was proof that it was a bad idea. I didn't want my son to get attached to someone, only to be disappointed when things didn't work out.

My ex obviously wasn't as concerned.

"Okay," Jeremy said, sounding confused as hell.

She was on her third boyfriend over the past three years, and it was taking a toll on him. It was one thing if she had someone stable in his life, but that hadn't been the case, and I didn't like it one bit.

Once he'd done his nightly routine and gone to sleep, I called Shona back.

"Hey, Duncan. Is everything okay?"

"Yeah, I just figured we haven't spoken in a while."

"That's true," she agreed. "So, how are things? Ms. Williams leaving wasn't great, huh? Especially with summer starting?"

"No, but that's fine. I've made new arrangements."

"Already? Wow, you always were very efficient."

"Listen, Shona—"

"Oh, I knew it. I can feel it in your voice. You want to admonish me."

"Not exactly, but I would like to ask you again to be a bit more discreet when it comes to your love life with Jeremy."

She sighed. "Damn it. I knew I didn't handle that very well. Honestly, I didn't even think he'd remember my ex."

"While he's there with you, will it be possible not to introduce him to anyone you're dating? It just confuses him."

There was a pause, and then she cleared her throat. "Duncan, I'm not introducing him to just anyone, okay? My ex and I were together for six months."

"I want to give Jeremy as much stability as possible. That's why I've never introduced him to anyone I'm dating." *Which is no one, so it's never been a problem.*

Shona cleared her throat. "Well, you know, maybe you should."

"What?"

"Listen, I think he's old enough now to understand certain things. He always tells me that divorced parents at his school are dating, or even remarried."

I blinked. "He's never shared that with me."

"Kids share different things with each of their parents, but from the way he talks, it's obvious that he does understand the nuances and differences between... you know... husband and wife or a dad who's just dating. I'm not saying you should introduce him to everyone you go out with, of course. But you're very hard on yourself, you know?"

"Always have been. It's the only way—" I replied.

"Oh, Duncan," Shona said on a sigh, interrupting my response. "It truly isn't. Just think about what I said, okay?" When I didn't say anything else, she added, "Is that all?"

"Yeah."

"Then have a great evening, Duncan."

"You too."

No surprise that we still had different views on this.

If I started dating, it would take a toll on Jeremy, I was sure of it. He'd feel slighted. Besides, the way I'd handled things these past few years had served us well, and it kept Jeremy happy. I wasn't going to start doing things differently now.

No matter how tempting Riley was.

CHAPTER NINE

Duncan

"You're doing a great job with this place," I said on Sunday morning.

We were all gathered at my parents' store. I still called it that, but I had to get used to the fact that it wasn't that anymore. At least not in the way it used to be. Dad had set up a bait and tackle shop downstairs, and Mom had transformed the upper floor into an art studio where she offered pottery classes and yoga. Much different than selling milk and Snickers when we were kids.

"Everyone ready for round two?" Chase asked.

Mom had decided she wanted to do some cosmetic changes to her studio—*again*. All my brothers had gathered here this morning, lending Mom our muscle and advice. Everything happened much faster if we did it as a group. Dad helped her as much as he could, but he was only a one-man show, so he couldn't leave his business unsupervised for too long.

We'd painted the room off-white as Mom asked, but we had to wait for the first coat to dry before applying the second.

Knox, Finn, and Wyatt were going to shellac the floors later that afternoon.

"Not so fast," Mom said. "Do any one of you boys want some brownies? They should be ready by now."

"Anyone else feel like they're five years old?" Finn asked.

Knox nodded while Wyatt and Griffin laughed.

She waved them off. "Oh, stop it. I want to spoil my boys. Being here and cooking brings back memories."

She was right. Only it didn't bring any good ones for me. All I could remember was my parents shouting at each other or bickering behind closed doors because Mom didn't want to disturb us while we were doing homework.

It was still bizarre to me that they were on good terms now. Hell, they even seemed to be flirting with each other, which was just plain weird.

I'd always thought that my parents' business was their own and that their divorce didn't directly impact me, but after the fiasco with Jeremy's mother, I had second thoughts. Maybe some things from back then had left some marks. It was one of the reasons why I simply didn't do relationships. It wasn't worth the risk of destabilizing the balance Jeremy and I had reached.

"Want to call Jeremy in here and ask him if he wants brownies?" Mom asked as we all went to the kitchen.

Mom still used the old kitchen from our childhood. She insisted there was no need to renovate it, since the clients wouldn't come in here. Knowing her, she'd eventually change her mind, but we'd help her when the time came.

"No chance. Dad's showing him fishing rods," I told her.

"I think I'm going to lose that boy to fishing, too, just as I did with you."

"Fishing is fun," I said, though I hadn't gone in years. It was something Dad did with Jeremy now.

"How's it going with Riley?" Mom asked.

I noticed the shift around the kitchen island as my brothers all trained their eyes on me.

For fuck's sake! If they started giving me shit in front of Mom, I was going to lose it.

"It's good. She and Jeremy really hit it off."

"I had a good feeling from the moment they met. She just lit up, like she truly couldn't imagine anything better than spending time with him. That's a rare thing when you're hiring help."

"I agree."

My son had had enough nannies that I could tell the difference when someone *wanted* the job or just needed it. I couldn't believe I'd been so incredibly lucky to find Riley. There was no way I could screw this up.

Though, technically, she was only the nanny for the interim until Maggie returned. After that, Riley was fair game.

What the hell? Where did that come from?

"Is she doing something with him tomorrow?" Mom asked.

Jeremy's school year officially ended yesterday, and he had some time off until summer school began after the Fourth of July.

"Yeah." Initially, I'd figured Jeremy could just spend time here with Dad at the store. But then Riley suggested that she could take him to a theme park. He wouldn't hear of anything else after that, so I gave in. "She's taking him to the park. He wants to ride the roller coasters."

"The boy loves roller coasters, but my stomach doesn't tolerate it," Mom said.

I grinned. "Yeah, Ms. Williams said the same."

"It's a good thing that you have a younger nanny for Jeremy. She'll be better at keeping up with him."

"Why would it matter that she's young?" Wyatt asked.

Griffin and Chase were trying to suppress grins. Knox and Finn didn't even bother. I glared at them all.

Mom smiled. "I think Jeremy can connect better to someone younger."

"You're right, I think so too. Though, once Ms. Williams is

back, we're still going to continue our arrangement. She's good for him, keeps him grounded."

"And makes you look fun in return," Knox said with a laugh.

"You know what? I actually agree. Since he's spending more time with Riley, he doesn't seem to miss me that much. Hasn't even asked once if I can take him out for ice cream," Finn said.

"We can always drop by uninvited," Knox told Finn. "Would give us a chance to meet Riley too."

I glared at them. Finn held up his hands in self-defense.

"What's going on?" Mom asked.

"Trust me, you do not want to know," Knox said.

She nodded once. "Fair enough."

"Really?" Wyatt said, clearly astonished. "You're going to give up so easily?"

"No, but some things mothers don't need to know," Mom said wisely.

"Hear, hear," Griffin said, laughing at me with a shit-eating grin.

What was it with my brothers? Sure, I'd been a bit possessive when talking about Riley, but that could be due to a number of things. For one, she was spending time with my son, so obviously I wouldn't want any of my womanizer brothers making things awkward.

And second...

There was no second point.

I couldn't lie to myself, especially not after our time in the pool.

We'd been completely professional since then, but it wasn't easy. She'd prepared dinner twice last week and had made an excuse for why she needed to leave both times. Then again, maybe it wasn't an excuse. The sexual tension between us was there.

Her work hours ended at six o'clock. She didn't need to spend evenings with her employer, which was exactly what I was —nothing more and nothing less. I wasn't going to take advantage of that. My strategy was to be around her when Jeremy was, too, so I couldn't even be tempted by *looking* at her in an inappropriate way.

Besides, she was nine years younger than me and probably wouldn't even consider dating me. I needed to keep that possibility in mind. We were at completely different stages in our lives, after all.

You're not dating anyone, Duncan. Why do you keep forgetting that?

"All right, I'm taking Jeremy to the city to buy some things for tomorrow," I said. "Mom, can you pack some brownies for him?"

"Sure. I'll also bring some for your dad. I've made some with pecans especially for him."

"Are you and Dad dating?" I blurted.

Mom froze in the act of putting tinfoil over the brownies. "Excuse me?"

"That's a good question," Knox said. There was an edge in his voice that I wasn't used to hearing from our youngest brother.

Not a single brother gave me shit or called me out on the question, which could only mean one thing: they were as interested in the answer as I was.

"You've been spending a lot of time together lately. We want to know what's going on." You could count on Griffin to always say what was on his mind. His honesty was refreshing. But he was also more impulsive than Wyatt, Chase, or me. That wasn't always good. At least not in business.

"I thought you would be happy that your father and I are on good terms."

"We are," Chase clarified.

"But we'd like to know if there's anything going on," I added.

Yes, it was their personal life, but still. If they ended up at odds with each other again, we'd have to pick up the pieces, and that was not a good time. Been there, done that.

"We're not dating, but...," Mom started. "Oh, it's weird to talk about it with my boys. I think we're flirting."

Knox winced. Actually winced.

Finn's jaw hung open.

"Yeah. No, you're right, that is very, very weird. We do not need details," Griffin said.

I agreed, as did the others. Suddenly, everyone looked for something to do.

I excused myself from the group, going downstairs with the brownies she'd packed for Jeremy.

Why the fuck had I asked that? I thought knowing might make things less weird, but I was dead wrong.

Jeremy and Dad were bent over a fishing rod on the counter. Dad was explaining to him how to replace the hook.

"Ready to go?" I asked.

Jeremy looked up. "Sure. Grandpa was just showing me what to do if a fish runs away with my hook."

Dad straightened up, ruffling his hair. "I've shown him a few times when we were fishing, but it's easier to learn the mechanics of it when you don't have adrenaline in your veins and a fish on your line. How was it upstairs?"

"We're making progress."

"Good, good. Do I smell brownies?"

"Yeah, she packed this for Jeremy. Mom's got a full tray upstairs. Some with pecans too."

"Damn, she's spoiling me. I'll close up here and see if she needs help with anything. Maybe we'll grab dinner afterward."

Fuck no. The logistics of my parents dating wasn't something I wanted front and center in my mind.

"Okay, buddy, let's go," I said. "We need to buy some things for tomorrow."

"All right. Bye, Grandpa."

After Jeremy hugged everyone goodbye, we left the store and got in the car. The whole drive, my son talked nonstop about fishing, Spider-Man, and God knew what else. Sometimes I think he just talked to talk, and I loved it.

We headed straight to the grocery store next to our condo building. Jeremy insisted on buying all sort of snacks for tomorrow. Since I didn't know the layout of the store, it took us a while to find everything even though the fancy-ass place was small.

"Dad, Riley said that if we find white truffles, she can make a veggie muffin snack."

"A what?" That sounded disgusting.

"We saw it on TV, on a cooking show."

I frowned. *Why didn't she buy them herself?* I'd given her a credit card last week to use for that reason.

I realized why when I looked at the price tag. She'd probably figured it was too expensive.

A little while later, we left the grocery store with two loaded bags.

Once I was inside the car, Jeremy said, "Dad? Can we drop the truffles at Riley's house?"

"Why?"

"So she can bake the muffins for tomorrow."

"Jeremy, she can just bake them in the afternoon. This is her free time. We can't encroach on it."

"She *told* me to bring them to her house if we bought them."

I found that hard to believe, so I decided to double-check with Riley. I called her right away, holding the phone to my ear.

"Hi, Duncan!" she answered cheerily.

"Riley, is this a good time?"

"Sure."

"I just went shopping with Jeremy. We got white truffles."

"Oh, that's perfect. Could you drop them by my house?"

That took me by surprise. "Really? I figured he misunderstood. You don't have to bake in your free time."

"I don't mind, honestly. And that way I'll have everything ready to go for tomorrow."

"All right. Then send me your address and we'll drop by shortly."

"Great." Her voice was strangely high-pitched.

After hanging up, she texted me her address. It was twenty minutes away.

I smiled to myself, curious to see her in her element.

I had no idea what I'd imagined, but it certainly wasn't the scene I witnessed as I pulled in front of a bungalow. First, the windows were open, and music was blasting out. Several women seemed to be fighting. No, wait. They were just trying to talk to each other above the music, not fighting.

Jeremy looked around. "Are we sure this is the place?"

"Yeah. Riley must have friends over."

"Are they having a party?"

It seemed like it. I knocked at the door. Of course, no one answered. I rang the bell, but you couldn't hear it over the music, so I texted Riley.

Duncan: We're at the door.

"They're here," I heard a voice yell above me. "Turn it all down and behave."

I laughed despite myself.

A few seconds later, Riley opened the door. Her face was completely red, and her hair was all over the place. She was so damn sexy that I couldn't look away.

Fuck me. How am I supposed to resist this woman?

CHAPTER TEN

Duncan

"I'm sorry. We were dancing, and I didn't realize you'd be here so soon. Hi, Jeremy." He just looked at her, shocked. "Come in."

"Are you certain?" I asked. "We don't want to disturb you."

"No, of course not. I also bought some things for tomorrow, Jeremy."

"Oh, can I see?" he asked, finally recovering his voice.

"Sure."

I looked curiously around the house. It was a very typical Californian bungalow.

Two women poked their heads in from a doorway. "Hi. We're Riley's roommates. I'm Christine, and this is Julia."

I didn't know she had roommates.

"I'm Duncan Sterling, and this is my son, Jeremy," I said.

"Wow, this is so cool. When I grow up, I also want to live with my friends." He looked up at me. "Dad, can I live with my friends now?"

"No. You have to be at least eighteen."

He nodded. "That's okay. I only have eight more years left."

Riley waved us forward. "Come on, the kitchen is this way."

She walked in front of us, and I was trying to look anywhere but at those long, tan legs. Though above them, her ass was delicious and calling to me in the tight white shorts she was wearing. *Damn it.*

"What snacks did you buy? Dad and I also went shopping," Jeremy said.

She smiled. "Snickers. I heard they were your favorite. I saw them on sale and thought they'd make your day."

His eyes lit up. "Can I have one now?" he asked.

Riley looked at me.

"No. You already had enough brownies in the car. Any more sugar and you won't sleep tonight."

"I promise I'll sleep, Dad," he whined.

"That's not how sugar works," I said patiently. "Remember? Then if you don't sleep well tonight, you'll be tired tomorrow."

He pouted but nodded. "Yeah. I don't want to be tired for the roller coasters. I don't want to fall asleep like a baby. Did you know some people faint?" he asked Riley eagerly.

"Yeah."

"I have no idea why," he went on.

"Not everyone's meant to go on roller coasters" was all I said.

Julia poked her head in. "Hey, Jeremy?"

"Yes?" he said.

"Riley said you like Spider-Man."

My son immediately perked up, as did I. She'd spoken about him with her friends?

"I've got a figurine collection I think you'd enjoy," she continued.

Jeremy looked up at me. "Dad, can I go look?"

"Sure." I usually didn't allow my son to go off with strangers, but they were Riley's roommates, after all.

He ran out of the kitchen before I even had time to add anything else.

Riley took the truffles from me. "Thanks for bringing these."

"Riley, you can buy anything you and Jeremy want with the credit card I gave you."

She nodded. "I just wasn't sure about these. They're exorbitant."

I couldn't get over how beautiful she was. Her sun-kissed skin and the blonde streaks in her hair made her blue eyes pop. She was simply stunning.

"Sorry to crash your Sunday. Are you going to bake now?" I asked.

"No, I'll do it tomorrow morning so they're fresh. We're going to the club after you leave."

Something about the idea of her dancing in a club triggered me. What if some dude came up to her and wanted to dance with her? What if he put his hands on her? The thought drove me crazy. "It's just the three of you who are going?"

"Yes. We're trying to take Julia's mind off her latest breakup. The girl doesn't have any good luck, I swear. Then again, none of us do."

I moved closer. She licked her lower lip but didn't break our eye contact.

"And why is that?"

"I don't know. I, for one, have been buried in work and school for the past few years. Law school isn't for the faint of heart, and that bar exam still gives me nightmares. Dating was something of an afterthought, and the guys I did go out with... weren't exactly what I was looking for."

"Which is what? What do you want in a man?" Why I was asking these questions baffled me. No, that was a lie. I wanted to know about her, about Riley, what made her who she was.

She averted her gaze. "I don't know how to put it into words. It's not a list of qualities or something." Then she looked back at me. "Just someone who makes me feel alive and wanted and cared for. Like I mean something to them, you know?"

She spoke with so much passion that I nearly kissed her right here against the sink.

"Anyway," she continued, "don't worry, I promise I won't stay out very long tonight. I'll be fresh for Jeremy tomorrow."

"What you do in your free time is up to you. I have no problem with you clubbing." I sounded like an angry bear.

"Your voice sort of contradicts what you're saying." Her smile was more of a smirk.

"It does," I confessed. Somehow, I was even closer to her now. She must have showered recently, because a faint smell of lemon came off her hair. It was damn delicious.

"Duncan," she murmured.

"I've been thinking about you constantly since that day at the pool."

She gasped. "Me too."

I tilted my head, looking from her lips to her eyes. "But you've refused to stay for dinner since."

She swallowed hard. "I thought it might be easier, you know?"

"What would be easier?"

"If I wasn't so tempted by you."

I forgot myself completely then. Forgot that there were three other people in this house—and that one of them was my son. Forgot that she was his nanny and completely off-limits.

I kissed her. She tasted like cherries.

I was a goner the second I pressed my mouth to hers. With both hands on her hips, barely keeping myself from bunching her shirt up so I could feel her bare skin, I kissed and kissed her until I was out of breath. And still, I didn't pull apart. A faint tremble went through her body. She moaned against my lips, then put her fingers on my biceps and dug in her nails.

"Riley, can you come here for a second?" Julia's voice filtered to us.

I came back to my senses, pulling away. Riley leaned back, pressing her lips together, then putting a hand on her chest.

"Why did you pull away?" The urgency in her voice nearly brought me to my knees.

"Julia called you into her room."

"Oh my God! I didn't even hear her."

In a fraction of a second, Riley's demeanor changed. She glanced around, clearly checking if anyone had seen us. Then she darted out of the kitchen.

I found a glass in the overhead cupboard and filled it with cold water before drinking it quickly. It would have been more efficient if I'd dumped it on myself, but this would have to do.

That's it, Duncan. Now you've done it. It was one thing to pretend that moment between Riley and me at the pool hadn't happened, but this was harder to ignore. Both the kiss and what she said before it—that she hadn't wanted to stay because I tempted her too much.

I was so screwed. I had to get my shit together.

Jeremy came running to me. "Dad, Julia's Spider-Man is awesome. I don't have that one. I hope I can find it."

I laughed but didn't do anything to curb his enthusiasm. It wasn't long ago that he'd been into Mario Kart, and now it was his Spider-Man phase. I was sure there would be others as he grew up, and I'd be there to support him all the way.

Jeremy led me down the corridor to one of the rooms. Julia and Riley were huddled over a shelf. "Anything wrong?" I asked.

"I accidentally knocked the shelf over, and it came off," Julia said.

"I can fix it," I offered.

Riley straightened up. "We've got it."

"The hell we do. Sorry, Jeremy," Julia said with a wince, then turned to me. "Yeah, we can do a lot of things, but we're not good at handling tools."

"Do you have a toolbox?" I asked.

Riley opened her mouth, clearly about to protest, but I cut in.

"You're baking for Jeremy in your free time. The least I can do is this."

Twenty minutes later, I'd fixed the shelf.

"Well, well, Duncan, you really have skills," Julia said. "Thank you!"

"No problem." I looked at Jeremy and clapped my hands together. "All right, it's getting late. Let's go, Jeremy."

"I'll walk you to the door," Riley said in a small voice. She'd avoided looking at me the entire time I was fixing the shelf.

I didn't want her to feel awkward at all, but I knew I wasn't going to make things better tonight. Quite the contrary. So when she walked us to the door, I said, "I'll bring Jeremy tomorrow at nine o'clock. Good?"

We'd agreed that they would take my car tomorrow, since it was more comfortable than the one Riley used on a daily basis to drive Jeremy around and the park was an hour away.

She sucked in her breath and then nodded. "That's great. Thanks."

"Have a great evening, Riley."

She smiled, "I will."

"Have fun. But not too much."

Jeremy looked up at me. "Why not, Dad?"

That effectively cut through the tension between me and Riley. Damn it, I couldn't keep myself in check even around my son.

Riley blushed, and I shook my head, replying, "It's just a saying."

Jeremy frowned but didn't ask anything else. I nodded at Riley just before we turned and went to the car.

After strapping Jeremy in, I went to my side of the car and got in. Riley was still standing in the doorway. I smiled at her, and even from a distance, I saw her lips curl in response.

I was certain of two things.

One: This was absolutely insane. She was completely off-limits.

Two: I couldn't fight my attraction to her anymore.

CHAPTER ELEVEN

Riley

"Girl, do you have any secrets to spill?" Julia asked the next morning. She was sitting at the kitchen table, looking like hell. We'd had a fun night dancing, but I ended up taking an Uber home long before they left.

"What do you mean?" I asked, though I wanted to shout, *"Yes, yes, I do. Duncan kissed me, and it was damn amazing."'*

"How do you look so fresh?"

"I didn't drink at all yesterday."

She rolled her eyes. "Boo. Yeah, now I remember. You were no fun."

"It's Monday, remember? I'm working and need to drive and be alert." The whole time we were dancing at the club, all I could think about was Duncan and our kiss. And how much I missed him. *This was nuts!*

"I don't know why I'm even awake. I'm going back to bed."

"You wanted to have coffee," I said, pointing to the machine. It was whirring, warming up.

She waved her hand. "No, I'll have it later. I still need, like, one more hour or ten of sleep."

I chuckled. "Fair enough."

I'd gotten up early and baked the muffins. They turned out delicious. I only ate one—a taste test of sorts. I'd packed the rest in Tupperware.

It was 8:50 a.m. My stomach somersaulted. I didn't have time for a proper breakfast, but I would grab something at the park. Duncan would arrive any second now. He liked to be punctual.

It was one of the reasons why I'd started preparing dinner fifteen minutes earlier than usual last week. I didn't want to risk him coming home before I finished, figuring the less we were around each other, the better. But clearly, that had backfired, because we both had a lot of sexual tension building up inside us.

Honestly, I didn't know what to make of it. Duncan was quite a bit older than me. Not that I knew exactly how much of an age difference there was between us, but I'd bet it was close to ten years, and that was a lot.

His life was set—he was divorced with a child, and he was successful in his career. He was *adulting*, and I was just trying to get my life started. But I couldn't deny how attracted I was to him.

I'd always been a bit of an old soul anyway. Mom said it was probably because I had to look after my sister often as we grew up. She always apologized about it, said it made me grow up too early, but I honestly hadn't minded. I'd loved taking care of my sister. Even now as an adult, I felt a bit older than my peers.

Boy, where did all of this come from?

I knew the answer to that—one swim in the pool, one hot kiss at the kitchen sink, one sexy look... and basically I was screwed.

As I waited for Duncan and Jeremy to arrive, I texted Mom yet another update so she wouldn't worry about me. At five to nine, there was a light knock at the door. I'd texted Duncan not to ring the doorbell, since Christine was still sleeping—and

Julia now too. I tiptoed to the door, opening it as quietly as I could.

"Surprise," Jeremy exclaimed. "We brought you breakfast."

"Quiet, buddy. My roommates are still sleeping. Come on, let's go to the back of the house and into the garden." I held my finger over my lips to make it more of a game to him, so he wouldn't think I was reprimanding him, and thankfully he got it right away.

I led them through the narrow corridor that opened up directly into the backyard. Jeremy tiptoed like he was a predator stalking his prey—God, he was cute! Our little patio area was small, but we had a portable cabinet we kept out here full of dishes. I took out three and put them on the table. It was big enough to seat four people comfortably.

"What did you buy?" I asked as they took out three glass jars.

"We didn't buy it. Dad and I made it. It's oatmeal. Dad asked me what your favorite food was, and I told him. So yesterday, after we left your place, we went by Walmart again, because that's where you said your favorite is, and we picked it up."

My insides simply melted. Duncan flashed me a gorgeous smile.

"Thank you!"

I was awfully touched, not only that he'd asked Jeremy my favorite food but that he'd gone to Walmart. He'd probably never been in one of those stores before.

"Wow, Jeremy, thanks for remembering. It looks great." I'd made it for him once last week, and it looked like he'd remembered every step. "You even remembered how to mix the fruit."

"I know. We took a picture, remember? And I showed it to Dad."

I blushed a little bit at Duncan.

"Let's eat and see if it's as good as it looks," he said, winking, and I melted yet again.

Sitting here, the three of us together, made me long for a family of my own. Growing up with my mom and sister, we were very close. I missed that kind of connection. Having roommates was just not the same by a long shot.

"I cut the bananas," Jeremy said.

I could just picture the two of them working side by side in the kitchen.

I smiled. "Good for you."

"Dad said that I might be allowed to cut more things, but it wasn't a real knife. It was just made out of plastic even though I'm not a baby," Jeremy countered.

"Of course not," Duncan said.

We exchanged a conspiratorial glance. It was hard not to give in to the impulse of imagining how my life would look if I were Jeremy's mom.

But you're not, Riley. You're his nanny. No matter how well the two of you get along, once you start your job at the law firm, you'll never see him or Duncan again.

Usually, my mood completely deflated when I reminded myself of the reality. But this time it didn't, and I blamed the absolutely delicious oatmeal for it.

"Whoa, this is good," I said. It had more honey than I usually put in. *Hello, new recipe.* I was going to start adding more honey too.

"We didn't find any agave syrup, so I just added more honey," Duncan said.

"It's much better." I grinned through a mouthful, then covered my mouth. "Sorry, that's so unprofessional. Thank you."

"You're welcome," he replied.

"Do you like it?" I asked both Jeremy and Duncan.

Jeremy nodded. "Yeah, it's sweet."

Duncan frowned. "It's certainly better than what I usually have, which is black coffee."

I shuddered. "Without any breakfast? Are you an alien?"

"No, I just usually don't like to eat in the morning. Wastes too much time."

"Really? The first meal of the day is so important," I chastised him.

"True, and Jeremy certainly eats his, but I just don't seem to find the time in the mornings."

"Well, I love breakfast because I love coming back here and enjoying the sun and the chirping birds while I take a few spoonfuls of oatmeal and wake up. It's like a little routine that makes every day start off on the right foot."

Duncan looked at me strangely.

Damn it, we were so different. Forget the age thing—we were just at other stages in life. This could never work out.

He was a single dad and needed to focus on his son. I was a lawyer just starting my career.

And yet I couldn't help but melt. They'd *made* me breakfast.

I smiled at Duncan, and he winked at me, making me feel hot all of a sudden. Did he want to talk about what happened last night? I wasn't even sure what to say.

"Okay, now that we're done, can we go?" Jeremy asked abruptly after he'd finished his bowl.

"Jeremy, what did I tell you? We need to wait for the others at the table to finish eating. Then you can ask."

"I'm done," I said, quickly eating my remaining two spoonfuls.

Duncan had already finished his, too, and was putting what he'd brought back into the bag as we rose from the table.

"Want me to load the bags you prepared for today?" he asked as I rinsed off the dishes in the outdoor sink we rarely used. I'd just leave them here for now and clean up later.

"Yes, please! I put everything on the front porch. We don't even need to go back inside the house. Let's go."

The three of us walked in step, and Duncan put the two bags in the back of the car as I secured Jeremy in the booster seat. After I closed the door, Duncan looked directly at me, and I sucked in a breath. The intensity in his eyes was mesmerizing.

"Call me if you need anything, okay? Or if he asks for something and you're not sure how to respond."

I nodded. "Sure. Don't worry, Jeremy and I will have fun."

He opened his mouth, then shook his head and said, "I can't start this now."

"What are you talking about?"

He smiled at me again. God, I loved those dimples at the corners of his mouth. They seemed even deeper than before.

"I'd planned to talk to you over breakfast but forgot Jeremy was going to be there, hanging on every word."

"You forgot?" I teased.

"Yeah. That's the effect you have on me."

"Oh!" My cheeks flushed.

"Yeah, oh. I'll think of something soon, though."

"Sure," I said, not really understanding what he meant. But I did several minutes later, while I was driving.

He wanted us to be alone. Heat coursed through me at the thought.

"I'm so excited," Jeremy said, snapping me out of my thoughts. "Did you know Ms. Williams doesn't like roller coasters? She said they make her head hurt."

"Some people do have problems with that."

"Mom doesn't like them either."

A cold shudder went down my spine. I looked at him in the rearview mirror. "She takes you to theme parks a lot?"

"No. Only when she visits."

"Do you talk to her often?"

He nodded. "Almost every night."

That was good. It was important for him to have a good relationship with his mother. I supposed the phone calls happened before he went to bed.

"And before school starts, I'll be with her in Dublin for two weeks."

"You looking forward to it?" I asked.

"Yes. I was there last summer, and it was really nice. Mom's boyfriend is nice too. But she says he's not her boyfriend anymore."

That was interesting. So, Jeremy's mom had a boyfriend. I was dying to know more, but it wasn't fair to question Jeremy about it. He was bouncing in the booster seat, smiling when he saw the first sign to the theme park. I'd never seen him so happy. I was glad that I'd offered to bring him here.

We had a blast the entire day. I loved the roller coaster just as much as Jeremy did. I looked ridiculous in a few of them that were clearly meant for kids, but when he'd hesitated, I told him that I secretly wanted to go, too, if he wasn't too embarrassed. He seemed relieved. Clearly, he needed to be able to feel safe with an adult in order to have fun. I was happy I'd caught on to that.

After a round on a particularly nasty roller coaster, we were both feeling a little unwell. "Want to sit down for a bit? I feel like my brain is whirling in my head," I said.

"Yeah, mine too." He was a bit green in the face. "This is why Ms. Williams didn't want to go on it last time."

I laughed. "You tried to talk her into going on that?" I couldn't imagine a sixty-year-old woman on that death trap. I had no idea how *I* survived it or why they even allowed kids on. But clearly it wasn't unsafe, just... unhinged.

Jeremy scooted closer to me. "Thank you so much, Riley. This was the best day ever."

I gave him a half hug.

"You're the best nanny I've ever had. Do you think you can visit me even when you start working your other job?"

I hesitated. "We'd have to check with your dad."

"I'm sure Dad will say yes."

"Oh, buddy, I'm not even sure how my schedule will be once I start working. I've heard that lawyers have to work until late in the evening every day."

His smile fell, and the light went out of his eyes.

Damn it, I didn't want to disappoint him. But wasn't it better if I prepared him now? The truth was that after these three months, I probably wouldn't see him or his dad ever again.

Now *my* smile fell.

"But we'll see," I added. "Maybe we can work something out." The light was back in his eyes now, at least. "Feeling better?" I was asking myself too. I wanted more.

Shit, what was I even thinking?

"Yes. Can I go on one last roller coaster before we go home?"

My brain was still spinning in my mind, and not because of the roller coaster. But I couldn't say no.

"Sure, let's go. One more round, and then we're done."

"Yes!" he cheered, then started tugging me in that direction.

CHAPTER TWELVE

Duncan

"I have a good feeling about it, but we should discuss it with everyone," I said.

Wyatt, Knox, and Finn were in my office, and we were debating the pros and cons of a property they'd found in Napa Valley. They'd spent the Fourth of July there while the rest of us were at our parents' place. Chase and Griffin hadn't had time to join us this afternoon.

"Sure, but we're going to fly out to check it out more thoroughly, and we wanted to touch base before that," Wyatt said.

I laughed. "You three are just looking for an excuse to fly to Napa Valley."

"Obviously," Finn said. "But if we can count it as a business expense, even better." Not that we had any need for it. We all had plenty of money, but we were conscious about finances anyway.

"What plans do you have for the weekend?" Wyatt asked me.

Knox and Finn exchanged a glance. They looked as if they were holding back laughter.

"Why do you ask?"

"Just wondering if you're going to make any more oatmeal breakfasts," Finn said. Knox burst out laughing.

"How long have you been sitting on that?" I asked my brothers.

"Oh, since we stepped into your office, but we figured it was best to end the conversation with it so we didn't hijack the whole discussion," Knox informed me.

"I see," I replied. "How do you even know?"

"From Jeremy, obviously," Knox said.

"Did he tell the whole family?"

"Not sure, but he told *us*, and *we* told everyone." Finn wasn't even apologetic.

My brothers were something, but I couldn't be mad at them. I was pleased that they all spent so much time with my son. Jeremy probably just blabbed it, and besides, he wouldn't know to keep it a secret.

"No plans, no," I said.

"But the question is, would you tell us if you had any?" Finn asked.

I sighed heavily. "Where's Griffin when I need him?"

Wyatt straightened in the chair, rolling his shoulders back. "What do you mean? I'm right here representing the middle group."

Growing up, there were three groups. Chase and I were the older ones, Griffin and Wyatt the middle, and Knox and Finn the younger ones.

I pointed from him to Knox and Finn. "Yeah, but you know you're more in their group."

"I'm affronted," Wyatt exclaimed. He was more cerebral than Griffin—usually, anyway—and they had a way to balance themselves out.

"Dude, what the hell?" Knox said directly to him.

"Yeah," Finn added. "Now *we're* affronted that *you're* affronted."

I laughed as they started to bicker. It was good to be surrounded by my brothers. Pity Chase wasn't here. I wanted to pick his brain on how he'd managed things with Hannah, hoping that might give me some ideas for my situation.

It was incredibly hard to stay professional when it came to Riley. I was constantly trying to tamp down my interest and my need for her. It was more than a physical thing. I liked talking with her. Riley wore her heart on her sleeve. She was spontaneous yet mature for her age and fun-loving. I liked that a lot—and Jeremy did too.

Riley had a fresh insight into things, and her natural sincerity appealed to me. I'd never been interested in anyone in this way. Things between Shona and I had been different. We'd had a great time together, but neither of us was in love with the other. That was why we'd never married. We'd tried to test the waters as a family, but we were honest with each other when it was clear it wouldn't work and broke up early on before it got even more difficult to do so.

As soon as I got to the office, I checked my phone. Riley had sent me a picture of her and Jeremy at the ocean. Since their time at the amusement park, she'd taken him to various places to "broaden his horizons," as she phrased it. Today was the beach, and I wished I was there with them.

Duncan: You look beautiful.

There went my legendary self-control.

Riley: Duncan...

Duncan: I know. I'm trying.

Riley: Really?

No, not really. I knew what was right. I knew what I had to

do, and yet at the same time, I couldn't do it. I couldn't keep myself in check.

But I promised myself that tomorrow, when she sent me the picture after she'd picked up Jeremy, I wouldn't flirt back.

But of course, that thought didn't last. Because the next day, she sent me a picture of the two of them at the Natural History Museum. She was wearing a white dress with a boatneck. I couldn't see her cleavage or anything, but damn if I didn't want to.

> Duncan: I wish I was there with you.

> Riley: I think Jeremy would enjoy it too.

I took a deep breath.

> Duncan: No, with YOU.

Fucking hell. It was time to admit that I wasn't going to do any better. I needed to talk to her face-to-face—alone. And I had a plan.

———

Riley

The next week passed by quickly. The tension between me and Duncan was building day by day. No matter how much I tried to steel myself, whenever I heard his voice announcing that he'd arrived home in the evening, my entire body reacted.

The dynamic between us had changed on a fundamental level. I didn't leave right away as before. I lingered during Jeremy's routine, and we mostly talked about his day. Sometimes

Duncan asked about my mom and sister. I didn't even care what we talked about, to be honest. I simply longed to be near him.

And that was dangerous.

"I'm so excited," Jeremy exclaimed on Friday.

"You haven't spent the weekend with your grandparents in a while, huh?" I asked.

"It's just with Grandma," he said.

I kept forgetting that Duncan's parents were divorced.

"She always makes homemade pizza and cake." His eyes were shining.

God, I wanted to hug him and never let him go, but then the front door opened.

"Daddy, I'm ready," Jeremy exclaimed, darting out of his room. His Spider-Man backpack was hanging off one shoulder. I hadn't gotten to zipping it up yet, so his stuffed giraffe and favorite car fell out. Chuckling, I grabbed them and headed toward the living room.

Duncan had picked him up in his arms. Sometimes Jeremy would insist that he was a grown-up boy and didn't want public displays of affection, but then sometimes he went looking for it. I assumed that, because he was going to spend the night away from his father, he wanted more affection than usual.

I walked up to them. "The backpack's ready," I said, stuffing the items back in and zipping it up this time.

Duncan glanced down at the zipper and smiled at me. "Thanks for that. Day went okay?"

I nodded. "Yeah, completely uneventful." My body buzzed. I couldn't understand how that happened when Duncan had only spoken a few words. But he'd *looked* at me, and apparently that was all it took these days.

"All right," he said, putting Jeremy back down. "Grandma is going to be here soon."

"I need to bring my magic pillow too," Jeremy said, darting toward his room.

The second Duncan and I were alone, I was even more on edge.

"As I was saying, my mom is picking Jeremy up soon. I'd like to cook you dinner."

My head snapped up as I looked straight at him, totally in shock. "Wow, Duncan... Um, I wasn't expecting this."

"It would do us good to talk," he said.

I bit my lip. "That's true. But I promised my roommates that I would spend the evening with them. We're having dinner and then going clubbing, and I don't want to blow them off. But you can come with us," I blurted.

He worked up a sad smile. "I don't go clubbing, Riley."

Right. I didn't want to turn him down, and yet I didn't want to disappoint my friends either.

"We'll have dinner another time," he went on.

"Thanks. I'm going to see if Jeremy needs help finding his pillow."

"Sure."

Just then the doorbell rang, and Duncan went to open it. His mother stepped in. "Hi, Riley. How's everyone treating you?"

"Great. Things are good. Jeremy is so excited for his sleep-over at your place."

She beamed. "Of course he is. And so am I."

"I'm just going to see if he's ready," I said. "He needed to get his magic pillow."

"Oh yes. Don't worry, Riley, I'll go." Susan walked straight to Jeremy's bedroom.

"I'll come with you," I said. "I want to tell him goodbye before I leave."

"Sure."

"Actually," Duncan said, "I have a proposition."

I looked up at him. My heart stuttered.

"Since Mom is taking Jeremy anyway, why don't I drive you home?"

I shook my head. "You don't have to do that."

"Oh, let the man drive you if he's offering to. It'll be quicker," Susan said from the doorway.

"All right," I said. My stomach was full of butterflies. I was super nervous, but I also was looking forward to spending a bit of time with Duncan even though it wasn't the way either of us had imagined.

Susan and I went to Jeremy's bedroom. He'd taken out half the contents of his closet and piled it on the bed.

"Jeremy, what's the meaning of this?" Susan asked.

He turned around, eyes streaked with tears. "I don't know where my magic pillow is. I can't leave without it."

My heart broke for the poor little guy. How could he be so inconsolable about a pillow?

"Jeremy, don't worry. We'll find it, okay?" I said.

He nodded. "I just don't know where it is."

"Let's go through things together. Where have you looked?"

"Everywhere," he said.

That was impossible, of course.

"I'll check as well, okay?"

I looked at the dresser, but it wasn't anywhere. Then I opened all the drawers of the tallboy next to his bed and glanced under the bed itself.

"I'm going to check in the playroom," I said.

"Okay," Jeremy replied between sobs.

The magic pillow was in the lap of his favorite giant panda bear. "Found it!" I called, then immediately headed back.

Jeremy ran toward me, grabbing the pillow from my hand as I stepped inside the room. He pressed it to his chest. "Thank you, Riley."

"Now, let's put everything back before we leave," Susan said. Her voice wasn't stern at all, but Jeremy immediately nodded and started folding his clothes.

Between the three of us, it took no time at all. When we returned to the living room, Duncan was already waiting by the door, car keys in hand.

"Dad, are you coming with us?" Jeremy asked suspiciously.

"No, I'm driving Riley home."

"Oh, okay. Let's go, Grandma," he said. "Bye, Riley. Bye, Dad."

After Susan and Jeremy walked out the door, Duncan shook his head. "Look at him. Mom comes and I'm like a second-class citizen."

"Don't take it so personally," I teased. "He's just happy to be with his grandmother."

After I gathered my tote, we left the condo too. Without Jeremy around, I was more nervous. I knew this was a dangerous path. I couldn't relax around Duncan and needed my guard up.

We were both silent on the way to the car, though I was aware of his every move. He was walking in step with me, and I was fighting every instinct not to lean in closer.

Once inside the car, I took a deep breath. It smelled like him.

Oh, this wasn't the best idea. Why didn't I make an excuse and leave when his mom arrived?

Because deep down, you do want to be alone with him, a little voice said at the back of my mind.

Damn it, that was true.

"Thank you for taking me home, Duncan. You didn't have to do that," I said as he started the engine. He'd initially prodded me to use the car he'd gotten for Jeremy's excursions anytime I needed it, but I didn't want to take advantage of him. Nor did I want anything to happen to the car on my watch. Occasionally, it was still a point of contention.

He turned to me. "No, but this was the only way I could spend some more time with you."

Wow, this was happening. We weren't dancing around each other anymore.

As I pushed a strand of hair behind my ear, he took my other hand, brushing his thumb over the back of it.

"Is this uncomfortable for you? Am I making you nervous?"

"No, not at all. I really want you to know that I'm not brushing you off tonight, but I promised them that I'd come."

"I understand perfectly. I'm a man of my word too."

My skin simmered at his touch, and not just the exact patch of skin where he was pressing his thumb. The heat was spreading everywhere, and I couldn't stop it. I didn't know how, and I also didn't want to. I didn't have any willpower left.

Letting go of my hand, he started driving, focusing on the road. "I should have told you when I first came up with the idea."

"Wait, you've thought about this? When?"

"All damn week. You don't know how often you're on my mind, Riley."

"I tried to leave quickly every evening, not that that actually happened..." Because I didn't want to. I liked the time we spent together.

"I didn't want that either. I enjoy spending time with you."

It was on the tip of my tongue to ask more, but I didn't. "We can set something up for next week. To talk more, I mean," I rambled.

Damn it, why was there no traffic? We were going to reach the house in no time, and it wasn't even that close. Was he driving that fast? I needed to spend more time with him.

"Yes, we will," he said. "Fuck, I can't believe I don't get to spend the evening with you." He drew in a sharp breath. His voice was even huskier than before.

"Come with us," I offered again.

"Don't tempt me." He swallowed hard, glancing at me. "I'm nine years older than you. How would that look, if I went with you and your friends? Clubbing isn't exactly my scene."

I didn't get it. It wasn't just twentysomethings who went to beach clubs. I bit the inside of my cheek, but I didn't insist. If he didn't want to join us, then I wasn't going to force the issue.

The car slowed down as we reached the house.

"Damn it," I said.

"What's wrong?"

"Don't you want to take a detour or something?"

He frowned. "What?"

I sighed. "I was hoping the drive would take longer."

He groaned. "Riley, stop right there, or instead of dropping you off, I will drive you right back to the condo for *dinner*."

The way he said the word made it clear that he had plans far beyond dinner. Sexy plans.

Ugh. Why did I agree to go out with my roommates?

Though right now, I wouldn't mind *in the least* if he whisked me back to the condo and did whatever he wanted to with me. But I didn't get a chance because Christine ran out of the house and opened the car door with a grin.

"Finally! We thought you'd never come home. Thank you for bringing her, Duncan." She winked at him.

"My pleasure." His voice sounded robotic.

"Thank you. I'll see you on Monday," I murmured as I got out of the car.

He just nodded.

Maybe this is for the better. Maybe we'll both cool off by Monday.

Somehow, though, I doubted it. Because there was more I wanted to learn about my boss too.

————

"You're not really having fun, are you?" Julia asked two hours later.

"What makes you say that?" I *was* counting down the minutes until I could make an excuse and go home. But I didn't want my friends to feel guilty, so I said, "Come on, let's do some shots."

Julia winked at me. We'd done two rounds, so I was already on thin ice. I thought having a drink or two would make me enjoy this more, but no such luck.

Objectively, it was nice. The music was pleasant, and I liked that it was in an open space. But in all honesty, this had never been my scene. Partying always felt like a waste of time, not to mention that I was always exhausted the day after. But I liked spending time with my friends, so I braved it for them.

After the third shot, Julia decided we needed a fourth one too.

I was going to get drunk if I continued at this pace, but oh, what the hell. This summer was the last one we had as college girls before we started our jobs. It was probably one of the last times we were going to do this, and I wanted to enjoy it even though I'd much rather have spent the evening doing something else.

Usually, I would have curled up with a good book, but now other things came to mind. I could have watched some cartoons with Jeremy and done his evening routine—though by this time, he'd have long been in bed. Then perhaps Duncan and I could have stayed up chatting, maybe while drinking a glass of wine.

Damn it. I should have forgone this evening to hang out with him.

"You're in deep thought," Julia said. "Do I want to know what you're thinking?"

I shook my head.

"Yeah, I thought so. I bet you're wondering why you're even here."

I pouted. "Is it that obvious?"

She laughed. "I just know you very well."

"I don't want to be a party pooper."

"Then let's dance."

And dance we did. But the four shots went right to my head, and I couldn't keep it up for very long.

"I'm going to sit for a bit," I informed them.

"All right," Julia replied. "Want me to sit with you?" She and Christine were dancing as if their lives depended on it.

"No, no. It's all good. You two have fun."

I went to the edge of the perimeter where they'd set up some low chairs and dropped into one of them. Out of reflex more than anything else, I took my phone out of my clutch, checking if I had any missed calls. Although, who would have called me at this hour?

I pressed the button that showed me the last calls and sighed, focusing on Duncan's name. Next thing I knew, I was calling him.

Holy shit. How the hell did that happen?

I tried to press the red button to end the call before it rang at all, but I kept missing the button, and then Duncan's voice resounded through the speaker.

"Riley? Is everything okay?"

I put the phone to my ear. "I'm so sorry. I called you by mistake. Just go back to sleep."

"I wasn't sleeping. Where are you?"

I licked my lips. "Still at the club."

"Everything okay?"

"Yes. I took a break from dancing and sat down. I've had four shots already."

"Jesus!" he exclaimed.

"Hey, what's with the judgy tone?"

"Not judging. I'm worried."

"I'd say you have no reason, but I'm not very good at holding my liquor. I don't get sick or anything, but I can feel myself getting a bit drowsy. Anyway, I was looking at the phone and got to thinking how much I would have rather spent this evening with Jeremy and then just with you alone..."

I stopped talking, covering my mouth with my hand. *Oh my goodness. I said that out loud?*

Maybe I just imagined it.

"Fuck, you're sweet."

Okay, I didn't imagine it. "I'm sorry I blurted that out. I can't stop thinking about you." Clearly, I couldn't keep myself in check. That was the unfortunate effect tequila had on me.

"Riley!" His voice was lower. "I've been thinking about you nonstop. Oh fuck..."

"I'm sorry I started this conversation. I don't want to make this uncomfortable. I should probably go home."

"I'll pick you up."

Tendrils of heat immediately went through me.

"You want to drive out here and pick me up? I can just Uber."

"I don't want you getting in a car with some stranger right now."

That made me laugh. "That's the point of Uber, and it's safe. It's—"

"I won't hear of it. I want to be the one to drive you home. Are your friends coming too?"

"No, they'll probably be here until the morning."

My heart was beating out of my chest. I was going to have some alone time with Duncan after all. Suddenly, I didn't want to fight him on this anymore. If he wanted to pick me up, who was I to say no?

"I'll text you the address of the club, if I can manage it."

"Just tell me roughly where it is."

I gave him instructions, and he said, "I'll find it. I'll be there as quickly as possible."

"Thank you, Duncan."

There was something between us—and it wasn't just chemistry. I didn't know what it was... but I wanted to find out.

CHAPTER THIRTEEN

Duncan

Five minutes after our call ended, I was in the car, speeding through the city.

Tonight had been a bust. Whenever Jeremy was away, I either hung out with my brothers or worked out for an extended period. But I hadn't wanted to do either. I could have worked because there was always something to do for the office. My to-do list was endless—I'd learned years ago that attempting to get it down to zero was a futile exercise and only led to frustration—but I rarely worked from home, and I hadn't cared to do it tonight.

After grabbing a quick dinner, I'd spent about half an hour on the treadmill, then moved to the weights section. And yet my mind was still on Riley.

I had to get a grip on myself, but not even a cold shower achieved that. I'd wanted her tonight. I'd been looking forward to this evening the whole week. Why the hell didn't I give her a heads-up?

Excitement coursed through my veins. I needed to see Riley, plain and simple, and I was going to stop fighting that fact.

Fifteen minutes later, I arrived at the address she'd texted me. There was a parking lot across the road. It was surprisingly empty, but then I noticed cabs and other cars only briefly stopping in front of the entrance and then taking off. Clearly everyone was Ubering, since they'd planned to drink.

The music was loud but not overpowering, since it was out in the open. I looked around. Riley had told me she was at the high table right next to the bar. I found her instantly. She looked absolutely stunning, wearing a short silver dress with a dipping back. She was barefoot on the sand.

Christine noticed me, and Riley immediately looked over her shoulder before turning around. Sex appeal rolled off her. Her hair was bound up in a high ponytail that came down in waves.

I walked straight toward her. I was so fixated on her that I didn't even realize her friends had left until I reached the table and it was just the two of us.

"Here I am."

"Thank you for coming."

I wanted to tell her so many things, but I didn't. Instead, I put a hand on her waist and moved to the rhythm of the music. She leaned into my touch, following my lead, exhaling sharply.

Because she was much smaller than me, her hot breath landed on my neck. It turned me on to no end. It was all I could do not to kiss her right now.

"You're a great dancer," she murmured, clearly surprised.

But I was just following my instincts. I *needed* to be close, and this was the perfect excuse. Then I turned her around, plastering her back against my chest, moving even slower. She was intoxicating.

I dipped my nose in the crook of her neck. "You smell amazing," I whispered in her ear.

She looked up at me sideways. Her lips were so damn inviting.

I closed the distance between us, kissing her the way I'd meant to all fucking week. She tasted like champagne. I didn't hold back at all. I explored her while we still moved to the rhythm of the music.

My entire body felt like a live wire, like she was fueling me. I couldn't get enough of her taste. I wanted to pin her against the table and kiss her until she wrapped her legs around me.

Fuck, why had I started this in public? I needed to touch her so damn badly, but I didn't want to make a spectacle of us.

I moved one hand from her hip up her belly, keeping it there. It rose up and down with her breath, which became more labored. I moved my palm farther up until my thumb rested on her sternum, my fingers on her left breast. Her heartbeat thundered beneath my touch.

I pulled back and cleared my throat. "Ready to go home?"

She nodded.

Fuck, I shouldn't have been kissing her. She'd had too much to drink.

You only came here to make sure she got home in one piece, Duncan. To make sure she was fine, not to take advantage of her.

Fucking hell.

"Yes, although now that you're here, I could be talked into staying. Actually," she said, clearly having a conversation with herself, "no, let's go home."

"I love the way you change your mind."

"I can't wait to be alone with you."

Christ, she was even more inebriated than I'd thought. Riley wasn't usually this forward.

You're the older one here, Duncan. You have to draw the line and enforce it, and you are the one who's sober.

"I'll take you home" was all I said. I put an arm around her waist as I led her out of the club and to the car.

"You're such a gentleman, coming across town just to pick me up."

"I wanted to make sure you're okay."

"I was, but now I'm doing even better," she said.

As we walked, it became even more obvious that she had some issues keeping her balance.

"Did you drink any more since we talked? Because four tequilas shouldn't—"

"I know," she cut me off. " I don't know why tequilas always made my knees weak. Or maybe that's you, with all those muscles wrapped around—"

"Fucking hell, Riley," I groaned.

"Oh goodness! Okay. Let's make a deal. Let's pretend on Monday that none of this happened, okay?"

I laughed. "If that makes you feel better."

"It really does."

"Then sure."

She's working for you. She's younger. What the hell are you even thinking?

I helped her into the car, then went around to the driver's side and climbed in. With a quick glance her way, I started the car and headed toward the main road.

I was certain that she'd fall asleep on the way, but she didn't. Instead, she simply looked at me and said, "This is so nice."

"What?"

She shrugged. "Feeling that you care enough to come pick me up."

I swallowed hard. "Of course I care, Riley. I want you to be safe." That contradicted my previous actions, since I'd mauled her right there in the club, but... "Whenever you need anything, just let me know."

"Why?" she whispered.

"You know why."

"Well, I don't. That's why I'm asking."

I drew in a deep breath just as we arrived in front of her house. "Let's get you safely inside."

She let out a huff that sounded like frustration and hopped out of the car by herself. I hurried to her side, putting a hand on her waist, but she wasn't swaying as much as before. I moved my hand around to her lower back as I gently guided her toward the front door.

As she opened it, she sighed and said, "I think I'm going to be sick."

"I'll walk with you."

"No, no. I don't want you to see."

We both went inside the house nonetheless, which she didn't protest.

After a moment, she took in a deep breath and said, "Nope, false alarm." Then she turned to face me. The house was semi-dark, the only light coming from one of the open doors. "You didn't answer me."

I was close to her—far too close. "Was the kiss at the club not answer enough?"

She shook her hand, biting her lower lip. "I need words, Duncan."

"I don't have them," I admitted.

She dropped her shoulders, tilting her chin to the floor. I put my thumb under it, lifting it so I could watch her.

"I'm not a man of many words," I said. "And everything that's gone on since I met you... it's not how I do things. I don't allow myself to..."

"To what?"

I wasn't even sure how to explain this to her, which was insane. My brothers often mocked me that I was very good at explaining everything, even unnecessary things. But right now, words failed me.

"I'm so attracted to you that I can't think straight, Riley."

Her face exploded in a grin. "See, that's what I'm talking about."

She put her hands on my shoulders. "You know, at the club, I thought I was making up in my mind how fantastic these muscles are. Even though I saw you at the pool. But they are quite exquisite."

I groaned. "Riley, if you keep touching me, I'll lose control."

"So, what's the problem?"

"You've had too much to drink, and I don't want to take advantage of that."

She pouted. "I liked you better when you said that you can't think straight. See, this is you being cerebral again. I don't like it. So much logic standing in the way of sexy times."

I laughed, and that seemed to bring her to her senses.

"Just another thing to strike off the list, okay? By Monday, this never happened," she said.

And that was the crux of the issue. I didn't want her to do anything she would regret.

"Riley, go to sleep, okay?"

"But I don't want to because if this evening ends, then this is all we had. A kiss. And I want more."

This woman, did she even know what she was doing to me? How much I wanted her anyway?

I kissed her forehead. "Go to sleep, beautiful. I'll be in touch tomorrow."

"You promise?

"I so fucking will."

CHAPTER FOURTEEN

Duncan

The next morning, I woke up early as usual and did a full workout before I had my first coffee. Last night was still on repeat in my mind. I'd been so fucking close to giving in to Riley.

But she'd been too far gone, and that wasn't how I wanted to do things anyway. It was futile to even think I could resist this attraction to her. Which meant there was only one thing to do: give in to it. Or at least admit it.

Well, I'd already admitted it when I mauled her in the club, so I was way past that.

The logical part of my brain was still fighting it. *She's younger. She's my son's nanny. I don't date.* And yet none of that mattered. None of it. I simply wanted Riley.

I texted her that afternoon.

> Duncan: Are you up? Do you have a headache?

> Riley: I'm up. Just a slight headache and a lot of embarrassment.

I immediately called her.

"No reason to be embarrassed," I said instead of hello.

"I could think of a few."

"Everything can be forgotten, as you said."

Fuck! I didn't want that. But she'd been the one who'd explicitly asked for it. If she wanted to forget everything, that's what we would do.

"Well, I technically said we should forget it on Monday. Today is Saturday."

"We can still forget if you want to."

"I don't!"

Hell yes. I felt damn victorious.

"If I weren't drunk, what would have happened last night?"

I considered the question carefully while I looked at the coffee machine, even though I wasn't really seeing it.

"Nothing," I concluded.

"Oh."

"I don't want to rush things, Riley. This is already happening at a maddening speed. I never want us to do something you would regret."

"So, where does that leave us?"

"What are you doing today?" I asked.

"Don't have plans, honestly. Although, I might go to a movie in the afternoon."

"I'll take you to the movie."

I wanted to spend time with her. I couldn't deny that to myself anymore. Just the two of us, where we could talk and Jeremy wouldn't be around.

"What do you want to see?"

"Well, there's a new science fiction movie coming out," she said.

"Let's go see it."

"Are you serious?"

"Yes, Riley. I told you I'd be in touch today."

"I know, but I wasn't sure if you meant it or... You know

what? Never mind. I don't want to look a gift horse in the mouth. Let me just check when it's showing. There's a theater a few streets away from here that's usually not at all crowded." She paused for a few moments, probably checking the show times. "How about six o'clock?"

"That works. I'll take you to dinner after that."

She squealed, and I grinned at the sound. I liked that she had no problems expressing her excitement.

"I'll pick you up from home," I suggested.

"We could just meet there. I need to stretch my legs."

"Your call."

"Yeah, let's meet there."

After we ended the call, I took a shower, dressing in jeans and a polo shirt before heading out. I hadn't been this excited about anything in a while. Adrenaline rushed through my veins at the thought of spending the evening with Riley. It felt right despite the fact that I still had my reservations. All those reasons I had for keeping myself in check still existed, but I was starting to brush some of them away.

Sure, there were a few years between us, but Riley was more mature than her peers. She'd taken a lot of responsibility on her shoulders at a young age. I think that changed her. And she wasn't going to be Jeremy's nanny for too long, so that argument wasn't going to hold up.

Jesus, Duncan, you're just looking for excuses, that's all.

I arrived at the address she gave me with about fifteen minutes to spare. She wasn't here yet, so I went inside and bought two tickets. I hadn't been to a movie that wasn't something for kids in a while, so I was actually looking forward to this. After buying the tickets, I headed over to the counter selling popcorn and nachos.

"You're early," Riley exclaimed.

I turned around and nearly swallowed my tongue. She had a short yellow dress on, and it looked fucking amazing on her.

"What snack do you want?" I asked her.

She turned to the counter. "Nachos with cheese and salsa and some popcorn too," she rushed out in one breath.

"Your favorites?" I assumed.

I walked next to her and was about to put a hand on her lower back, then changed my mind. If I did that, I was going to maul her again, and that wouldn't do.

She nodded. "They are."

"I'll have the same," I said.

Five minutes later, we both entered the theater with enough food for five people. The room was only half full. We had excellent seats with a gap between our row and the next one in front of us. Plenty of legroom.

Riley was captivated the entire movie. Every time I looked at her, she was staring at the screen as if her life depended on hearing every word. She was adorable.

Once the movie ended, we threw away the empty food cartons. I had no idea how we'd managed to finish all of it.

Riley sighed. "What did you think?"

"I really liked it."

"I love science fiction movies. They sort of transport me to other worlds."

"Do you like to read science fiction books too?"

"Funnily enough, no. Usually, I read either fantasy or mystery. Sometimes romance, too, but not science fiction. That's something I enjoy most on a big screen."

"I want to take you out to dinner," I told her.

She pouted. If she continued to do that, I was going to capture that mouth.

"I'm too full."

I laughed. "Yeah, me too," I admitted, then stepped closer and touched my fingers to her cheek. "But I want to spend the rest of the evening with you."

"So do I." Her eyes sparkled as they looked into mine.

"Want to take a walk on the beach?"

"Yes, yes, yes!"

"We could watch the sunset too."

"I'd love that. It's fifteen minutes from here."

"Nah, let's take the car. Otherwise, we'll have to come back for it. We'll walk enough once we're there."

It only took us a few minutes by car to reach the beach. It was one of the reasons I loved living in San Diego. I didn't visit the beach very often, but I liked having that option. I'd never been to one in this area, though. I was surprised that it was almost deserted—just an older couple walking next to the water, holding hands. There were no surfers either.

"I love this salty smell," she said as we walked on the sand.

"So do I."

"Oh look, tacos," she exclaimed, pointing to a food truck at the edge of the beach. "I thought I was too full, but I can always make room for tacos."

I chuckled. "Your wish is my command."

She blushed slightly. Fuck yes, I loved that. "Come on, let's get you some tacos."

There was no line at the food truck, so we walked right up to the window to order.

"I want some with carnitas and chicken," she said.

"Just pork for me."

"Right away," the vendor said.

Riley rubbed her stomach. "I'm going to have a food belly, but I don't even care."

"You're damn gorgeous no matter what, Riley," I said.

She whipped her head to me, eyes slightly wide. "Something's changed," she whispered. "You speak more... openly. Did you lower your filter because I totally ran my mouth last night?"

I grinned. "That, too, and I lost the battle."

She blinked. "What battle?"

"With myself and all the reasons I had in my mind to stay away from you."

"Tacos are ready," the vendor said, interrupting us. The guy had atrocious timing.

After I paid, we took the food and moved a few feet away to a high bar table. We immediately devoured them.

"You're right. It's always a good time for tacos," I agreed.

Riley was eating with the same passion she'd eaten the nachos earlier. She nodded, grinning.

I could watch this woman do anything. Eat, watch a movie, or just read a book. I was captivated.

After we finished, I threw the cartons in the nearby bin and then grabbed her hand, moving her farther away from the stand so we could be alone.

"Hey, where are you taking me?"

"Away so that guy can't hear us or interrupt us."

"Oh, that's right. You were saying that you've lost the battle. So, what were those reasons?"

"Riley, look... Since Jeremy's mom and I and broke up, I didn't want to bring anyone into my son's life. Shona—"

"Your ex-wife?"

I shook my head. "We were never married. We were in a relationship, and we both wanted to make it work for Jeremy's sake. But then when it became clear that it wasn't going to be possible, we simply went on different paths."

Her eyes filled with compassion. "It's so nice that you did it amicably."

"It was what was best for him, and there's no bad blood between us. Though we do have some differences of opinions. For example, she has no problem dating, whereas I never wanted to confuse my son."

"Oh. I understand." She sounded slightly disappointed.

I swallowed hard. "But with you, it's different."

"How?" she whispered.

"Because this isn't just attraction, Riley." I took in a deep breath. "It's bigger, it's more powerful, and ignoring it is not the right thing."

"I completely agree. So, what else was on that list? It sounded like it was a number of things."

I frowned. "Does it really not bother you that I'm older than you?"

She rolled her eyes. "I thought it might, in the beginning. But it's not so important."

"Nine years is a lot."

"Yes, but it doesn't *feel* that way. Honestly, I don't care about it at all. I've never been like my friends. Not even in high school or college."

"But there are many differences that come with that age gap. You'll be starting your career soon."

"And I can't wait for that. But I don't think any of that means that we should..." Her words faded.

"Keep ourselves in check?" I finished for her in a teasing voice. "Behave?"

"Yeah, that. I think we've moved too far past behaving anyway."

I tilted closer to her and covered her mouth, exploring her slowly. Then I put my hands on her back, deepening our connection. I kissed her until she whimpered. I'd been craving another taste of her, had dreamed about it last night and woke up this morning with a fucking hard-on. I'd imagined how exquisite it would be to feel her mouth again. The reality was even better than that.

Soon, the kiss wasn't lazy anymore. It was fast and desperate.

I groaned, straightening. "I can't stop."

"Then don't."

"I fucking should, Riley. Because—" I kissed her forehead, feeling her shudder under my touch. "—I want us to watch the sunset."

She pulled back, looking at me. "Are you serious?"

"Yes. I want us to just enjoy this. Take our time."

She smiled. "I like this side of you so, so much."

I waggled my eyebrows. "You haven't seen anything yet. Let's sit on the sand and just watch it."

Since the beach was practically ours for the taking, we found a place that was farther away from the taco truck. I sat down behind her, keeping my arms wrapped around hers.

"This is so nice," she whispered. "I love sunsets on the beach."

"Me too," I said as we kept our eyes on the horizon. "Jesus, I haven't done this in I don't even know how long. It's a privilege to watch it with you."

"And you know how to say cool things," she whispered.

As we watched the sun disappear completely, something buzzed.

"Oh, that's my phone," she said. She reached into the small black bag she'd set next to her on the sand and took it out. "It's my sister. I never reject a call from her," she added apologetically.

"Don't do it on my behalf," I said. "I also don't ignore a call from the family." I liked that we had that in common.

She answered the phone immediately. "Hey, sister!"

Her face instantly transformed, and I knew something was wrong before she said one word.

CHAPTER FIFTEEN

Duncan

"Oh, my God. Right. Well, stay where you are, okay? Is there anyone else with you? Can you call the police?"

The police? What the fuck is going on?

"Then just stay indoors and don't open up, okay? It doesn't matter if he fires you. He should have fixed the fucking cameras. Be there soon to pick you up."

She was shaking when she hung up.

"What's wrong?"

"My sister works at a gas station. Someone just robbed the place, and the owner has no camera." Her voice broke. "I need to pick her up."

"Let's go together."

"What do you mean?"

"I've got my car. We'll drive there together. Do you want to call the police?"

"She already did."

"Is she okay? Did he do something to her?"

"He had a knife, but he just waved it around to scare her, thank God."

Riley was shaking badly. I kept my hand on her shoulder all the way to the car.

"Where exactly does your sister work?" I asked her once we were inside.

"I'll put the address here." She typed it into my app.

"That's a seedy area."

"I know. And she lives there too," Riley said in a small voice as I drove off. To my dismay, her eyes watered. "That's why I was hoping to get the job right away instead of waiting for the stupid bar exam results. I want to be able to help her out so she doesn't have to live in that godawful place. She's working three jobs to put herself through school. It sucks. I've done it for five years, and I don't want my little sister to go through the same thing."

She'd clasped her hands together in her lap, and I covered them with mine. She was shaking even worse than before. I'd never felt a connection as deep as I did to Riley. The fact that she didn't want her sister to face the same spoke volumes about her.

"I promise we'll figure this out, okay? Don't you worry. First, let's go check on your sister. Don't blame yourself."

"I should have convinced her to move in with me, but she's so stubborn."

"She didn't want to?"

"No. She said that, since she's eighteen, she should be able to get by on her own."

"San Diego is an expensive city."

"That's why she found that hellhole to live in. I even offered to give up my room at the house and move somewhere else, or even share it, but she wouldn't hear of it."

I'd never heard Riley so distressed.

"Listen. No matter how much we care for people, we can't force them to do what we think is best. All we can do is support them."

"I know," she said, wiping away her tears.

"Please don't cry. I want to make you feel better."

She turned to me, smiling. "Thank you for driving me there. I promise I'll get my shit together before I'm back to work on Monday."

I stared at her. "Riley, I'm not going to leave you to deal with this alone. We'll figure out things together."

She just stared at me, but at least she didn't fight me on it.

We arrived at our destination twenty minutes later.

"Where are the police?" I asked.

"I don't know, but that's her boss's car." She pointed to a fucking Range Rover.

What the hell? The man didn't even bother to repair the cameras, but he was driving a Range Rover? I was seeing red.

I parked the car, looking around carefully. The area seemed deserted.

Riley jumped out before I'd even turned off the engine. Damn! I followed her quickly inside the store. A woman who looked a lot like Riley stood behind the counter. Range Rover guy seemed no older than midtwenties with very short hair and three rings in his left eyebrow.

"I don't care. Your shift is until midnight," he was saying as we entered.

"I'm too shaken. Honestly, I don't think I can stay here for that long."

He shook his head. "I can't believe you called the fucking police."

"What is going on?" I asked.

Riley immediately went to her sister's side.

He turned to me, face red. "What is this? Who are you?"

"I'm her sister," Riley said, rolling back her shoulders.

"You asked your *sister* over? This is your place of work. What the fuck?" he growled.

"You can't talk to her like that," I said.

He straightened up and puffed out his chest. "Who the fuck do you think you are? This is my business."

"Yes, and clearly you have no idea how to talk to your employees. She was robbed. You can't expect her to continue working."

"Nothing happened to her, but the guy did take some of my cash. She'll have to work for free until she makes it back," he sneered.

"No, she won't," I said. "That's not how this works."

"It fucking does if she wants to keep her job."

"No. I'm a lawyer," Riley said.

The guy froze. Fuck, was I proud of Riley.

"You haven't even taken steps to ensure your employees' security because you're too cheap to repair that camera. She's not liable for anything except suing your fucking ass."

"She wouldn't do that."

"Oh yes, she would. You know why? Because she'd have a lawyer pro bono."

I'd never seen Riley like this. She'd been so lost in the car, but now she was 100 percent confident.

"You don't need this job, do you? What with your fancy-ass lawyer sister. Why the fuck would you even take it?"

"You say one more word and I'm going to knock your teeth out," I told him.

I didn't give a fuck if that made things worse or not. He couldn't treat anyone like that. I despised people who thought their employees were their servants and expected them to put his profit above everything else, including their health and safety.

"All right, fine. I changed my mind. You can leave," he said, looking straight at Riley's sister. "Don't bother coming back."

She was red in the face, and for a split second, I thought she might burst into tears, but instead she cleared her throat.

"You know what? My pleasure. Everyone warned me not to

take this job, but I was stubborn. But I'm not going to risk my life for $8 an hour."

She looked up at Riley and said, "Let's go."

Both of them rounded the corner. The guy looked like he wanted to do something, but I stepped in front of him.

"Shut your fucking mouth."

He jerked his head back. "Out of my store."

"Gladly," I snapped.

He looked behind me at Riley and her sister. "What the fuck am I supposed to do? Man my own counter?"

They didn't bother to reply.

I snorted, walking right behind them with quick steps. I didn't want them to be alone outside for a split second.

Once we were all in the car, I turned around to look at her sister and then at Riley, who was sitting next to her, holding her hand.

"Paula, are you hurt?" Riley asked her.

Paula shook her head. "No, he didn't do anything to me. I'm just shaken and pissed off."

"Of course you are," Riley said. "I can't believe that asshole. You are not going back there even if he begs you to, understand?"

"I'm not planning to," Paula said. "But I'll have to find something else quickly so I can pay my rent."

"We'll think about this in the morning, okay? This is Duncan, by the way."

"Jeremy's dad?" She dropped her head back against the seat. "Oh my God, I'm sorry you had to see all that."

I smiled softly. "No problem."

"Uhh... I don't live far from here."

"Don't you want to come to my place?" Riley asked.

Paula shook her head. "No. I love your roommates, but I can never relax around them. I feel like they always look weird at me when I'm there, like I'm encroaching on their space."

Riley jerked her head back. "What? You never told me that. I'm sure they'd understand the situation."

"Don't insist. I just want to go home and sleep."

"All right, I'm your driver for the evening," I said, trying to lighten the mood. "What's your address?"

The second she told me what it was, I understood why Riley wasn't so thrilled. It wasn't exactly a dump, but it wasn't safe.

Five minutes later, we arrived in front of a small building that looked to house about five or six apartments. Riley and I walked Paula to the door. I kept looking around, keeping an eye out for anything suspicious.

"Are you sure you don't want me to stay with you?" Riley asked.

Paula turned around and sighed. "Duncan, please help me."

I cleared my throat. "Actually, I don't think that's a bad idea."

Riley looked over her shoulder at me with a very grateful expression.

Paula glared at me. "Yeah, no. Damn it, you're not helping at all." She turned to face her sister. "Riley, I just want to process this on my own, okay?" Paula put her hands on Riley's shoulders. "And you know I do that best when I'm alone."

"You're even more stubborn than me," Riley said, kissing her sister's cheek.

After Paula closed the door, Riley sniffled. "Can we go?" she whispered. "I don't want her to hear me."

"Sure."

I put an arm around her shoulders and led her out of the building. I surveyed the street, but it was completely deserted, and I couldn't see any headlights. She got into the car quickly, and I hurried into the driver's seat.

Riley was dabbing at her eyes when I started the engine.

"Damn it, I was so scared," she said.

I took her hand, kissing it. "I'm sorry."

"And I tried to hold it together for Paula, but it's just... He could have hurt her, you know?"

"But nothing happened," I said.

I had unbelievable respect for her. Watching her back at the station and even at Paula's apartment, I couldn't even tell she'd been scared or that she'd been holding in tears. Clearly, she had practice at being strong for her sister.

"I can take care of that moron, make sure he won't bother her again," I said.

Riley swallowed hard. "That's really nice of you, but I don't think it's necessary. I can't wait to finally start as a lawyer. She'll never take a job that puts her in danger again." She yawned and sank lower in her seat. "I don't want to go home. The house is empty. Julia and Christine went clubbing again."

"You're coming with me," I said.

"What?" She jerked her head up. "No, that's not what I was implying. I'll be fine."

"Riley, you're in no state to be on your own."

"My roommates will be there... eventually."

"They're at the club. You need a good night's sleep. They'll come back late and make noise."

She hesitated for a moment, then sighed heavily. "Honestly, I don't really want to be by myself tonight. I suggested staying with Paula as much for her benefit as for mine."

"Besides, I'm better company than drunk roommates," I replied.

"I have to say, you're very convincing." She gave me a small smile. "I'm all yours tonight, Duncan."

CHAPTER SIXTEEN

Duncan

I held Riley's hand while I sped through the city. When I arrived in my parking lot, she got out of the car before I even managed to walk to her door. Clearly, she couldn't stay put.

As we headed to the entrance, I placed my arm around her shoulders again. She leaned into me completely.

She didn't say one word while I led her upstairs. But once we stepped inside the apartment, she turned to me. "Duncan, you think this is a good idea? I'm sorry, I didn't think this through at all. Jeremy—"

"Jeremy is with my mom," I said slowly.

"Oh, right, I forgot." She closed her eyes and took in a deep breath. "God, I'm all over the place."

"Riley, relax. I have everything under control."

The fight went right out of her. I felt the tension releasing from her body.

"You want a drink?" I offered.

She nodded vigorously. "I think it might help."

"I think so too." I took her hand, leading her into the

kitchen. She sat on one of the breakfast chairs. "What do you want? I can open a bottle of wine."

"I think something stronger might be better."

"Bourbon on the rocks?"

"That sounds good," she said, resting her chin on one palm.

I poured my best bourbon and added two ice cubes before sliding it to her. She gripped the glass with both hands, taking a huge sip.

"Not so fast," I advised.

"You're right. But I can practically feel my legs relaxing."

"That's good." I walked to the other side of the counter, standing next to her. When she looked up at me, I put my hand on her cheek, and she sighed.

"Thank you for coming with me tonight."

"You didn't even need me. You were amazing back there."

She swallowed hard. "Yeah, but that was because you were there. I don't know how to explain it. Somehow, just knowing you were around made me feel stronger. Like I was drawing my strength from you. Does that make sense?"

"Yes, it fucking does," I assured her.

"I was angry but also so scared. I kept looking at my sister for any signs that she was hurt while putting the douchebag in his place."

"And you so fucking did. I'm proud of you."

I brushed my lips against hers. I was so damn hungry for her. I needed to explore her, but first I had to get everything out of the way.

Taking the glass of whiskey out of her hands, I placed it on the counter, then deepened the kiss. She moaned against my mouth, moving closer to the edge of the chair, leaning into me. I parted her legs, stepping between them. Fuck, I needed to kiss her until I made her come. I wanted this woman with every fiber of my being. I craved her—her nearness, her body.

I moved my mouth down her neck, tracing the column down to her cleavage, then pushed out the tip of my tongue, licking the skin on her breasts. She got even wilder, putting her hand at the back of my head, pressing me into her. I smiled against her skin.

"Duncan," she pleaded.

I nearly lost control then and there. I straightened up, looking her in the eyes. "Riley, if I keep kissing you, I won't be able to hold back."

"Please don't. I want everything with you," she said.

"Are you sure? You're very sensitive tonight. You've been through a lot."

"I know, but it doesn't matter. I'm sure of what I want."

"And what is that?" I double-checked. I needed to hear her say it in her own words.

"You. I want you, Duncan."

Her words triggered something inside me. I was going to make her the happiest woman tonight.

"Are you sure?" I asked one last time. I needed the answer to be an absolute resounding yes.

She leaned closer, sealing her mouth over mine as she placed her hand on the zipper of my jeans, cupping my cock. Even through all the layers of clothes, I groaned. That was the answer I was looking for. Feeling her hand over my erection was insanely good. It didn't exactly bring me satisfaction, but it gave me a taste of what was to come.

I kissed her lips and her neck again. I wanted to get her out of her clothes, but I didn't want to do it here. If I saw her naked in the middle of the living room, I'd fuck her right here against the bar. She deserved more than that, so I led her into the bedroom. I also took the glass of whiskey with us. I had plans for it.

"You can still change your mind," I said because I wanted to give her every opportunity possible to voice any doubts.

The last thing I wanted was for her to feel rushed into this. I could wait a few weeks more, or at least another night when she wasn't so overwhelmed from everything that happened earlier.

"Duncan, I want you. Nothing will change that."

I kissed her hard, exploring her with my tongue. Pushing the dress up to her waist, I drew my fingers over her long, soft legs. Her skin was amazing. I couldn't wait to kiss, lick, and explore it, but so far, we both liked the effect my hands had on her. Her skin changed from soft to sensitive. I purposely didn't touch her buttocks or between her legs, not yet; I wanted her to need my touch so badly that she begged for it.

I paused long enough to pull her dress over her head and realized she wasn't wearing a bra. The dress must have had one incorporated or something, because her breasts spilled out, and I suddenly became even harder than before. In fact, I had to undo the button of my jeans because it was too painful.

"You're fucking beautiful, you know that?" I said, cupping her left breast and lowering myself until it was in my face.

I sucked the nipple into my mouth, and she cried out my name as I palmed her other breast. She was feisty, and I fucking loved it. I sat on the bed, pulling her between my thighs. I was still face-to-face with her chest, but I also had good access to her pussy. I touched her inner thighs before cupping her pussy over the fabric of her panties.

She gasped, rocking her hips back and forth, rubbing herself against my fingers at her own pace. Her panties were wet—I needed them drenched. I kept moving my fingers, watching her gorgeous face.

I dipped my other hand into the whiskey glass, taking out one of the ice cubes. She was so focused on the friction between her thighs that she wouldn't anticipate this at all. That would only make the pleasure more intense.

I placed the ice cube under her clavicle, sliding it down to her navel. She cried out, pushing herself even more into my hand. I sucked one nipple into my mouth. She completely drenched her panties the next second.

Fuck yes. That was exactly what I wanted—for her to be completely wet before I slid inside her.

I kissed down her body, stopping when I reached her navel, taking my mouth off her.

"No! Why?" she protested.

"I want to see your pussy."

I yanked her panties down with too much force, because there was a ripping sound. They didn't fall apart, but I was certain I'd damaged them. Riley didn't seem to realize it.

She was shaved clean. I was close to exploding in my pants. I couldn't wait to bury my tongue inside her. Sitting her at the edge of the bed, I kneeled in front of her.

"I want to taste you right now."

I pressed my tongue on her opening, and she moaned so loud that I knew she wasn't going to last long. She would come right away.

As she writhed on the bed, I realized I still had my jeans on. *Fuck, what was I thinking?*

I pushed them down just enough for my erection to hang free, then focused on Riley. She rocked back and forth on the mattress, her thighs shaking. She was very close to an orgasm. It filled me with pride that I'd brought her to this point so quickly.

I alternated between sucking her clit and massaging it with my thumb while I pushed my tongue inside her. She seemed to enjoy both equally. I wanted to give her everything she needed— my fingers and my tongue.

I knew she was about to come before her gasp filled the room. She frowned, and the corners of her mouth turned downward, almost as if she was in pain. But I knew she was simply overwhelmed by pleasure. She dug her nails into the mattress. When she pushed her hips off the bed, I knew it was time.

I pressed the flat of my tongue against her clit and slid one finger inside her. I'd always thought Riley was beautiful, but her orgasming on my tongue was truly a sight to behold.

She thrashed around wildly. I held both thighs with my hands and worked her with my mouth, nipping her clit again and again until her cries calmed down and her ragged breaths filled the air.

I'd never felt this kind of satisfaction. I was hard as hell and completely on edge. When her breathing normalized, she opened her eyes.

"I need you, Riley."

"Yes. Please. Please. I need you right now too."

"I need to get a condom," I said.

She pressed her thighs closer to my head and asked, "Did you get tested recently?"

"Yes, I'm clean."

"Okay, because I got tested not too long ago. And I have an IUD, so we don't need a condom. Unless you want one."

"I so fucking don't." I rose to my feet, putting a knee on the mattress. "Are you sure about this?"

"Please, I want you."

I only had enough self-control to push my jeans farther down so I had some flexibility in my knees, and then I yanked one leg out. I didn't bother with the other, just climbed on the bed next to her.

She attempted to open the buttons of my shirt. I heard a ripping sound, too, but I didn't care. She'd only managed to undo them until she was at my navel, and then I rubbed my crown up and down her entrance as she put her hands on my ass.

She took in a sharp breath, then glanced between us. "You're huge!"

"That's why I wanted you to be ready, Riley. To be completely soaked for me."

"I am. I think I can take you in."

I slid in a few inches. "Fuuuuuck." She was so damn tight. I forced myself to breathe in and out. The sensations were overwhelming. I hadn't expected to feel this way from the very beginning.

"Can I push in more?" I asked through gritted teeth.

"Yes, yes. But just a bit for now."

"Don't worry, Riley, I'd never hurt you. I give you my word."

"I believe you," she whispered.

I slid in another inch. She gasped. "This is so good. I need more."

I watched her intently as I moved so slowly that it was fucking torture. But anything was better than hurting her. I'd go through fucking hellfire before I saw any harm come to this woman. I still had a few inches to go.

"More! I want more! I want all of you."

I entered her all the way to the hilt. Her cry split the air, but it was one of pleasure. I didn't move for almost a minute so she could get used to me, but then I couldn't hold back anymore. I thrust my hips with precision. She clasped the pillow above her head.

"Oooooh!"

I wouldn't have believed she'd come again so fast. I didn't manage to brace myself. When her inner muscles clenched around me, I nearly came too.

Watching her lose herself to me a second time so soon was exquisite.

I wasn't going to show her any mercy. I'd make her come until she couldn't take any more. My own orgasm pulsed through me, but I was determined to bring her over the edge a third time.

As she started to calm down, I reached into the glass and took what was left of the ice. It wasn't much, but it was enough for what I needed. I let it slide between our bodies. Riley's eyes were open in shock as I plastered my chest to hers. The cold and hot sensation was delicious. Her skin broke into goose bumps.

I pushed myself up on my knees and put one of her ankles on my shoulder. She planted the other one on the mattress. Then I lifted her ass, putting a pillow under it. I rolled my hips forward, and she cried out.

"How is this even deeper?" she gasped.

I could feel my orgasm coiling through me already. Knowing I didn't have much time left, I pressed two fingers on her clit and moved them slowly. It was too sensitive, so I didn't want to press too hard. She came just as hard as last time.

I relished watching her come. Five seconds later, my own release took over. Pleasure ripped through me—it started in my cock but spread like wildfire.

I lowered the leg that was on my shoulder and then hunched over Riley, driving inside her like a madman. I wanted to ride this wave out completely. My vision went dark for a few seconds, and when I regained it, I realized I couldn't make out any sounds.

Then my senses sharpened again, and I took in everything about this moment: the way my body succumbed to the climax —and to *her*. The way Riley opened up beautifully without holding back. I loved how her face changed and the cries coming out of her. I couldn't do anything except move in and out of her slowly. I was unable to break our connection until I was so spent that I lay on top of her and kissed the side of her neck. Her skin was warm and salty.

A few minutes later, we went into the master bathroom and cleaned up quickly, then climbed right back into bed.

"I love this mattress," she said. "It's soft but somehow not too soft."

"It's got a foam cushion on top," I explained.

"Oh, it's a *fancy* mattress. Better not get used to it," she mumbled, her voice heavy with sleep.

She immediately dozed off, but I didn't, so I kept watching her. I wanted to tell her many things, but no way would I wake her up. She was the first woman to spend the night in my bed, and I wouldn't mind if she got used to it. For so long, I'd denied myself this. I'd managed to convince myself that it wasn't something I needed, but I so fucking did.

I didn't need just anyone, though.

I needed Riley.

CHAPTER SEVENTEEN

Riley

I woke up the next morning at eight thirty sharp. The problem with having the same schedule for years was that I was used to getting up even when I wanted to sleep in and enjoy a lazy Sunday with the gorgeous and sexy man next to me. To my astonishment, Duncan wasn't sleeping. He was watching me with a wry smile.

"Hey. How long have you been awake?" I asked.

"Ten minutes, give or take."

I turned onto my stomach, hugging the pillow with both hands, watching him. "So, you've been staring at me all this time?"

He twirled a strand of my hair around his finger. "I wanted to do a lot more, but you looked so peaceful, and I didn't want to wake you up."

"Well, now I'm awake, so you can do everything you want to me."

Duncan laughed. It was different than any of the laughs I'd heard from him before. It was more relaxed.

I'd felt a wall come down between us last night, and I wasn't ready to explore that. I was, however, ready for more sexy time with him. It had been amazing; the man had skills. I'd never experienced anything quite like it in bed.

"I'm wide awake. I don't even need caffeine. I know some people need it to wake up, but I don't. Especially not when I have a sexy man next to me. I think the pheromones rolling off you have an interesting side effect, because I'm usually not *this* chatty in the morning."

He kissed the tip of my nose, then went down to my neck, then my ear.

"I'm glad you're happy, and that you don't regret last night," he said while he ran his fingers up and down my spine. He cupped one ass cheek, then the other one.

"Of course not. It was absolutely perfect," I confessed.

I sucked in a breath. Could he tell I meant that this went deeper than just the three orgasms he gave me? He'd opened something deep inside me. I'd felt more alive than ever before. I didn't know how to put it in words... or if he even wanted to hear it.

I was his son's nanny, after all.

Why was I so emotional?

Was it because—

"Oh my God. My sister." I bolted into a sitting position. "I totally forgot about what happened. How is that even possible? Do you know where I put my phone?"

"Your purse is in the other room," Duncan said.

I leaped out of bed and made a beeline for the kitchen, feeling self-conscious that I was walking around naked. Not because Duncan could see me but because I spent time with Jeremy here. Somehow, this felt wrong.

I immediately spotted my purse on the counter and took out my phone.

"Wow!"

"What happened?" Duncan said. He walked toward me with quick steps. He was naked too.

"I don't have any messages from Paula."

"Riley," he said softly, taking my phone out of my hands and setting it back in my bag. Then he turned me around, putting both hands on my neck. "It's early. She's probably sleeping."

"You're right," I whispered and closed my eyes. "I like feeling your hands on my neck. It's calming me." I opened my eyes. "Like last night. You touched the small of my back, and somehow that kept me relaxed while all that shit show was going on at the gas station." That wasn't too much of a confession to make, right? Telling Duncan that I felt safe around him?

Then I remembered that I'd made a similar confession last night and he hadn't run away. Granted, he'd yet to get into my pants at that point, but somehow I didn't think that was his end goal. Duncan Sterling wasn't like any of the guys I'd dated in college, thank God. I could connect to him in ways I'd never been able to with anyone in the past.

"Give your sister a few more hours, okay? I'll take care of you in the meantime, make sure you have a great start to the day. Then I can take you to see her."

I nodded, pushing my hair behind my ears. "That sounds like a solid plan. I do want to see her. Wait... you said you wanted to take care of me first?"

He grinned easily. "Yes."

I hadn't seen that type of grin on him before. It was more seductive than his usual ones.

"Okay. And just so you know, my caffeinated drink of choice is green tea."

"Got that. What do you want to eat?" he asked.

I narrowed my eyes. "What is this, a restaurant?"

"I'm a single dad with a boy who could eat more than three adults. So yeah, I have skills in the kitchen. I can make you an omelet, waffles, pancakes, avocado toast. Or oatmeal."

"No oatmeal today. That seriously seems like a waste of stomach real estate when you have all those options ready to be had. I want all of the above." I felt so at ease around Duncan. God, this man was everything I never knew I wanted. He completed my soul. He and Jeremy.

Careful there, Riley. You just spent a night together, nothing more.

"All right, but first let's get dressed. It's always a hazard to cook naked. I've burned myself a few times."

Something inside me shifted. *Crap. Does he do this often? Have women over when his son is away?* It had never occurred to me.

Duh. The guy is older, experienced, and has physical needs just like anyone else. Of course he has women over for sex.

Shit, I'm an idiot.

"What happened?" he asked, coming to stand in front of me. "You kind of disappeared. Your eyes looked vacant."

"Nothing." I glanced at his shoulder, unable to meet his eyes.

"Riley... something is off. You don't even want to look at me, so I'm assuming it's about me. And it's not good. Did I say something to upset you?"

"No. It's silly, honestly." Besides, who cared if he had sleep-overs? It wasn't like he and I were going to walk down the aisle or anything.

And why did that thought bother me?

"Riley," Duncan exclaimed.

Finally, I looked up at him and instinctively knew he wouldn't let this go. "Nothing. I just... I thought about all the women you must have made breakfast for."

His eyes went cold. He dropped his hands and took a step back. "And how did you come to that conclusion?" His voice was flat.

"Because you said that you... I mean... you implied that you often cook naked." I was stumbling over my words, laying bare a side of me I'd hoped to keep hidden. One that was vulnerable and jealous.

"Hey," Duncan tilted my chin, making me look at him. "I don't appreciate you jumping to conclusions like that."

"Okay." That wasn't what I'd expected. I figured he'd try to let me down gently by skirting around the subject.

"And for what it's worth, you're the first woman I've ever had here in the condo. In my bed." His fingers moved along my jaw, and I realized what he'd just said.

The knot in my chest unfurled just as quickly as it had formed. In fact, my entire body felt weightless.

"Wait, Duncan, are you serious?" I asked.

"Yes. I wouldn't lie to you about anything, much less about this. I think you know that about me by now." He looked sincere, and he'd never made me ever think he wasn't truthful about anything.

I dipped my head. "I'm sorry. I don't know what to say."

He stepped closer, touching my face again. "Babe, when you want to know something, ask me. Don't just assume the worst."

I touched his chest. "I don't know why I did that." I was digging a hole for myself and knew I'd better stop while I was ahead because I had no idea how to climb out of it.

"Why haven't you brought anyone here before?" I asked, trying to disguise my shock.

"Because I had rules for myself for years, and I never strayed. I never felt the need to break them for anyone. Until you."

"Duncan," I murmured, putting my hands on his abs and then moving them up slowly, stopping near his pecs. His heart was pumping furiously.

"You mean a lot to me, Riley. I've never had to fight myself more than since meeting you."

I sucked in a breath. "Do you regret losing the battle?"

"Not even a bit," he said, and I smiled.

He captured my mouth, lifting me up by my ass and pressing me against him as he walked with me through the house.

His touch meant so much more after what he'd shared with

me. I was the first woman he'd had in here. I was bursting with happiness.

Once we reached the bedroom, I slid down him, brushing against his fully erect cock. I jerked my head back, looking between us. "Duncan."

He laughed. "See? All I need is you naked against me and this is what happens."

I squeezed it tightly. He dropped his head back but then immediately straightened up. "Nope, not now. Let's get dressed. I'm making you breakfast and then dropping you off at your sister's."

I looked at him with narrowed eyes. "No sexy interlude?"

"We'll see. Maybe after breakfast."

"Mm-hmm." I loved his bossy side.

After we dressed, we returned to the kitchen. I didn't bother putting on my panties because they were stretched out of shape.

In the kitchen, Duncan took out the batter and eggs and a million other things. We were side by side, but I was watching him more than doing anything. It was fascinating. He had a system, and he was efficiently moving through it.

"Wow. You weren't kidding when you said you have skills. Did you always know how to cook?"

"Yeah. Ever since we were little, we'd help Mom around the kitchen. It was just something we did. I don't know why. I think it was one of our favorite spots, mostly because cooking was always Mom's happy place. My parents rarely fought when she was behind the stove. Anyway, once Jeremy and I were on our own, I had to seriously up my game."

I touched his arm, grateful that he'd chosen a shirt with short sleeves. "Want to tell me about it?"

"I'd been with his mother for a very short time when she got pregnant. We decided we'd try our best to make our relationship work."

His voice was tighter as he put the batter in the waffle maker. We'd yet to finish the avocado toast and the omelet.

"We threw in the towel a year later," he continued. "We were fighting constantly, and then we both decided that it was better if we separated. We never married; I think, deep down, we both knew it wouldn't work out. We decided that I'd have primary custody of our son. In the beginning, she lived in San Francisco, so she met with Jeremy more often, but then she moved to Dublin. Her job took her there, so now he mostly vacations with her."

"Are you two on good terms?"

"We're co-parenting the best we can. Despite the time difference, she really does her best to talk to Jeremy every evening, but it's not the same, you know? I want to fill both roles, but it's not possible. He's nowhere near as emotionally close to his own mother to talk to her about everything. My mom tries her best, but..."

His body had tensed up as he talked. I kissed his bicep. "You're doing a great job, Duncan, trust me. Jeremy's a happy kid. He feels and knows that he's loved."

"Does he mention anything to you?"

I loved that he was so in tune with his son. It made me want him more.

"Not anything in particular, just that he loves you and that you're besties. He loves his uncles too. Finn the most, though that can change to a different uncle depending on the week. He mentioned his mom once to me but hasn't said anything since. Just that she lives far away and they talk on the phone."

"You'd tell me if he said anything that, you know, I should know about?"

"Of course. But I truly think you have nothing to worry about."

"Well, we're all doing our best, and I don't regret any of the decisions his mother and I made."

A few seconds later, he took the waffles out, putting one on each plate. "Breakfast is ready."

"This is so decadent. I've never had a food festival like this before," I said as we carried the plates to the table.

"Really?"

"I've always had oatmeal. It's cheap and filling. Growing up, my sister and I ate our biggest meal at school. Lunch was everything. In the morning, we had a hurried breakfast at home before Mom went to work, which she had to do seven days a week."

"Damn, that's tough," Duncan said. He touched my forearm, brushing his thumb up and down.

"I know. That's the other thing I want to accomplish once I start earning the big bucks. I hope Mom will be able to get by without working nonstop. It's always been rough, but now she's getting older, and it's hard on her body. She tries to play it cool, but her knees and hips are bothering her more than a few years ago. But once I start at the firm, I'm going to knock everyone's socks off. I'll work my way up to partner, and then I can spoil Mom and my sister all day long."

"I'm sure you'll kick ass."

I munched on my avocado toast. "Oh my God, this is great." I wasn't sure what he'd put in it even though I'd watched him prepare everything. I then asked, "And why do you say that? That I'll kick ass?"

"You've got a lot of determination and grit."

"That I do, in spades. A lot of people complain about the work hours, but if you think about it, ever since I was sixteen, my days were twelve hours long. Sometimes fourteen. I mean, this is honestly the most relaxing period of my life. And the only reason I'm not taking a second job is because you're paying very generously. And looking after Jeremy is important to me. I don't want to be exhausted by the time I pick him up because I've been working somewhere else."

"That's *exactly* why I pay so much. I didn't want anyone doing that."

"You think of everything, don't you?"

He nodded. "I try to."

I moved from the avocado toast to the waffle. "I love this breakfast," I said. I ate slowly, enjoying every single mouthful.

After a few minutes, I realized Duncan was watching me eat.

"I like seeing you this happy," he said. His thoughtfulness made me feel special.

"Well, I'm easy. All I need is a few orgasms and this amazing breakfast," I teased.

He smiled. "I can do that."

CHAPTER EIGHTEEN

Riley

After we finished and had put everything in the dishwasher, I intended to seduce this sexy man. Not that I thought he needed much seducing, judging by how quickly he'd gotten hard earlier. It wouldn't take long to get him exactly where I wanted him.

But just as I was ready to move this into the bedroom, the screen of my phone lit up with a message. I knew without even checking that it would be from my sister. Julia and Christine wouldn't wake up before noon today, if even by then.

I was right. Paula had sent me a message.

Paula: Hey, sis, are you up?

I called her right away. "Good morning, sleepyhead. How are you feeling?"

"I'm good." She sounded like she literally just woke up and texted me first thing. "Do you have plans today?"

"I'm going to drop by your place."

"Oh thank God! I was going to ask you if you could meet up."

"Want me to drop by in, like, I don't know, thirty minutes or something with breakfast?"

"You're my favorite person ever."

"I love you too," I said.

"All right, then. Let's hang up because I need to shower if I want to look presentable when you come. Love you."

"I'll spoil you today, you'll see."

After hanging up, I turned around, looking at Duncan regretfully. "No time for a sexy interlude after all. You're not mad?"

"Babe, family first. Go and help her," he said. "You're a great sister."

"I really think she needs me today."

"No doubt. I'll drop you off."

"I need to buy some breakfast for her too."

"There are lots of waffles left. Why don't you just take them with you?"

I could have swooned. *Is this man not the most thoughtful?* "She'd love that."

Duncan grabbed a Ziploc bag and put the waffles in it.

Lord help me, I was truly finding a man holding a Ziploc bag sexy. This single dad had warmed his way into my heart.

"Okay, then, we're ready to go," I said.

I was feeling a bit weird, walking commando around the city, but I didn't want to stop by my place and put on panties. I'd promised my sister breakfast, and I was going to deliver.

Once we reached the front of her building, Duncan said, "Her place doesn't look better in daylight."

"I agree. I hate that she lives here; I'm always worried about her." Eventually, I wanted to work something out so she could take over my lease once I started my new job. At that point, I should be able to afford another place.

"I'm walking you upstairs."

"Duncan, that's not necessary. The place looks dingy, but

there have been no incidents during the day. That I know of."
My sister had a habit of not telling me when really bad stuff
happened. "Actually, maybe it wouldn't be so bad if you come up
with me."

We both got out of the car at the same time. Duncan was
next to me in an instant, arm around my waist. He kept looking
around. The area was deserted except for the three homeless
guys two blocks away who we saw on the drive over, but they
didn't pay attention to us.

Just like yesterday, the elevator wasn't working, so we trudged
up two flights of stairs.

"You don't have to come up," I told him. "These stairs are
insane."

"It's the least I can do. And it'll count as my cardio for the
day."

I snorted. "As if I'd believe that you got that hot bod just
because of some cardio."

"I didn't say I wouldn't hit the weights afterward." I could
hear the grin in his voice.

"What else are you doing today?" I asked him as we went up.

"I'll probably do some laps. If I hurry, there won't be anyone
in the pool. The rest of the neighbors typically show up in the
afternoon. Although sometimes I do see some of the single
moms. Though none of them swim."

I stopped walking and turned around, smiling from ear to ear.
"And you have no idea what they're doing there?"

"Suntanning, I guess."

Oh my God. Duncan was so naive. He seriously didn't
know?

"Here's an idea," I said. "They might come just to watch the
show."

"What show?" he asked, bewilderment obvious across his
features.

"You swimming. You're a hot, sexy guy."

He wrapped both arms around my waist. The bag of waffles

was dangling at my side. "Really? You think everyone's out to get me?"

"I hope not. But they are for sure out to ogle you. And I don't blame them. But just so you know, you're super irresistible when you do the butterfly stroke. Maybe you can put a helmet on or something so you look like a dork and lower your sexiness factor. But I don't think it'll work." I could tell he was getting a kick out of my antics.

"You're so damn adorable and funny. I love that about you."

I bit the inside of my cheek. "Really? I've been told my humor might be a bit too much, so I was trying to tone it down around you." Duncan was still my boss, after all, but we'd moved past that to... what was this?

Don't get all philosophical Riley. Just enjoy it.

"Well, don't. I like sassy, fun Riley."

"Excellent, because it's really hard for me to not be me."

We both laughed, and I couldn't help but to think how strange this situation had become.

Technically, he was my boss, and I was sleeping with him. But I wasn't going to work for him for very long. Regardless, I wasn't prepared to let go of what we had; I wanted to see where we could end up. If the three of us could find happiness.

He pushed my hair to one side, kissing my neck before we resumed climbing the staircase. When we reached Paula's door, it swung open before I even rang the bell.

"Finally. I was afraid something happened—oh, hi, Duncan," she said. My sister was clearly only at coffee number one, because her forehead was full of creases. Her eyes widened, and she jerked her head back so forcefully that she nearly stumbled.

"This is where I leave you," Duncan said. He handed my sister the Ziploc bag. "This is your breakfast. I hope you have syrup. Have fun, you two. Call me if you need anything."

"Thanks, Duncan," I said, then stepped inside as he went down the stairs.

The second the door closed behind us, Paula cleared her

throat. "What was that? What is this?" She pointed to the waffles.

"Ah, I should have probably given you a heads-up."

"It would have helped. I did put two and two together last night, although I figured maybe he'd come with you because you were still working when you got my call. I did wonder why you were wearing this dress. And oh my God, you're wearing it today too. You're doing the walk of shame!" she concluded.

I laughed. "Did you even finish coffee number one?"

"No," she said. "Isn't it obvious?"

We went into her kitchen. It was tiny, just a stove and a minuscule countertop. She grabbed the half-empty cup from the edge of the sink and downed it in one shot.

"Let's see if this helped. So, you *are* doing the walk of shame?"

"Sort of, although I'm not really ashamed." I blushed.

"I can't believe it."

"Let's talk about you first. What happened?"

"Please, what is there to talk about? I live in a shithole, work at a shithole, and got robbed. End of the story. Can you believe he actually sent me a message last night saying he expects me to show up at work today? After he fired me."

I stilled. "Tell me you're not going back there. Paula, you can't."

"Hell no. I know I'm stubborn, but I'm not stupid. That place is unsafe. I'm not taking any night jobs in gas stations anymore. There's a reason there are so many openings. No one wants them, and now I know why." She blew out a frustrated breath, making herself a second coffee.

"Waffles?" I asked, pointing to the bag. She seemed to have forgotten about them. My sister truly wasn't a morning person.

"Yes, please. I was going to eat some oatmeal, but this looks so much better."

"They're delicious, trust me."

Paula paused while getting the syrup from the cupboard and asked, "Why are they in a Ziploc bag?"

The corners of my mouth lifted. "Because Duncan made them, and he bagged some for you."

Her face changed so fast, it was as if she was in a cartoon. Her jaw dropped, and I could almost see her eyes bulge.

"Let's sit down," I suggested. I brought over her plate and utensils, and we sat on the wooden chairs at the small table.

She put the bag of waffles, syrup, and the coffee in front of her. "You had breakfast already?" she checked.

"Yes."

"So these are all mine."

"Knock yourself out."

She looked at me for a few seconds before saying, "So, you're sleeping with him, huh? But he also made you breakfast, which means you two are... I don't know... going out? Tell me what happened. I want to know what's going on."

"I can explain some of it. I literally had the hots for him from the second I started the interview with him." I loved my sister. I could tell her anything—this was a judgment-free zone.

"Hey, I don't blame you. I mean, he's superhot. But he's kind of old, isn't he? Not that he looks it, but he's got a kid and a good job, right?"

"He's only nine years older than me. But when we're together, I don't notice the age difference."

She winced. "Sorry, that sounds like a million years to me."

I did understand her point of view. When I first started college, I would have considered an almost-ten-year gap monstrous. "He's a good person. I love watching him with Jeremy. One day, I was with Jeremy in the pool, and Duncan joined us. Honestly, sis, I basically melted."

"I can see that. I mean, he's hot with clothes on. I can imagine that in swim trunks, he's even hotter."

"Yesterday, we went to see a movie, and—"

"And then I called," she said. "I would say I'm a cockblocker, but clearly that didn't keep you from getting down and dirty."

I laughed. "He was very considerate with me. Last night and this morning too."

"All right," she said. "Let me drink another coffee, and then we can make plans."

I spent the entire day with my sister. We went to the beach and enjoyed the sun, and then we looked at some jobs. I offered to put her in contact with some of the places where I'd waitressed, and she agreed, thank God. I also tried to talk her into moving out, but she flat-out refused.

One thing at a time. When it came to Paula, I had to pace myself. She'd only said yes to changing jobs, though I didn't have to do any convincing. But she wouldn't agree to move any time soon.

Paula dropped me off at my house in the evening and I made myself a salad—Paula and I ate junk food all day on the beach, and it was high time for something healthy. As I sat on the small couch in the backyard with a bowl of salad in my arms, I wondered where everyone was.

Knowing my roommates, they probably went to some kind of party. That was a part of their usual schedule on the weekends. They went out on Friday evenings, slept until late, and then went out on Saturday again and on Sunday too. I'd always been the party pooper because I worked throughout my entire law school program. Most of my waitressing shifts were Saturday and Sunday because no one wanted those hours.

Even when I did go clubbing, I usually returned shortly after midnight, sometimes even before. The last few years of law school, I'd really noticed the change in myself. I enjoyed the blissful silence of our small yard. Yeah, my life was amazing and even becoming better.

My phone beeped, and I saw a message from my sister.

> Paula: Just got home safe. I think I'm going to sleep again. We ate so much that I'm not even hungry.

Then I saw other messages. Oh my God, Duncan had texted me today. I hadn't seen them before. I had three texts from him.

> Duncan: Hey, gorgeous, how are you doing?

> Duncan: You were right about swimming.

> Duncan: Text me whenever you've got a free moment.

That was four hours ago. I typed back quickly.

> Riley: Hey, sorry, I just saw this. I wasn't ignoring you. I was right about what?

He replied a second later.

> Duncan: About the reason so many single women head out to the pool when I'm there.

I burst out laughing so hard that I nearly dropped my bowl of salad.

> Riley: How could you tell?

> Duncan: Because I started talking to one, and she full-on flirted with me.

My laughter died in my throat. *No. What the hell? Just no!*

I'd never felt jealousy like this. It simply raged through me. Someone had flirted with my man.

Whoa, hold your horses, Riley. He's not your man. He's Duncan Sterling, hot, successful woman magnet, and you don't know if you're even exclusive.

But he'd told me this morning that I was the first woman he'd brought to the condo. That had to mean something, right?

I took in a deep breath and then texted back.

> Riley: I don't know if I should tell you this, but I feel weirdly jealous.

A weight lifted off my shoulders once I put it out there. All the guys I'd dated in the past were never serious and liked to play games. Of course, they were younger, less mature—as was I, for that matter. But things had changed.

> Duncan: You don't have any reason to be jealous. You're the only one I want in my bed, Riley.

This was the precise moment that he confirmed that he was nothing like anyone I'd dated before. He was a man through and through, and he knew exactly what he wanted—and that was me! *Squeeee!*

This was so different from my past relationships. The guys I dated had FOMO—their fear of missing out was too big. Or maybe they were just all assholes.

> Duncan: The only one.

I smiled at my phone, putting the bowl of salad on the table. This wasn't going to be easy or straightforward because he had Jeremy. I vividly remembered when he told me that he wouldn't introduce a woman to his son until Jeremy was at least sixteen. So, whatever this was between us may not have a future.

But that didn't matter, at least not right now. I was happy as a clam with what we had.

CHAPTER NINETEEN

Duncan

In the afternoon, I picked up Jeremy from my mom's place at four o'clock. She usually liked to have Sunday evening free, and I respected that. Besides, I already missed the little guy so damn much that I was glad to have him back.

"How was your weekend?" I asked when we were both in the car.

"It was great. Nana taught me how to bake muffins. We can try at home too. I got the recipe."

"Sure we can," I told him. "What do you want to do tonight?"

He was sad for a few seconds, which told me that he wanted to ask something that he expected me to say no to. I looked at him in the rearview mirror.

"Dad, can we go to the zoo?"

And my insides died.

I'd been there more times than I could count. And I knew for a fact that he'd been there with Riley this week. Still, he was pleading with his eyes.

"Sure, buddy. Why not? We can stay for two or three hours and still be home in time for dinner."

"Yes! Thank you. You're the best dad in the world."

"The zoo it is," I said.

I tried to muster up enthusiasm, but the best I could bring myself to do was smile and ask him what exactly he wanted to see there this time. I loved spending time with my son, but trips to Disney or Legoland or the zoo were at the very top of my shit list. I couldn't hype myself up for them, hard as I tried. Especially not when I was doing it for the millionth time. But I wanted to make him happy. I'd promised myself a long time ago that I'd listen to what he wanted and needed and do my best to fulfill it. He wanted quality time with me in a place he liked, which happened to be the zoo.

We found a parking spot easily enough because they had a huge lot. As we walked to the entrance gate, he was already bouncing with joy. Once inside, I spotted a few familiar faces, but that was par for the course. Jeremy wasn't the only kid who liked to come here repeatedly.

We strolled on the main path, stopping in front of each animal's display. There were quite a few people gathered in front of the zebra park.

"Did it have its baby?" Jeremy asked excitedly.

"What?"

"The zebra was supposed to have a baby soon. Riley kept checking the zoo's website for updates."

"I think you're right," I said as we approached. There was a huge sign in front of the zebras' area that read "Baby Z is here."

"Dad," he said, looking up at me, "do you think Riley will want to come here?"

I lowered myself onto my haunches so I was face-to-face with him. "Jeremy, today is Riley's free day. It's not fair to ask her to come here and work on Sunday too."

"But she would love to see the baby, Dad. She told me. And she said that she doesn't consider me a job. I asked her about it."

I frowned. "What do you mean?"

"Well, sometimes Ms. Williams tells me that 'If your dad didn't pay so well, I wouldn't be caught dead here.'" Jeremy said this so matter-of-factly, I had to rewind what he'd just said. I couldn't believe it.

I barely stopped myself from cursing. *What the actual fuck?* I'd always thought Ms. Williams was a bit set in her ways, but who in the hell would make a kid feel like he was a chore?

She was not fucking coming back as a nanny. My mind was made up.

"And then I asked Riley once if she would like to still do stuff with me if you didn't pay her, and she said yes." His eyes were almost glassy.

If Riley was here, I would kiss her senseless.

"Still, buddy, it's not fair to ask her to come here on a Sunday evening."

"Please, Dad, let's try. If she has plans, she'll tell you."

He had a point, of course, but I didn't want to put her in that position. I was feeling more uncomfortable about it now, primarily because she and I were dating. I didn't want her to think I was taking advantage of her because we were having sex. That would be wrong on so many counts.

But I couldn't let my boy down.

"Fine, I'll call her. But you have to understand that she might have something else to do."

"Okay."

Riley's number was in my favorites, and I immediately punched it. I figured maybe she was preparing to go out with her friends again. Hell, maybe she was already somewhere in another beach club, dancing.

Hell no. The thought of men salivating around her was enough to make me see red.

But she was fresh out of college and barely out of that clubbing scene, so who was I to be angry? I kept forgetting we were at different stages in our lives. I was thirty-three and she was twenty-four—when you were young, that age difference probably seemed like light-years apart. Of course she could be out clubbing. But damn it, I didn't like that one bit.

"Hey," I almost barked when she finally answered.

"What's wrong?" she asked in a panicked voice.

I cleared my throat.

"What are you doing?" I asked her. There. Now I sounded more normal.

I looked down at Jeremy, who was tapping his right foot impatiently.

"Um, not much. I'm home, reading."

That was good. Damn it, I was hoping even more than Jeremy that she'd join us. "Listen. Have you looked at the zoo's website recently?"

"What? No. Oh my God. Is there news?"

I couldn't help but smile at the excitement in her voice. How could this bring her so much joy? "Yeah. Jeremy and I are here, and we're happy to inform you that the baby zebra is as well."

"Wow! Wait, let me grab my laptop. They've got a live cam." I could hear her typing in the background for a few moments. "Oh! So cute. It was supposed to come next week. It doesn't need intensive care or anything. I'm so glad."

"What do you say about joining us?"

"What, at the zoo?"

Jeremy jumped up. "What did she say?"

"Is Jeremy right next to you?" she asked.

"Yeah. And he really wants you here."

"How about you?" she whispered.

I sucked in a deep breath. "So do I." If Jeremy wasn't here, I'd tell her just how fucking much. She belonged here with us. With me. I felt it in my bones.

"It's going to take me about forty minutes to get there."

Something reared in my chest. It was almost like a small explosion, combined with relief. "We'll be here waiting for you," I said.

Jeremy cried out, jumping up and down, pretty much expressing what I felt.

"Thank you," she said.

"I'll pay for your Uber."

"What? No, Duncan. Come on. I can afford that."

"But I've asked you here."

"Hey, it's my free time, okay? I can do as I please, and if I happen to want to go to the zoo to see the baby zebra, that's on me."

I didn't want to start an argument in front of Jeremy, and I was beginning to understand that when it came to Riley, I had to be careful about which battles I fought. "Fine. Let us know when you're nearby."

Once she disconnected the call, Jeremy jumped up and down again. "I told you she wants to come, Dad! I told you! I like Riley."

"So do I."

He looked up at me and said with a toothy grin, "When I'm with her, it almost feels like I have a mom."

It was like a physical blow to my stomach. My elation drained instantly, giving place to worry as we stepped away from the zebra so others could see it.

"Jeremy, you have a mom." It was a weak reply, but what else could I give him?

"You know what I mean. Someone who's here and does mom stuff with me."

I gritted my teeth. I'd always been determined to give my son everything he needed, but it was time to admit that I couldn't replace his mother, as hard as I tried.

"Come on. Let's sit down," I said, sitting on the bench between the zebra enclosure and the neighboring restaurant. "Jeremy, is there anything you would like us to do together? That would make you feel like you aren't missing out on things?"

"Hm. I don't know. I'll think about it." He dangled his feet under the bench and gripped the edges, looking down. "I just, like, really like Riley."

Just when I thought I'd gotten a grip on fatherhood, Jeremy got older and I had to deal with a new layer of complexity. I was always playing catch-up. I could read the stock market no problem and deal with any crisis that came up at work. But my son always kept me on my toes and managed to surprise me. He was growing up too fast.

"Let's buy a snack so we can all share it when Riley comes," I suggested.

"Yes!"

"What does she eat when you come here?"

"I'll show you. She likes two specific carts, one that sells ice cream and one that sells popcorn, and she always eats it together."

"Okay," I said, assuming she ate a sweet-flavored popcorn with ice cream. Weird combo, but whatever. Then it turned out to be even weirder. She liked salty popcorn with ice cream. I double-checked with Jeremy three times.

"You're sure?" I asked the fourth time.

"Dad!" He stomped his foot, letting out an exasperated sigh. "I told you."

"All right." I was tempted to message Riley and ask if this ridiculous combination was what she really liked, but then I'd ruin the surprise. If worse come to worst, we could always throw away the salty popcorn.

Jeremy wanted ice cream too. I usually didn't allow sweets before dinner, but I was breaking far too many rules today to stick to this one. I wasn't a hypocrite. I wasn't hungry at all, so after I paid, I carried Riley's ice cream and popcorn, and we went to wait by the entrance to the zoo.

CHAPTER TWENTY

Duncan

She'd shared her location with me on the phone. Jeremy and I stood next to each other, looking at everyone who came in. Now that it was late afternoon, the crowd had thinned.

I sucked in a breath when Riley arrived. She had on a thin blue dress, something she would probably wear at the beach. I imagined her relaxing in her bed with a book. How easy it would be to slide that dress off.

I sucked in a breath and pulled myself together as Jeremy and I walked over to her.

"Surprise!" Jeremy said. He immediately wrapped his arms around her waist.

She returned his hug without hesitation. The sight did something to me, though I wasn't ready to admit what it was.

"Hey, we bought you ice cream and popcorn." I handed her both.

She looked at the bowl, then asked, "It's the salty kind? Oh my God. You really remember my favorites, huh?"

All right, I had to give Jeremy more credit. The guy had a good memory.

"Yes." He looked up at her and then said, very unhelpfully, "Dad didn't believe me. He asked like five times."

Riley giggled. "I know it's a bit weird, but it actually works with the salted caramel ice cream. You're welcome to try."

"I'm good," I said. "Thank you for coming, Riley."

"Of course. I'm happy you guys called."

"Dad was afraid we might overstep the boundaries," Jeremy cut in.

Riley and I exchanged a glance. Yeah, we'd set whatever boundaries we'd had on fire already. But that had been different —just between her and me. We hadn't discussed how we were going to behave around Jeremy. I'd been too consumed by her to think about anything else.

"Can we go see the zebra?" he asked.

"Let Riley enjoy her food."

She had a system. After taking the popcorn from me, she held it with her forearm to her belly so she could still hold the ice cream in the same hand and eat it with the other one. She took one spoonful of ice cream, and the next mouthful was one of popcorn. Weirdest combination I'd ever seen, but she was so damn happy.

We walked straight to the zebra's enclosure as Riley ate her snacks. She even knew a shortcut, so we were there in less than ten minutes. The crowd had dispersed here, too, reminding me that the zoo was much better at this time of the day. The only downside was that the animals tended to be less active later in the day.

The zebra and its foal were currently lying down. The baby had its head on its mother's belly.

"Oh my God. It's so cute. Can you take a picture of me and them?" she asked, expertly taking out her phone from her bag and handing it to me.

"Sure," I said. "Jeremy, do you want to be in the picture?"

"Yes, please." He was thrilled at being included.

He didn't pose next to her but rather wrapped his arms around her waist from the side, pressing his head against her rib cage.

"Smile," I said, positioning the phone so I caught both zebras and Riley and Jeremy.

"Come on, let's give your dad a toothy grin," Riley said.

They both grinned at me, then started making silly faces.

I snapped a few pictures.

"Let's look and see which ones we want to keep," Riley said. "I bet it's the third one. We always seem to get the hang of things by then."

I couldn't believe they had their little habits. When had that happened? Riley hadn't been with us for that long, and yet she was already so important to both of us.

She crouched so I could hold her phone at Jeremy's level. Once they could both see it, I scrolled to the right.

"I want this one," Jeremy said, pointing to the second one I'd snapped where they were both flashing their teeth.

"Okay. Then that's the one I'll keep too," Riley said.

As she rose to her feet, I handed her the phone back. I touched her fingers, squeezing them. Her eyes widened. The next second, the popcorn tumbled all over the ground.

"Oh my goodness," she said, jumping back.

"Don't worry, we'll clean it up. Nothing happened," Jeremy said.

That was exactly what I told him every time he had an accident, ever since he was a little kid. I'd always made it my mission not to yell at him or make him feel bad when accidents happened. They were just that, accidents. There was no reason to lose my shit over it.

"Um, I-I'm sorry. I didn't..." Riley started licking her lips. She was blushing. Because I'd touched her hand? Damn, it made me feel good about myself.

"I-I'll clean up," she said.

"No. You enjoy your ice cream and snap all the pictures you want of the baby zebra. I'll pick it up and buy you a new popcorn."

She shook her head. "You don't have to do that."

I winked. "Come on, your zoo experience wouldn't be complete."

They stayed in front of the zebras as I cleaned up the popcorn and headed to the cart. I could hear Riley sharing trivia about zebras with my son. I wondered if this was what Jeremy meant by doing mom stuff. I was determined to give him a good childhood, but was I failing him somehow? How could I be better?

When I returned with a fresh batch, I noticed that Jeremy was quickly shifting his weight from one foot to the other. I knew the signs.

"Riley, here's your popcorn," I said.

"Thanks."

She took it from my hands as I looked straight at my son. "Jeremy, do you need to go to the men's room?"

He nodded. "Yes, I really do."

"I didn't notice," Riley said.

"Want me to go with you?" I asked him.

"No, Dad," he said indignantly, standing up as straight as he could. As if he wanted to make himself taller. "I'm a big boy. I know how to go."

"All right," I said, pointing to the restroom that was right next to the zebras' enclosure. "The men's restroom is actually right around the corner. I can go wait with you."

"No, Dad. What will everyone say? Can you and Riley wait *here?*"

"Sure," I said. I wasn't sure why I was even offering. He'd been insisting on going to the restroom by himself since he was five years old, and I always waited by the door. He ran straight toward it, which meant he needed to go badly.

Afterward, I turned to Riley, who was looking down at the

popcorn. I couldn't keep myself in check a moment longer. I brought a hand to the side of her face, caressing her jaw and making her glance up.

"Riley?" I asked. "Why are you avoiding looking at me?"

"I'm not sure how to do this. I figured we'd talk and sort things out before I came to work tomorrow, or... I don't know..."

I nodded and then stopped touching her. "I don't have a plan," I admitted, which was insane. I was the man with a plan. It was my thing. It was what I was good at. And yet right now, all I knew was that I needed to touch her more than I'd needed anything in my life. And I also wanted to give Jeremy the best childhood possible and not confuse him. I couldn't see how those two things could happen at the same time.

She touched my wrist and then my forearm, moving slowly to my elbow.

"Are you fondling me?" I asked, stunned.

"I don't think it counts as fondling if it's not the ass or, you know, a sexy part."

"It so fucking does," I said, then stepped even closer, bringing my mouth to her ear. "Because it turns me on."

"What? Touching your arm?"

"No, you. Whatever you do. Eating, breathing, smiling. Especially that fucking smile. It slays me."

"Duncan..."

I brought my lips to the corner of her mouth, only intending to breathe in the scent of her skin. It was delicious. My damn pillow was starting to smell like that, and I was seriously considering not washing my bedsheets again so they would keep her scent.

I moved my mouth farther to the right. Her breath was shaky. Her lips were soft and warm and so damn inviting, and I captured them without a second thought. I hadn't realized how much I needed to kiss her until I'd tangled our tongues. I reached one hand around the back of her head, running my fingers through her hair. This kiss was exactly what I needed.

A loud noise startled us. She'd dropped the second bucket of popcorn too.

"Oh my God," she said, looking down, then started to laugh. "No way!"

"You know I'll just buy you another one."

"No, I think this is a sign that I shouldn't have any more. I mean, one dropped bucket is one thing, but two? It's basically saying, 'Stop eating, Riley. You've been stuffing your face the whole weekend.'"

"What are you talking about? You are damn gorgeous."

"That's because I usually don't stuff my face."

I moved closer. "You're beautiful. Don't fight me on that, or I will prove to you exactly how sexy you are to me."

She narrowed her eyes. "We're in public."

"So?"

"And Jeremy's in the bathroom."

That did the trick. I looked at the mess and crouched to the ground at the same time, putting the spilled popcorn back in the bucket.

"You dropped it again?" Jeremy said, sprinting toward us from the restroom.

What the hell had I been thinking, kissing her like that in public when Jeremy was just a few feet away? I couldn't do this. It was unfair, both to my son and to her. He needed to grow up in a stable home. And Riley deserved so fucking much more than a stolen kiss at the zoo while he was in the restroom, or a night in my bed when I could get away with it. She deserved everything, and I didn't know if I could give that to her.

I tossed the popcorn in the trash can and then faced Riley. She bit her lip, avoiding my gaze. Could she tell from my expression what I was thinking? Or was she thinking along the same lines?

"Let's head toward the exit," I suggested. "They're going to close soon."

Jeremy pouted but nodded. We walked toward the exit with

him between us. I glanced at Riley from time to time, but she seemed determined to avoid my gaze. I needed to have a serious conversation with her, but it couldn't be right now. I wanted her undivided attention, and I needed us to be alone.

"I can drop you off at home," I said once we got out.

"No, that's out of your way. And you're going to miss Jeremy's bedtime if you do."

"That's true," I said. "Then I'll order you an Uber."

"Really?" The corners of her mouth twitched. "Why do we want to start that argument again?"

Jeremy snatched his head up, and she pressed her lips together. Her tone had been flirty, and he could tell that it was different than usual. We were walking a very fine line.

"Riley," I said in a determined voice.

"Fine," she replied.

"Thank you." I knew she didn't like splurging, and I had asked her to come here, so this felt like a fair deal.

I turned to Jeremy. "Buddy, we're going to wait here until the Uber picks Riley up, and then we're going home, okay?"

"Sure." He turned to face her. "Thank you for coming tonight, Riley."

"Of course. I'm glad you guys thought about me."

"I did," Jeremy said proudly, "not Dad."

I laughed and glanced at Riley, giving her a look that indicated otherwise. I'd been thinking about her more than I wanted to admit.

Her Uber arrived a few minutes later, and her jaw dropped. "What did you order, Uber Luxury?"

"What do you mean?"

"This is a Mercedes!"

"I always order the most comfortable option."

She opened her mouth, but I narrowed my eyes, and then she closed it again. If she was her usual sassy self, Jeremy would pick up on something for sure.

"Thanks. Both of you have a great evening."

Jeremy was busy investigating the magnets we'd bought earlier today. He didn't even glance up. I kept an eye on him while I tilted closer to Riley.

"Thank you for joining us, Riley. It was the highlight of the day."

Her lips parted slightly as she lowered herself into the car, and I closed the door.

As the Uber drove away, I turned to Jeremy. "Come on, buddy. We're ready to go home."

———

After a quick dinner, and despite my fears that the ice cream would give him too much energy, he went out like a light at eight thirty. The excitement of the day had probably counteracted the effects of the sugar.

I paced the living room, unable to relax. I needed to talk to Riley. Ideally, I'd do that face-to-face, but I wasn't going to leave my son alone at home.

I was seconds away from calling Mom or Finn and Knox and asking them to come watch him, then stopped myself. First, they'd realize I was up to something, and I didn't want a million Sterlings weighing in on this. I didn't actually want anyone's advice. And second, Jeremy himself would be scared if he woke up and I wasn't here. He'd think something bad had happened. I didn't want to put him in that position.

Damn it! I couldn't believe that I was desperate enough to even consider calling my family. No, I wasn't going to see Riley tonight, but that didn't mean I couldn't call her.

I went outside on the terrace. I had too much energy coursing through my body to sit on the couch, so I stood at the edge, looking down at the pool.

"Come on, Riley, pick up."

She answered after a few rings. "Hey." Her voice was soft.

"You were asleep?" I asked.

"Yeah, I don't know how that happened. I came home and lay on my bed to read and must have zoned out. I even dropped my Kindle on my chest."

"Then go back to sleep."

"No, if I sleep now, I'll wake up at three o'clock in the morning What's wrong? Did something happen with Jeremy? Does he not want to sleep? You could try persuading him by saying that Mr. Beagles is going to visit him in his dreams."

"You know about that?" I said, stunned. He'd lost Mr. Beagles years ago.

"Yeah. One day, he told me that sometimes he dreamed about him, and then I made up this whole thing that Mr. Beagles is out there somewhere and visiting him in his dreams. So the more he sleeps, the more he'll visit him."

"You're amazing," I said, and that was the honest-to-God truth. Jeremy had had many nannies, but none had taken the time to understand his worries and come up with ideas to comfort him. I didn't want to ruin this for him.

And yet, Riley and I needed to talk.

"Riley," I said.

She groaned. "You don't have to say it."

"You don't even know what I was about to tell you."

"Something about how this can't happen because you don't want to have to sneak around with me in bathrooms or outside them. And, most of all, because this would be complicated for Jeremy."

I closed my eyes. She was right. I was going to say a variation of that. But now that she'd said the words, they all felt like excuses. Nothing that wouldn't be manageable.

"I want you, Riley" was all I said.

She gasped. "Oh wow. That did not go the way I thought it would."

"Everything you said is true," I admitted, putting my hand on the railing and looking down, "but I still want you." I paused and then added. "I need you."

"Really?" Her voice was a mere whisper.

"I don't know how it happened. I just know that it's true. Of course it's complicated, but I'd never forgive myself if I didn't at least tell you this."

"Well, tell me more, because I definitely like what I'm hearing. I'm not dreaming, am I?"

"You're so fucking not. If I were there, I'd prove it to you. I'd touch you until you'd beg for me."

She giggled. "Well, now I know I'm not dreaming because I never have dirty dreams."

I sucked in my breath. The idea of her having dirty dreams was enough to make me hard. I groaned.

"What was that?"

"We should talk about this face-to-face."

"Oh, okay. What do you propose?"

"A date," I said.

"Really? But how? When?"

I swallowed hard. "My youngest brother wants to take Jeremy away for the weekend on Friday."

"Okay, then, Friday it is," she said. "In a minute," she called out.

"What's that?" I asked.

"My roommates want to talk to me."

"See you tomorrow?"

"Yeah. See you."

I was already counting down the days to Friday.

CHAPTER TWENTY-ONE

Riley

On Monday afternoon, Duncan arrived just before I headed out. I grinned and almost wanted to jump him before realizing that Jeremy was there as well. Crap. Why hadn't we discussed how to handle this? Then again, what was there to discuss? I just had to act like a normal human being, not a teenager.

"Hi, Riley," he said, then looked around. "Where's Jeremy?"

"In the bathroom, washing his hands and getting ready for dinner."

"Which means I can do this," he said, then pressed me against the wall and kissed me senseless.

Well, at least I wasn't the only one acting like a teenager. I figured that made it okay.

On Tuesday, we learned to behave... or at least that's what I thought. And when he asked me to stay for dinner, I flatly refused because that was just playing with fire.

We managed the same on Wednesday.

But then on Thursday, we didn't. When he arrived at home, Jeremy was in the shower. He'd played in the mud outside and was under strict instructions to clean himself properly, which I relayed to Duncan.

"So, that means he's going to need a while, huh?" Duncan asked.

"I guess. He just went in."

"Good. I need to kiss you so fucking much."

Then he lifted me onto the kitchen island, kissing me hard and deep, even more desperate than on Monday. We both had so much pent-up energy from behaving for two days. I pressed my thighs against the sides of his hips until a low groan reverberated in his throat. My torso was pegged to his, so I felt it throughout my body.

"Can't wait for tomorrow," he said.

"I can't either."

Then, for some reason, I became a bit jittery. I wasn't ready for us to talk about this. I couldn't see what would come out of it. I mean, we both knew our respective situations. I was starting my law job in less than two months. And he was a single dad focused on his son. That was never going to change, and it didn't have to. I just couldn't see how I could fit into their lives.

Why, oh why did I want to become a lawyer and be stuck in an office all day, dealing with all those uppity suits? I loved spending time with Jeremy. He was hands down the best kid in the world.

But being a lawyer would allow me to take care of my sister and Mom. That would make it all worth it.

Despite my reservations, I was looking forward to tomorrow because the man was a damn good kisser, and I was dying to have him all to myself again. I'd seen a different side of him last weekend. I'd seen Duncan the man, not Duncan the dad. And while I liked both a lot, I really, really wanted to experience some more of Duncan the man.

He stepped back, helping me down from the kitchen island, just as we heard the bathroom door open.

"You have excellent timing," I said.

I wanted to ask him more about tomorrow, but I didn't get a chance because Jeremy ran toward us wearing nothing at all and saying, "There's a spider on my towel. Hi, Dad."

Then his eyes widened, and he ran back into the bathroom.

I looked at Duncan.

"Okay, what just happened? Why did he run away? Does he have you kill spiders?" he asked me.

"Yeah. I'm the designated insect killer around here."

"Funny, because he tells me that he can do it himself because he's a big boy when it's just the two of us," Duncan said.

I chuckled. "Maybe he wants to impress you. Oh, and he trusts me enough to be vulnerable with me. That's so cute."

Then I said, "Let's go kill that critter before it scares him even more."

I walked in front of Duncan, and he squeezed my ass. I looked at him over my shoulder. "What are you doing?"

"I believe you call this fondling."

"Yeah, it is," I said.

"Then you've got your answer. Fuck, I can't wait to get you alone."

I smiled, focusing on my steps.

"Let's get that spider first."

————

On Friday, Duncan's brother Knox arrived earlier than I'd expected, which was fine by me. My plan was to hurry home and change—I wanted to look perfect when Duncan picked me up.

I'd imagined all the brothers to be similar to Duncan, but I couldn't have been more wrong. Knox was laid-back and quick with a joke. I also had a feeling that he knew way more about me than I knew about him.

"So, how do you like working with my brother?" he asked.

"He's a great boss," I said.

"He is, isn't he? Very exacting as well."

"If he wants things done a certain way, that's not bad."

"So, I heard you plan to be a lawyer."

I jerked my head back. "Really? How?"

"From my brother. He likes to talk about you," Knox said.

"Oh, okay."

"Yeah. Especially because he doesn't seem to be aware of it. After our meetings are over, he somehow ends up talking about you."

My jaw dropped.

He wiggled his eyebrows. "Am I putting you in an awkward position?"

"Yes, a bit."

"Sorry. It's a habit of mine. Actually, it kind of runs in the family. Duncan has better manners than us. The rest of us are a bunch of Neanderthals."

"I see."

This conversation was completely bizarre.

Knox grinned. "I hope I'm not scaring you away."

"No," I said, "I'm just stunned that you're so... not like Duncan."

"Ha! You can say that twice. No, I am not. Between you and me, I'm so much better."

I laughed. "I'd say it's debatable, but obviously I'm biased."

Knox whistled. "You're a good sport, Riley."

"I appreciate that. So, what exactly are you going to do with Jeremy?"

"I've got a full weekend planned for him, but I'm afraid it'd make no sense to lay it all out. Knowing him, he'll convince me to do something else, like to go on roller coasters again."

I beamed because there was a lot of affection in Knox's voice. I liked that Jeremy was so well-loved by all members of the family.

"What are you still doing here?" Duncan asked, coming out of the elevator.

Knox looked over his shoulder, and his face exploded into a grin.

"I'm waiting for Jeremy to retrieve his favorite toys. And I was getting to know Riley here."

Duncan stopped right next to me. "Don't annoy Riley."

"It's too late, brother," Knox said, folding his arms over his chest. "I already introduced myself as a Neanderthal, and now I have to live up to that intro."

Duncan looked at me. "I'm sorry for whatever he's said."

I laughed. "Nothing too bad. Is it true that you're the only one with manners in the family?"

Duncan's eyes closed as if he couldn't believe what I just said. "He said what?"

Knox jerked his head back. "No, man. I meant it in a way that sounded boring, but apparently, Riley appreciated it."

Duncan shook his head. "I should have known that you'd bolted from that meeting for a reason."

"Ah, the rest of you had it covered, and besides, when else would I have the opportunity to meet Riley one-on-one?"

Wait, what? He'd left a meeting early to meet me?

"Right. I'll go see if Jeremy needs—"

I didn't finish the sentence because Jeremy came barreling toward us, holding his favorite bus under one arm and an inflatable bear in the other one.

"I'm ready, Uncle."

"That you are, buddy." Knox looked at the toys but didn't chastise him at all. I liked him even more with every passing second.

I avoided looking at Duncan, feeling more on edge than any other time we'd been together.

"All right, then. Let's go," Knox said. "Duncan, I'd promise you that we'll be good, but you know me. I don't like to lie. I am absolutely incapable of behaving."

Jeremy looked up at him, grinning. Knox was uncle of the year.

"All right, bud. If you want, I can hold one of these." Knox held his hands out toward the toys.

Jeremy took a step back. "No, I want to hold them."

"Then I'll just take the backpack," Knox said, grabbing it and throwing it over his shoulder. It looked comical since it was much too small for him.

After a brief goodbye, they both headed toward the elevator. Just before going out, Knox waved at us. I felt my cheeks go up in flames the second the doors closed.

Duncan and I went back inside the condo and closed the door.

"Riley, is everything okay?" he asked. He swallowed hard, not taking his eyes off me. "Are you changing your mind?"

"About what?

"Our date."

My eyes widened. "No. Why would you think that?"

"Because you seem nervous."

"No, it's just that I was hoping that the first time I'd see you tonight was when you picked me up from home and I'd be wearing a knockout dress."

He smiled before starting to laugh. "Sometimes I forget how adorable you are. You're gorgeous just as you are."

"We should hurry up. I don't have too much time to get ready."

"Or," he said, coming closer and splaying his hand around the back of my neck, "we can just go directly there."

I gasped. "No way! I mean it. I look terrible."

"You look gorgeous," he said.

"I want to dress up."

He grinned reluctantly, straightening up and lowering his hand. "Right," he said. "Okay, then. Let's go." He pointed toward the door. "After you."

As we headed to the elevator, I realized that Duncan was walking a few feet behind me. "What are you doing?" I asked.

"Keeping my distance. Who knows what will happen otherwise."

Guess where he couldn't keep his distance, though? In the elevator.

I was making a concerted effort to stay away, leaning against one of the walls. It took all I had not to tempt him. What on earth was happening to me? After all, I'd been the one who insisted that I wanted to change, yet now I wanted to entice him.

Good Lord. I was terribly confused about what I really wanted.

CHAPTER TWENTY-TWO

Riley

The drive took longer than usual because there was a lot of traffic. I was starting to get anxious; I wanted to wash my hair and style it, but now it looked like I'd have to cut corners.

I'd kept my fingers crossed the whole way that my roommates wouldn't be home because they were for sure going to pounce on Duncan while he waited. But then I groaned when I stepped inside the house. Both of them were here.

"Hey, Riley," Julia said, and then her eyes widened. "Duncan."

"He's going to wait for me while I get ready."

I pinned Julia with my gaze, trying to communicate silently that she had to behave. I wasn't sure if I'd succeeded, though. There was no way I could pull her and Christine to the side and warn them without Duncan overhearing, so I had to hope for the best. I knew I should have texted them.

"Don't worry, we'll keep you company," Christine said.

Hell, this was going to be a bloodbath, but still, I had full confidence that Duncan could hold his own.

I hurried into the shower. I usually liked to take my time—I was like a frog in the water—but right now I washed my hair at top speed and decided to forgo the conditioner because I was supposed to leave it in for five minutes, and I absolutely did not have the time. However, I regretted it the second I started to comb my hair. It had so many knots that I lost as much time detangling them as I would have if I'd simply let the conditioner do its work.

Then the hardest part came. I'd spent half the day thinking about which outfit to wear tonight. I'd decided on wearing a white-and-pink dress and white sandals, but now of course I thought that was a completely silly idea. I needed something to make a statement.

I took out a red dress that I hadn't worn in forever. I'd bought it once at a sale, figuring that eventually I'd have a reason to wear it. Tonight was definitely that reason. I paired it with black sandals that had straps. They looked 100 percent sexy. The dress had a heart-shaped décolletage and fit snugly on my body. I accessorized it with half-moon earrings and a matching necklace, then sprayed on my favorite perfume, Hugo Boss Seduction, before heading out of the room.

"So, Duncan, you want to do shots?" Julia asked.

I closed my eyes. *Oh, Julia. Way to scare him away and think we're a bunch of sorority girls or something.*

"I'm driving, so no drinks, but thank you," Duncan replied smoothly.

I stepped inside the living room, loudly announcing, "I'm ready. Let's go."

Julia and Christine both stared at me. "Okay, this is the fastest you've ever gotten ready for a date." Christine grinned at Duncan. "I think that's a good sign, Duncan. Means she couldn't wait to go out."

"Or," Julia said, "she couldn't wait to get him away from us."

I pointed at each of them in turn. "You're both right." Then I looked at Duncan. "Ready to go?"

He didn't reply, just lowered his gaze slowly, then glanced back up.

Holy shit. I felt tingles all over my body.

"Let's go." His voice was a bit rougher now.

I sent an air-kiss to Julia and Christine. The latter winked at us in a manner that reminded me of Knox.

Duncan put a hand on my back. Usually, he put it at the small of my back, but now he placed his fingers higher, right at the point where the dress ended and my bare back started. I straightened up instantly, as if an electric charge had shot through me.

The second we stepped outside, he said, "You smell amazing. You *look* amazing."

"Thank you."

He opened the car door for me, and I sat down. He looked away quickly as he closed it.

What was that? Why didn't he want to look at me?

He got in the car and drove away immediately, without even glancing at me.

"Duncan?" I asked.

"Hmm?" That one syllable was loaded.

"Everything okay? Are you upset?" My stomach tightened at the thought. What did I do to make him upset?

"Why would you think that?"

"Because you're not looking at me."

He groaned. "Riley, you're so damn beautiful tonight that I'm not even sure how I'll get through our date without mauling you. For now, my goal is just to get to us there."

I swallowed hard. *Wow, okay.* "I hope my roommates didn't drive you too crazy," I said to change the subject. "I heard something about shots when I came out."

He chuckled. "Don't worry. They're young. I get it."

His words didn't quite sit well with me, but I didn't know why. What he was saying was true. And he didn't say it with contempt. But then again, I was young too. The way he said it made it sound like he thought it was a problem—that we were in two separate worlds.

This wasn't the first time I'd thought as much, that we were at different points in our lives. But I thought we'd moved past that and matched up well.

We arrived at the restaurant twenty minutes later. It was in the Gaslamp Quarter on top of a redbrick building.

"Let's see what the fuss is about. It's one of the best places in town," he said proudly.

"You've never been here before?"

He shrugged. "Nope, but I've asked around. I wanted to impress you."

I leaned into him. "You've impressed me already. Don't you know that?"

"Doesn't mean I can rest on my laurels." He kissed the side of my head before adding, "Come on, let's get out of the car."

"But don't we have to park?"

"They have valet."

That's when I noticed a guy in a uniform wearing a chapeau walking toward us as we got out of the car.

"Hi, my name is Duncan Sterling. I have a reservation here this evening."

"I'll park your car, sir, and then I'll leave the key with our hostess. Just tell her when you need your vehicle, and I'll have it brought around for you."

"Thank you," Duncan said, then took my hand. "Shall we?"

I nodded. I'd never been to a restaurant that had a valet. To be fair, I'd never been to anything that even looked nearly this fancy.

We took an elevator up to the rooftop. A hostess waited by the doors when they opened.

"Good evening," she greeted us.

"Duncan Sterling. I have a table for two," Duncan said.

"Certainly." She looked down at what I assumed was the reservation list.

"You might find the reservation under Knox Sterling."

She glanced back up at him and smiled. "Oh, you're his brother."

Duncan nodded. "Indeed."

"This way, please."

As we followed her, I glanced around the restaurant. This place was amazing. It looked like a botanical garden with plants everywhere. It felt like we were in a forest, each table somehow hidden in greenery.

When we sat down at our table, I swear I could almost forget there was anyone else around, although I could definitely hear chatter.

Duncan looked at me, smiling. "You like it, huh?"

"I love it." Then I asked, "So, Knox found this place? And you still gave him so much shit this evening?"

"Hey, he had no right to show up like that and pounce on you."

"He didn't pounce. He was just... I don't know. I've never met someone like him."

Duncan groaned. "Anyway, Knox is very much aware of what is *in* and what *isn't*. He's investing a lot in the restaurant business and also likes to go out to the best places. I'm probably the most knowledgeable Sterling brother in the kid-friendly restaurants, though that's not what I wanted tonight." He touched my cheek with the back of his fingers. "Tonight, I wanted something special just for the two of us."

I felt my cheeks heat up again. I had no idea why I was blushing so much tonight.

"I've been looking forward to this evening so much," I said in a breath.

"So have I."

A moment later, the waiter arrived with two menus, then recited the daily specials.

"We can start with drinks," he finished. "Madam?"

"I will have a mojito," I said.

It was one of the specials. Apparently, they had a secret recipe.

"And I'll have a Buona Sera," Duncan said.

We ordered food as well. I chose the chicken and scallops with hummus, and Duncan went with something similar but with additional harissa sauce. I was impressed with the menu. It was fusion cuisine as far as I could tell, a mix of different oriental foods.

Once the waiter left, Duncan said, "Why do you look so amused?"

"I remembered how smoothly you turned down Christine and said you wouldn't drink because you're driving. Then again, you're always smooth."

He groaned. "Not always. Not when it comes to you."

I bit my lower lip. "Well..."

I stopped because the waiter returned with our drinks. The mojito was red. *All right, this definitely looks different than what I'm used to.*

Duncan and I clinked glasses, and then I immediately took a sip. I'd suspected that the red color came from some sort of strawberry juice, but it was melon.

"Hey, this is really good."

Duncan nodded. "I've got to give it to Knox. He knows his stuff."

"See, you can tell him that you've been too hard on him."

"Never," Duncan said. "It will only go to his head."

I laughed. "You can't have that, can you?"

"Fuck no. We all rely on one another to keep us grounded."

"How so?" I asked.

He shrugged. "Early on, when we started the business, we realized that a lot of people are going to blow smoke up our asses and inflate our egos. That's dangerous. You lose sight of who you are and what really matters. We promised one another not to allow that to happen."

"That's very smart," I said. "I like that you and your brothers are a team."

"We really are. Mom and Dad are extremely good at keeping us in line as well."

"So, I'm a bit confused. Your parents are separated, right? Because Jeremy sometimes mentions doing stuff with each of them individually."

"They're divorced, but lately they've been getting closer, even before my brother gave them the store. They're almost flirting, which is a bit weird, if I'm honest."

I nodded. "I bet."

"I'm happy for them no matter what they choose to do, but it sometimes feels like I'm the third wheel."

"Do you often go to the store?" I asked.

"Sort of. We're helping Mom put the finishing touches on her section. I don't know if I mentioned, but they each have their own businesses. They tried to use a construction company, but it didn't work out. Initially, she wanted a particular color scheme, then changed her mind. It's all right, though."

I was going to melt. Duncan Sterling was the man of my dreams. And quite frankly, until now, I didn't even know I had a type. But maybe I didn't. Maybe my type was simply Duncan Sterling.

"What are you thinking?" he said. "Your expression changed."

I sighed. "Up until right now, I didn't think I had a type."

"A type?" His voice had a dangerous edge.

"You know, a type of man I'd go out with."

My voice faded because his eyes turned feral.

"You're going on dates with other men while we—"

"No!" I said. "No, I didn't mean right now. I meant before."

He swallowed hard, cupping my jaw with his hand. Tingles traveled all over my body, alarmed at what he was processing.

"Good," he said. "Because you belong with me."

I licked my lips. "Okay."

Yep, he was a hundred percent my type.

"Tell me about you, Riley."

"What do you want to know?" I asked.

"What's something you love but haven't done in a long time?"

"Oh, that's easy—camping. I love camping."

He stared at me. "You're serious?"

I nodded vigorously.

"What exactly do you like about it?"

"Being surrounded by nature."

"You can do that in a hotel too."

I shook my head. "It's not the same. You're closer to nature when you're in a tent. Don't tell me you don't like it."

"It's not one of my favorite things to do. Jeremy loves it, though. Dad takes him often."

The corners of my mouth twitched. "But you don't?"

"No. If I can get away with not going, then I'll take advantage of it."

"You didn't even like it as a kid?" I asked.

"No. Dad is also a fan of the outdoors, like you. I liked going fishing with him but not spending the night in a tent." He took a sip of his drink. "So, where do you like going camping?"

"Nearby. I've been to a few of the parks around here. They're wonderful. Although one of my dreams is to travel outside the US, I've never been."

CHAPTER TWENTY-THREE

Duncan

I could lay the world at her feet if she wanted me to. I could take her everywhere she wanted, experience the world next to her.

"What are you thinking about?" she asked.

I leaned forward. "Too many things. Some of them might scare you."

She scowled. "I doubt it."

I put my hand on the table, palm up, and she immediately placed hers in mine. "The thing is, Riley, some of those thoughts scare me too."

She sucked in a breath. "Why?"

"Because I've never had them before. With anyone. Not even Shona, my ex. Everything is different when it comes to you."

"What do you mean?"

"For instance, I've always been able to override my instincts."

She frowned. "That's not possible. Instincts are just instincts."

"The mind is a powerful tool. But when it comes to you, everything is different."

"That bothers you?"

"Not one fucking bit."

I feathered my thumb along her palm, moving farther up to her wrist. She sucked in a deep breath.

"Riley," I said in a low voice.

"Yes?"

"What about having that second drink at home?"

"Thank God. I thought you were never going to suggest it."

This woman! We were in sync, craving to be alone. I didn't want anything else holding her attention—not the food, or the waiter, or the view. I wanted it on me and me alone.

I'd given them my credit card on arrival, so we left quickly. During the drive, she fiddled with her thumbs in her lap.

"Riley, are you having second thoughts?" I asked cautiously.

"No. Why would you think that?"

I covered her hand with mine. "Because you're nervous."

"Oh no, not at all. I'm just giving my hands something to do so I don't, you know, maul you right here. Talk you into parking somewhere so I can jump your bones."

Now that she'd said it, the idea was forming in my mind. I could pull over somewhere.

No! She deserves better than getting mauled in the back seat.

We arrived at my building a few minutes later. The parking lot was empty; there wasn't much activity at this time of the evening. There was no one in the elevator either. And if I thought it took a lot of willpower not to pull the car into a dark corner, it was nothing compared to the self-control necessary not to kiss her here in the elevator.

The condo was dark when we stepped inside. I didn't even bother to turn on the light, just kissed and kissed her, walking her through the room until we bumped into the wall. This woman had a hold over me that I couldn't explain. It didn't matter that I'd started my evening with the best intentions. I'd intended for us to stay out in the city for hours, yet here we were. My need for her was greater than anything else. It over-powered every thought.

"Duncan," she murmured as I kissed down her neck.

Her dress had driven me crazy from the second she'd come out of her room. The way it molded to her body should be illegal. It didn't dip too low, but it pushed her breasts together, and she looked so fucking irresistible in it. I honestly had no idea how I managed to keep myself in check while we were at the restaurant.

But now I didn't have to hold back; I could explore her to my heart's desire. I wanted to get her into bed, fast. I took her hand, stepping away.

"No! Why did you do that?" she asked.

"Because I want you in my bed tonight. I don't want to fuck you against this wall, and it's a real possibility if we don't get moving."

She giggled. "Okay."

I led her down to the master bedroom and closed the door even though it wasn't necessary. It was just the two of us tonight, so she could scream so it carried through the walls. I didn't care if the neighbors heard.

I kissed her again, moving her closer to the bed. I undid her zipper, intending to push down her dress, but it wouldn't budge, so I yanked it over her head instead and threw it next to the bed. She wasn't wearing a bra, and her breasts were so damn exquisite. I touched her nipples, and she tilted her body forward, pressing them into my hand. I lowered myself until I was face-to-face with her chest, then took one nipple into my mouth, twirling my tongue around it. At the same time, I pushed her leg up. She instantly understood what I wanted and put her leg on the bed. I nearly lost my self-control when I realized she was already wet. This woman wanted me.

I played her pussy like a harp while I continued to suck her nipple before moving to the other one. She was getting wetter with every stroke. She gasped when I brushed her clit with my thumb, and I knew she was ready for more. Fucking hell, so was I.

I pushed my hands down, gripping my cock. I needed this so damn bad, but I wanted the taste of her pussy too. I wanted to feel her come on my tongue.

Lowering myself to my knees, I dipped my tongue inside her. She gasped and nearly lost her balance. In the dark room, she hadn't seen me. I'd been about to turn on the lamp on the night-stand, but this was better. Our senses were heightened. I nudged her clit with my fingers while I dipped my tongue in and out. Her body was completely soft.

I couldn't take this much longer. I needed more. I needed all of her.

Rising to my feet, I replaced my tongue with two fingers.

"Lie down on the bed," I said.

I guided her down as she sat on the bed first and then moved farther to the center of it, lying down. I fought the instinct to turn on the light, wanting to relish this. I might not be able to see her, but I was acutely aware of her reactions. They were exquisite.

I kissed a straight line from her clavicle down to her pubic bone and then nudged her clit with my nose before going back up. At the same time, I moved my hands all over her body. Her breath hitched when my mouth went from the lower part of her breast straight to the upper part, completely ignoring her nipple. She sucked in a breath, clearly bracing herself for what I was about to do next.

I liked surprising her. Tonight was different than the last time. We were both in a completely different state of mind. Then, part of me had always worried that she wasn't ready and that it wasn't the right time. But not right now. Everything felt fucking perfect. Having her scent against my sheets again was all I'd wanted.

I kissed down her body again. Now, I wanted my mouth on

her. I'd made up my mind. But then she unexpectedly turned on one side.

"What are you doing?" I asked.

"I want your cock."

I damn near exploded. *Fuck yes.* I positioned myself so we could easily sixty-nine. And then I was on her. When she took my cock into her mouth, I nearly forgot my damn name. It felt so impossibly good. I dipped my tongue inside her as she swirled her tongue on my crown. And then I nipped her clit.

She exploded instantly, clamping her lips around my cock tightly.

Fuuuuuck. I nearly exploded, too, but I paced myself, fighting to keep my hips in place. Every instinct wanted to thrust. I kept pulling her clit between my lips until her entire body convulsed, and then I felt her calm down. I pulled back, and so did she.

"Oh my God, that was fast," she said. "Why did you move away?"

"I want to be inside you, Riley. I need it so damn bad."

"I need it too."

"Get on your knees," I commanded while I reached over to the nightstand, turning the light on. Feeling her was exceptional, but I wanted to see her too.

Her face was red and flushed, and it spread down to her neck and chest. And then I saw that gorgeous ass up in the air as she positioned herself on all fours in the middle of my bed. She looked over her shoulder, moving her body lightly back and forth. She accidentally brushed her pussy against the length of my cock and gasped. "Oh my God." She buried her head in the mattress.

"Riley, what are you doing to me?" I said.

I slid inside her the next second because I couldn't take this anymore.

She groaned against her hand. I nearly came when I realized that she was biting her own arm. "No, I want to hear you. I want the whole city of San Diego to hear you. Don't hide."

"Duncan, I don't think I can..."

My whole body was on edge. "Do you trust me?" I asked.

"Yes." Even though her voice wavered, there was strength in it.

"You can trust that I'll make you come again, and you're going to enjoy it."

"Okay," she whispered.

I pulled back a few inches, then pushed in with all I had. Her cry resounded through the room. The fact that she followed every single command turned me on to no end. I liked hearing her unrestrained passion.

Her groans reverberated through her body, and I soaked them up. It seemed as if this union went far beyond satisfying each other's desperate need for release. I felt close to her when I was very deep inside her. I unleashed all her pleasure, like I had a key to her body. I was the only one who could do this to her.

In this position, I had my hands free. I touched her upper thighs and then the side of her hips, then leaned slightly forward and grasped both of her breasts. They overfilled my palms in this position, and I discovered that she liked me to circle both her nipples while I slid in and out of her. Her cries changed slightly, as if they came from somewhere deep inside her.

When she reached one hand to her side, groping blindly around her thigh, I realized she wanted my hand. I interlaced my fingers with hers, and she squeezed them hard. She was close, and so was I. I knew I was going to succumb to my climax only seconds after I felt hers. It was just what I needed to tip over the edge.

I cupped her right buttock and then slid my hand past her upper thigh and onto her pussy. Once again, I played it like a harp, focusing on her clit. She groaned so hard that I knew she was going to give in soon.

I was lost even before her orgasm rolled in. For a few seconds, I didn't realize what was going on, and then I felt us falling forward. I rolled onto my back, holding her on top of me.

Her back was plastered to my chest. Her head was lying next to mine, my nose pressed against her cheek. I held her ass high up in the air, and I pounded inside her. I was relentless.

Fuck, why didn't I think about this position before? It was excellent. I could feel the rhythm of her breath; her own pulse seemed to become mine. We were one, and I had fantastic access to her clit. I pressed three fingers against it, moving them in circles. She rewarded me with her loudest moan yet. It was a throaty sound, and it reverberated through both our bodies. I tugged at her earlobe and kissed the side of her cheek that I could reach. Then I gave her my own release.

My grunt of pleasure took me by surprise. Heat spiraled through me, capturing every cell and every muscle. I put my ass down on the bed. Even like this, I kept thrusting inside her. I had to take one hand away from her clit so I could hold both of her hips as I moved her up and down.

When I felt her fingers against my cock, I realized she'd replaced my hand with hers. My orgasm intensified even more while her own cries become fainter and fainter as she calmed down. Gradually, so did I, but I kept her on top of me, inhaling her perfume.

This is the best night of my life.

CHAPTER TWENTY-FOUR

Riley

The next few weeks flew by quicker than I'd hoped. The clock was ticking—I didn't have that much time left with Jeremy and Duncan. But I was determined to focus on the positive. Jeremy and I were having a lot of fun together, and Duncan was so swoon-worthy that I wasn't sure how any other man could hold a candle next to him.

Paula had a new job, and she seemed to be happy there. Which was why when she called me on a Wednesday afternoon, just as I was heading out to pick up Jeremy from summer school, I instantly knew something was wrong. She wasn't one to call in the middle of the day. I answered right away.

"Hey. What's wrong?" I asked.

She sighed. "Don't panic."

My heart leaped into my throat. "What's wrong?" I repeated.

"My shit ex-boss kind of lost it. He called, demanding I go back to work."

"He did what?" I ran my hand through my hair, cursing under my breath.

"He's coming here. Not even sure how he got my address."

"Why?" I asked.

"To talk. And I know this is bad timing, but I could really use some of that sass you gave him last time, you being a lawyer and everything."

I nodded even though she couldn't see me. "I'm on my way."

"Thank you so much." The relief in her voice was clear. Then Paula asked, "Hey, have you talked to Mom in a bit? You haven't told her anything, right?"

"No, Paula, I haven't mentioned it, but you should. You know Mom will finagle it from one of us eventually."

She sighed. "Yeah, I know. I just wanted to get settled first before I mentioned my drama. Hey, does she know about Duncan?"

"She knows I work for him." *And no, she doesn't know we're together, and I want to keep it that way for fear of getting a lecture about not eating where I sleep or whatever the saying is.*

"But not the rest, right? I just don't want to ruin your parade unknowingly," Paula said, which I appreciated. Both of us usually spoke or texted with Mom weekly and tried to not worry her with things she'd have no control over.

We talked more about her shitty boss, and I could have slapped myself for not having taken up Duncan on his offer to make sure he wouldn't bother Paula again. Clearly, I hadn't done the job properly.

After hanging up, I remembered that I was supposed to be picking up Jeremy.

"Shit. Okay. Breathe in, breathe out. Riley, you've got this."

I took in another breath and called Duncan. To my relief, he picked up immediately.

"Hey," I said.

"Riley? Anything wrong?"

Shoot. I knew I didn't sound like my normal self. But I wasn't going to hide this. Duncan and I had moved past that, and I knew he'd want to know.

"Yes, um..." My voice shook. "Paula is having some issues with her ex-boss. She asked me to go over to her place and help out. Any chance you could pick up Jeremy?"

"What kind of issues?" he asked.

"He belittled her on the phone, and now he said he's going to drop by her place."

"What the actual fuck? He's harassing her, that fuc—" he bellowed.

I couldn't believe he was getting so indignant on behalf of my sister, that his protectiveness extended to her as well.

I interrupted him, saying, "I know. That's why I want to be there."

"I'll come too."

"What?" I asked sharply.

"I'll ask one of my brothers to pick up Jeremy."

"You really don't have to do that." It was one thing to be protective of her, but I didn't want to drag him into this.

"I don't want the two of you alone with him. I don't like him one bit."

"Neither do I," I admitted. "I'll meet you there, okay?"

"Do you want me to pick you up?"

"No. It's faster if we both head there."

"Got it."

I was feeling a bit guilty that he was taking off in the middle of the day and that someone else was picking up Jeremy. But I couldn't deny that I was happy he was joining us.

I hurried to my sister's, forgoing public transportation and taking an Uber instead. When I arrived, Duncan's car was already in front of her building. Honestly, he and I needed to have a chat about speed limits. He couldn't have arrived too long ago, though, because he was standing in front of the building's entrance, phone in hand.

"Duncan," I said, hurrying toward him.

He looked up from his phone. "I was about to call you." His mouth was set in a thin line. Frown lines marred his forehead.

"Is everything okay with Jeremy?"

"Yeah. Griffin got him."

"I'm really sorry—"

"Riley, you don't have to apologize about anything. Come on, let's go to your sister's apartment. I forgot which unit it was."

"Number 3."

I pressed the button, and the front door buzzed a second later. We hurried inside, going straight to her place. As we approached the door, I heard voices coming from inside.

Damn it! The guy was already here. I'd hoped to arrive before him so my sister could give me more details.

We didn't bother knocking. I just opened the front door.

"Christ. What the hell are you two doing here?" Her boss was outrageously belligerent, just like last time.

"The better question is, why are *you* here?" Duncan bellowed. "We told you to stay the fuck away from Paula."

"You have no real basis to come here and demand that she go back to work for you," I said as coolly as possible.

He glanced at Duncan, then at me. "You know what? I've looked you up. You're not a licensed attorney, so don't think you can put up that same spiel you did last time. You're a liar, just like she is."

Paula rolled her eyes.

"I'll have my license this month."

I had no idea how I was being so calm, but I suspected it had something to do with having this mountain of a man next to me. I'd always been sassy and strong, but having him next to me made me feel grounded in a way I'd never experienced before.

"Riley might not be a lawyer yet, but I've got an army of them at my beck and call."

The guy sneered. "Really? Is that so? And who the fuck do you think you are?"

"Duncan Sterling."

His eyes narrowed. Sterling Investments was a huge company. Even a slimeball like him would have heard about it.

"Yeah, right," he said with disbelief. "The fuck you are."

Duncan stepped closer to him. "You leave here right now, or we're going to sue you into the next century."

"For what?"

"The list is endless," I said. "Stalking, for which she has witnesses." I pointed to myself and Duncan.

"Not providing safety and security at work," Duncan added through gritted teeth. "You name it."

Paula wasn't saying anything. She simply crossed her arms over her chest, tapping her foot.

He looked between all of us and said, "This conversation isn't over."

"Yes, it fucking is," Duncan said. "Now get the hell out."

Duncan stepped closer to him. The guy winced. My heart was in my throat. I hoped it didn't come to a physical altercation because it would definitely count against us.

Finally, he stomped out of the room. I blew out a breath of relief when the door closed behind him. Paula started shaking. I put an arm around her shoulders.

"Are you okay?" I asked.

"Yeah, I'm just glad that he left."

"What the hell did he even want?" Duncan asked in a harsh tone. He rolled his shoulders and shook his head, as if he needed to expel the adrenaline from his body.

"He said that the last few people he'd hired all quit after a few days and that I was his longest-lasting employee. It all started good on the phone, you know? Friendly. He almost convinced me to go back to work. He was so charming; he can really be nice when he wants to. Then, when I asked if he planned to install cameras, he totally turned on me. And then he showed up here."

"All right, you can't stay here anymore," Duncan said. "And no argument allowed."

My sister looked straight at him and then back at me. "You know what? I think I really shouldn't."

Will you look at that? She ignored me when I wanted her to, but Duncan convinced her with one sentence. I would definitely remember this for the future, whenever I have a hard time convincing her again. *Sheesh.*

"I don't think he'd show up here again," Paula said, "but I also don't want to risk it."

"And the place is a shithole," Duncan said in a stern voice. "There were plenty of guys looking for trouble outside."

She nodded. "Yeah, I know."

"How about we move you to my place now?" I wanted to strike while the iron was hot. "I can help you pack."

Paula laughed. "Sure. It's not like I've got a ton of things. And my lease is month to month and up next week anyway."

That was news to me. Maybe she'd been listening to my pleas after all?

"Don't worry about any of those logistics. I'll have someone take care of that stuff if you have any problems," Duncan said in that take-charge manner that I loved.

There really wasn't much to help her with. All her belongings fit in one suitcase. The apartment had been furnished, so she wouldn't be taking anything with her.

Less than an hour later, we were on our way to the house. I messaged Christine and Julia so they weren't blindsided when they came home in the afternoon and my sister was there. This wasn't unexpected, though; I'd spoken to them about the possibility of Paula rooming with me for a while, and they'd been very supportive.

Once we arrived, Duncan took her suitcase out of the trunk and brought it inside the house. He'd rolled his sleeves to his elbows sometime in the past few minutes, and the sight was absolutely exquisite.

"Do you want something to eat?" I asked Paula once we were inside the house.

"Um, yes, actually, I'm starving. I didn't have much for breakfast and didn't manage to get lunch at all."

"I'll make something really quick," I said, disappearing into the kitchen.

I needed a few moments on my own—though not too many because I didn't want my sister to get suspicious. Like Duncan, I also had adrenaline flowing through my body, and I needed to expel it. I did that best when I was on my own.

———

Duncan

Paula sat down on Riley's bed. "Thank you so much for showing up there today."

"No problem. Anything you need, let me know."

She smiled. "You sound like my sister. No wonder she likes you so much. And I like you, too, Duncan."

I winked at her. "You'd better not think I'm doing all this out of the goodness of my heart. I'm hoping to win some points."

She laughed. It was good to see her relaxed. "I'm not buying that. I think that's exactly why you're doing it—out of the goodness of your heart."

"I always take care of family." I wanted her to understand how important Riley and she were to me. "I know Riley's glad you decided to move in with her. It'll give her some peace of mind too."

"Yeah, I should have done so when she first suggested it, but don't tell her that." She smiled, adding, "She'll get all 'big sister' on me."

We laughed, and I could see how similar the two were, both independent and self-sufficient.

"I'm going to go check on her."

"I was going to suggest just that," Paula said. "She put up a tough act back there, but I know Riley. It takes a lot out of her."

"I know," I said.

Her eyes widened. "You really do, huh? You're great for her, Duncan."

That was good to hear.

I stepped out of the room, walking to the kitchen. Riley was putting toast, cheese, and ham on a platter. Her hands were shaking slightly, as were her shoulders. I went to her without saying anything and simply put an arm around her waist. She stilled instantly.

"I'm here with you," I whispered in her ear.

She turned around and buried her face in my chest. I put a hand at the back of her head, massaging it lightly.

"Thank you, thank you, thank you," she murmured. "Both for coming with me and convincing my sister to move here."

"I didn't need to do much convincing," I said. "She agreed fast."

Riley looked up at me with a happy smile, but her eyes were glossy. Had she been crying?

"You used that mysterious voice. Of course she agreed," she said. "I hope she picked up on the serious and not the sexy part." She wasn't making much sense, but I didn't interrupt her. "Anyway, you did help, trust me."

"My pleasure, Riley."

"Huh. See, you're using it again. And it's working."

"Good, because I meant what I said about the lawyers. That moron is trouble. At Sterling Investments, I have some of the finest lawyers in the city. I can ask them to deal with him."

She bit the inside of her cheek. "But is that okay? To use them for personal issues?"

"Fuck yes. I'd do anything for you. They work for the family as much as they work for the company."

Her eyes softened. She muttered, "The family," and then smiled again. Her body was less tense than it had been before.

"Okay," she said. "If it's not too much trouble."

"It's fucking not. I mean it. I'd do anything to help you out, to help Paula out. Whenever either of you needs anything, I want you to know, Riley, I can help. Always."

She gave me a wry smile. "You're so sure about that, huh?"

"Yes. I know you two are very capable, but I can make things easier." Money and influence had a tendency to do that. I had vast resources at my disposal, and I didn't mind using them for Riley and Paula. "Now, I have a proposition for you. Take care of your sister, and then I'll take you away and care of you."

"She might need me the whole day."

I shook my head. "She's going to be happy knowing you're taken care of."

Riley stepped closer to me, laying a hand on my cheek and then my shoulder before drawing it down my chest.

"What are you doing?" I asked.

"Checking that you're real. That you're really standing here, saying all these beautiful things."

"I'll do so much more. I'll show you."

I cupped her face, and her breath turned ragged instantly. I loved that I had this effect on her. That her breath quickened when I was near, no matter what.

I tilted over her, kissing the curve of her neck. "Let's take care of your sister."

I spent the whole afternoon with Riley and made several phone calls to our lawyers, not wanting to waste any time. Paula volunteered all the information she had on the guy. The lawyer agreed to start soft. There was no point asking for a restraining order just yet, but they could give him a good scare.

I'd dealt with slimeballs like him before. A display of power usually sent them scurrying away.

CHAPTER TWENTY-FIVE

Duncan

The next day, I met my brothers in the afternoon. Knox and Finn came back from yet another trip to Napa Valley. We were all in favor of buying the property. The only risk was someone else snatching it from us. Everyone had smug smiles when I entered the meeting room. I assumed that meant they had good news. Griffin, Knox, and Finn were sitting on one side of the table. I sat next to Wyatt and Chase.

"What's new?" I asked.

"You tell us."

Now that I was paying attention, I realized Chase's smile was smugger than everyone else's.

"What are you talking about? I'm not the one who flew to Napa. Did you email me a report and I didn't look at it?" I asked. I'd been busy with Riley the whole day yesterday, and then Jeremy. I didn't even check my mail.

Finn blew out a breath. "No, man. It's not about Napa. Everything's fine there. We've spoken already to the realtor and put everything in motion. He's going to keep in touch and let us know as soon as he puts in an offer."

"Okay, so the vineyard is still available. That's good." I was building something with my brothers again. It was exhilarating. I hadn't realized it before now, but I'd missed this: the thrill of a new joint project.

"So, why exactly are we meeting, then, if things are already in motion?" I asked.

Knox laced his fingers and put them on top of his head. Finn grinned. Wyatt laughed. Griffin shook his head. Chase's smile was even smugger.

"Well, the meeting *was* on the calendar," Finn said lazily.

"And we thought it would be an excellent opportunity to give you shit," Chase continued.

"About what?" I asked, bewildered.

"We've heard through the grapevine from our lawyers that you asked them to help with Riley's sister," Griffin said.

"Yeah."

"Ha!" Chase exclaimed.

"What exactly do you think I asked them for?" I was starting to realize what his smug smile was about. He thought I was going to do something stupid like he'd done with Hannah.

"I don't know. You tell us."

"Yeah, we're very excited to know," Wyatt added.

"Dude, I tried to get them off your case," Griffin said, "but they wouldn't stop."

"Thanks for having my back. Riley's sister's boss kept giving her headaches. I simply asked them to formally scare the shit out of him by sending him a cease and desist."

Chase was on the edge of his chair. "And?"

"And that's it," I said.

"Aw, man. Damn it."

I couldn't help myself; I burst out laughing. "I can't believe it. You thought I was going to pull some shit like you did?"

Chase sighed. "I'm not proud to admit, but yeah. That was exactly what I was waiting for."

Wyatt shook his head. "I told you that Duncan's got a good head on his shoulders."

"Hey!" Chase snapped. "I do as well. I just lost it when it came to Hannah."

It was my turn to smile smugly. "Well, I didn't. Case closed. Now, let's get back to Napa Valley."

"Yes, let's," Finn said. "But I will just say one last thing on this topic. You haven't lost your head *yet*. There's still plenty of time for that, and I'll be here to cheer when that happens."

I chuckled. "Good to know I can always count on you."

"Since Napa is a done deal and we skipped Monday's meeting, how about doing our usual brainstorming now?" Chase suggested.

"Great," Knox replied. "I love our brainstorming sessions. It puts my brain into a creative mode, and then it stays like that for the rest of the week."

Wyatt turned to him. "We're supposed to think about the ideas *before* and just pitch them here."

Knox grinned. "No one said that, brother. We agreed to share ideas in this room on Monday mornings. I like to fly by the seat of my pants."

Griffin burst out laughing, pointing at Wyatt. "And you didn't catch on until now?"

Knox stared at Wyatt.

"What do you mean, catch on?" Wyatt looked around the table. "Everyone else knew?"

"Obviously," I said.

"Some of the ideas he comes up with are outlandish," Chase informed him.

I was usually the tactless one in the group, but Chase gave me a good run for my money.

While everyone pitched in with ideas, I took out my phone, looking up nearby locations for camping.

"What's that?" Griffin asked, leaning over and glancing at my phone. "Why are you looking up camping?"

I immediately turned the phone face down. "That's none of your business."

"You're finally taking Jeremy camping?" Wyatt asked.

"Maybe. Riley also mentioned that she's into it."

There was silence among my brothers, and then Griffin fist-pumped the air.

"Man, I did not see this coming," Wyatt said.

"Yep," Knox replied. "I called it."

"Yeah, but you were the only one with insider information," Griffin said.

Knox shrugged. "It's not my fault that the rest of you aren't creative."

"What are you talking about?" I asked.

Wyatt put both elbows on the table, looking at me intently. "We would really like to meet Riley. So would Dad."

"She'll be there at our water polo match," I informed them.

We played once a year, at the pool near my condo building. It was fun. I expected this year to be no different.

"Excellent. I was betting on that," Griffin said.

"You all talked about this?" I asked.

"No," Wyatt replied. "That's not our style. I actually thought that these bozos were making this out to be more than it is. But you're the most unpredictable of us Sterlings."

I opened my mouth.

He shook his head. "That wasn't up for discussion."

Chase was looking straight at me.

"I like surprising her," I said. "I want to do something she'll enjoy."

"So this, between the two of you, is serious?" Chase asked.

"It's the most serious I've ever been about a woman." Saying that felt insanely good.

"Holy shit," Griffin exclaimed. "Does Jeremy know?"

I shook my head. "No, we're keeping this under wraps."

"How on earth did you manage that?" Wyatt asked.

"It's not easy," I admitted.

"But do you plan on telling him?" That came from Chase.

"Riley and I haven't discussed it yet. And I don't want to pressure her in any way. I also don't want to confuse Jeremy."

"What do you mean, confuse?" Griffin asked. There was an edge in his voice. My brother was protective of Jeremy. All of them were.

"I don't want him to get his hopes up. After all, he's never met a woman I went out with, and she's his nanny."

"Not for long, though, right? So problem solved," Knox said breezily.

I cocked a brow. "How do you know that? You only talked to her for a few minutes at the condo."

"Oh, I got that from Mom. Riley's only there until she starts her job as an associate."

I was already searching for a new nanny. Ms. Williams had informed me that she wanted to permanently retire, and that was for the best. It also meant I didn't have to deal with firing her after the things she'd said to Jeremy.

"See, you're going to be off the hook then," Finn said. "Jeremy will have another nanny."

"And you can continue to date Riley without worrying that it might impact him," Griffin said.

I realized at that moment that no matter how helpful my brothers wanted to be, there were so many nuances they missed. It wasn't all black-and-white with a kid. Just because Riley wouldn't be his nanny, it didn't mean that he wouldn't care about her. I could already tell that the bond he had with Riley was far closer than what he'd had with any of his previous nannies. That wasn't just something kids forgot.

"You know, this is a good thing. Jeremy's given hints ever since Chase and Hannah got together that he'd like you to meet someone."

Wyatt was more logical than the rest of my younger brothers, but he didn't understand kids either. Sure, Jeremy might say that to anyone who wanted to hear him, but what he imagined happened when two adults got together was entirely different from the reality of a relationship. Things didn't always end up with the couple riding off into the sunset, as in Chase's case. In my personal experience, relationships were messy and could potentially end up in disaster, or at least a lot of heartbreak and collateral damage.

And honestly, Riley was young—not that I noticed it so much when we were together, but whenever I saw her roommates, it hit me like a ton of bricks. Would she even want an exclusive ongoing relationship with me?

"I appreciate you all looking out for me and Jeremy, but I wasn't asking for advice," I said in an even tone.

"We weren't giving any," Chase said.

"Just our straightforward, obviously unwanted opinions," Wyatt continued, bouncing off him.

I usually liked hearing them. Chase had more experience than the rest of us with relationships. But none of them could understand my particular case.

"How about we get back to business?" I suggested.

Griffin groaned.

Wyatt nodded. "Yeah, you're right. That's why we meet every week. This isn't gossip hour."

"No, we can gossip next week after our water polo match," Finn said with a shit-eating grin.

"Excellent," Wyatt exclaimed with an uncharacteristic grin of his own.

I just shook my head.

Even though we continued to talk shop, my mind was on my surprise for Riley. I was going to enlist her sister's help. Paula had been only too happy to give me details, and she was a wealth of information. I still had to figure out all the logistics. Most of all, I had to figure out Jeremy. But one thing at a time.

After our meeting, I noticed I had a missed call from Shona.

She rarely called me; we usually spoke after she and Jeremy had their nightly conversation. She'd also had sent me a text.

Shona: Hey, call me when you can without Jeremy around. I'm making some arrangements for the vacation and want to prep some surprises for him.

I called her right away. "Hi, Shona," I said, closing the door to my office.

"Oh, good. I'm putting together a shopping list. He's still in his Spider-Man phase, right?"

"Yeah, he is."

"And you still think he'll be in it by the end of the summer?"

"Definitely. This has a stronger hold on him than his previous passions."

"All right. And he still loves the zoo?"

"Yes."

"Apparently, he shares his passion for animals with Riley."

"That's true. Riley's been monitoring all the babies that are coming in the next few months. She keeps looking at all the cameras."

Shona gasped. "Oh my God, Duncan."

"What?"

"Is there something going on between you and Riley? I did think that it sounded that way from what Jeremy told me, but I wasn't sure. Well, knowing you, I figured the last person in the world you'd go out with would be your son's nanny."

Her words felt like a punch in the gut. "She's not going to be his nanny for too long. She starts her full-time job as a lawyer soon."

"You're not denying it."

"I'm not." I didn't want to keep this from Shona. She was Jeremy's mom and had a right to know.

"Oh, wow. Well, good for you."

"What?" I didn't expect this reaction.

"I hope things are going well. Jeremy doesn't know yet, does he?"

"No. I'm looking for the right moment to explain everything to him."

"So, this is serious?"

"Yes," I replied.

"Goodness. When you move, you move fast," she said.

"It feels right," I confessed, "but I want to tell Jeremy under the right circumstances."

"Well, I, for one, think he'll be thrilled."

I was certain that he would be. He cared about Riley, but still, no matter what Shona and my family thought, this required tact. Of course Jeremy could understand the notion of a parent dating, but I still wanted to do this as carefully as possible.

"Duncan, I honestly am very happy for you. Just make sure you give the relationship a chance, okay?"

"What's that supposed to mean?"

"You and I didn't work out because it wasn't meant to. If it weren't for Jeremy... well, you know what I mean. When we decided to try to be together for his sake, we both knew it wasn't going to be a success. At least, deep down, I did. But before I got pregnant, I always got the feeling that you held yourself back. I don't know if it was because of the way your parents' marriage ended or something else, but you always seemed to keep me at arm's length."

I couldn't disagree because she was right. It wasn't something I'd done consciously, but I'd done it nonetheless.

"So, if Riley is important to you, don't stand in your own way, okay?"

"Okay."

CHAPTER TWENTY-SIX

Riley

"I hope Uncle Finn and Knox win today!" Jeremy exclaimed.

Duncan groaned. "Hey! You know I'm your dad, right? You're supposed to be on my side."

"Not todayyyyy," Jeremy chanted.

"When is everyone arriving?" I asked.

I was on pins and needles. Apparently, all the Sterlings played a water polo match every year. Duncan had asked me to stay, and I'd said yes. I was looking forward to meeting everyone, although I was a bit nervous. We were waiting for them at the pool.

"Soon."

"Your neighbors don't mind?" I asked Duncan. We were both keeping an eye on Jeremy. He insisted that he wanted to go down the slide a few times before everyone arrived.

"No. Actually, a lot of them come to watch."

I smiled, wiggling my eyebrows. "Let me guess—some of your single neighbors?"

He narrowed his eyes. "I'm trying to remember... I think you're right. Mostly women come."

"I can't imagine why," I teased him before adding, "So, when everyone arrives..."

"They're going to be rowdy and obnoxious, and you'd better not pay attention to whatever my brothers say."

I frowned. "Why not?"

"Because they tend to give me shit at every turn when it comes to you. They can't wait to meet you."

I sucked in a breath. "They know I'm here?"

He frowned. "Yes. Why do you think I asked you to stay? I wanted to give you a chance to meet the family as well."

Holy shit. I hadn't put two and two together. But honestly, the past few weeks had been busy, and I was scattered. It took a while to settle Paula into my place. I bought her an air mattress that was surprisingly comfortable. I didn't have time to look for another place to live for myself, but I was going to get to it soon. Right now, I was helping Duncan search for my replacement.

"You should have seen them when they got wind that I'd put the lawyers on Paula's case," he said with a twinkle in his eye.

"They know about that?"

"Yes. There aren't any secrets in my family. Not that I tried. I wanted them to know that you're important to me."

Oh, that made me so blissfully happy. We hadn't talked to Jeremy about any of this yet, but that was quite all right. It was better to wait until I wasn't his nanny anymore.

Just the thought of it made me uneasy. I hated that I had to search for my own replacement.

"I see the party's already started," a loud voice said.

I turned around and saw a stunning guy walking right toward us.

"Riley, nice to meet you. I'm Finn. You know, I was wondering if my brother would be brave enough to ask you here with us today."

I laughed nervously. "Why wouldn't he?"

"Oh, he might be afraid that we're not going to shine the brightest light on him or something."

"Finn," Duncan said in a warning tone.

Finn winked at him. "Don't worry, we've got your back. We want Riley to hang around, after all." He smiled enigmatically but didn't add anything else, as Jeremy yelled, "Uncle Finn!"

He was on top of the slide but then turned around and came back down the ladder.

My heart lurched in my throat. I'd told him so many times not to climb back down. It was tricky enough when you went up. It was a slippery death trap when you tried to descend it.

He jumped down the last three steps and then ran toward us, hugging Finn.

Knox arrived just then. "Why isn't everyone already in the pool?" He had a huge grin on his face when he noticed me, but then his eyes darted to Jeremy, and he said, "Riley, nice to see you again."

I had a hunch that he would have teased me and Duncan just as much as Finn, but they were reining themselves in for Jeremy's benefit. Aw, that endeared them to me.

Several more people arrived. I only recognized Susan. There was an older man among the group as well, who I assumed was their father.

Duncan was right next to me. Finn and Knox had stepped to one side with Jeremy. I swear I only blinked and the two of them had gotten rid of their clothes, putting them on one of the lounge chairs. They already had swim trunks on, and they jumped into the pool with Jeremy.

The group approached us. "Riley, this is Bruce," Susan said, pointing to the elderly man.

"Nice to meet you."

"How do you do, Riley. I've heard a lot about you." He glanced from me to Duncan, then to the rest of the guys. The brothers, I assumed. Susan and Bruce headed toward two chairs closest to the slide.

"I'm Chase," the nearest brother said, putting his arm around the only woman in the group besides their mother.

"Hi, I'm Hannah," she introduced herself.

"She's mine," Chase said.

That was hands down the best intro I'd ever heard. Not "my wife," "my fiancée," or "my girlfriend," just "mine." I gathered that there was a possessive streak running in their DNA.

"Nice to meet you, Hannah."

"This is my first rodeo with the polo match too. I don't play. Do you?" she asked.

I shook my head. "No. I'm here to keep an eye on Jeremy."

"And to meet you," Duncan added.

I blushed.

"My brother didn't give you a heads-up about us?" one of the other men cut in. "I'm Griffin, by the way."

"Hi, Griffin," I said. I felt myself blushing even more.

"I did give her a heads-up," Duncan said in a more serious tone.

"But I actually think a warning would have been necessary," I replied, holding my head high, though I was still blushing.

Griffin yawned. "Sorry, everyone. I went to bed late last night. Might not be at my best today."

"What did you do?" Duncan asked.

"That's private," Griffin replied.

"No, it's not, dude," Knox said from the pool. "You do know that every time someone tags Sterling Industries on Instagram, all of us see it, right? Your date last night was hot."

Griffin blinked. "What the hell? People are tagging the company? That's fucked-up."

"It's the first thing that comes up when you type 'Sterling,'" Knox explained.

"You might want to be careful," Duncan warned.

Griffin groaned. "Please tell me you're not going to be on my case all day, Duncan."

"No, he won't," I assured him. "He wants to win. He'll focus on that."

Damn, was that too cheeky of me? Duncan was still my employer, after all.

The guy next to Griffin threw his head back, laughing, before saying, "I'm Wyatt. And you can go toe-to-toe with us. That's good."

Chase looked at Duncan. "Good choice, brother."

Hannah started laughing. "Oh, Riley. They can be a handful."

"They are," I said, feeling more of my sass coming back. I liked the guys. "I thought only Knox was a bit much, but clearly that applies to all of you."

"Heard that," Knox said from the pool.

I snapped my head in his direction. When had he swum toward us?

"Yeah, he's got like a sixth sense when people talk about him," Griffin informed me, as if reading my thoughts.

"Good to know."

"What do you mean, I'm *a bit* much? I'm a lot much," Knox said.

"My bad," I replied, fighting to keep a straight face.

He shook his head theatrically. "Come on, everyone. We've got a game to play. And if we time this right, we'll have all the single gals in the complex join us in the afternoon."

Duncan grinned. "Knox, knock it off."

"I swear to God, you warn me one more time not to hit on your neighbors—"

"Sounded like you needed a reminder."

"No, I didn't." He glanced at me. "Riley, help me out."

I jerked my head back. "No, I won't. I'm with Duncan on this one."

Duncan's smile was totally smug.

Wyatt burst out laughing again. "All right, everyone, let's get this game started."

———

The next few hours were a veritable muscle fest. The guys were all hot as hell. There was no other way to describe them. They were tall, with broad shoulders and endless muscles, and moved with grace in the water. They were playing three against three. Jeremy was the referee.

"Can you even play water polo with just three people?" I wondered out loud.

"Oh, don't worry. My sons make their own rules," Bruce said. He, Susan, and Hannah were sitting side by side on chairs.

"They seem good at it," Hannah remarked.

While keeping an eye on the pool, I headed to the shade where Knox and Finn had left drinks in a cooler. Susan came with me, and we each took a Diet Coke. The fridge upstairs was stocked with beer, wine, and mixers, but Duncan said they'd only start mixing cocktails after the game was over, which I thought was smart.

"It looks like Duncan, Griffin, and Wyatt will win," I said as we stood in the shade, and I took a few sips of my soda. It was much cooler here than under the umbrella.

"You don't mind being here on a Saturday?" Susan asked, eyeing me.

"No, not at all. I really love my job."

"Hmm. But you're also looking forward to starting your new job, right?"

I nodded. "Yes, I am very much looking forward to that." I sighed, looking at the pool. "I'm going to miss Jeremy, though."

"And Duncan?" Susan asked, sounding surprisingly sassy.

I swear I blushed from the top of my head to the tips of my toes.

"Of course, although I'm spending most of my time with Jeremy." I wasn't sure what else to say. I didn't want to make things awkward.

"You know, Duncan's different when he's around you."

"What do you mean?" I asked quickly.

"He's relaxed, and even his body language is more open. He was never like that around Jeremy's mother. I was afraid from the very beginning that things wouldn't work out for them, but they did try for his sake. And Jeremy's closer to you than he's been to any of his nannies."

That filled me with so much pride. My face exploded in a grin. "I'm so happy to hear that."

She looked at me with a soft expression on her face. "You love that boy."

I swallowed hard and nodded. "Yes, I do. So very much."

"He likes your company so much, he's even bailing on spending evenings away with me," Susan said.

"Oh, I can't possibly compete with you or Bruce. Jeremy absolutely loves his time with you."

"He does. Bruce is a very good grandfather."

The affection in her voice took me by surprise. Not many people spoke with so much candor about their ex-husband.

"How is seeing him at the store every day?" I asked, then immediately added, "I'm so sorry. I don't know why I asked that. I don't want to pry."

"No, it's fine. Honestly, that's the question on everyone's lips when they find out about it. It's surprisingly easy. We're living the life we always hoped we would. Each doing our own thing without much monetary pressure." Her eyes clouded as she looked at the pool. "But I will forever be sorry that my boys had to go through our shit-show years with us when they were so young."

"Raising kids is hard."

She nodded. "We were overwhelmed. Neither of us is originally from California, so our parents couldn't help with the little ones. That's why I'm so adamant about helping my kids with theirs."

"Oh, that's something my mom would say," I said, putting a hand on my chest.

"Jeremy said she doesn't live nearby, right?"

I shook my head. "Not as close as I want her to. I have big plans, once I start my job, to look after her and my sister."

She snapped her fingers. "That's right. She's here."

I nodded. "Yes, she's in college."

"You know, I don't think anyone would mind if she joined our family events," Susan said, winking at me.

"Oh, wow. Th-Thank you," I stammered, because that was a truly lovely offer. Only it seemed like far too much. Duncan had already done a lot to help Paula. That moron of a boss hadn't bothered her again. But her joining us at things like this... well, Duncan and I weren't there just yet, but I didn't have the heart to tell Susan that.

"All right, I need to put some more sunscreen lotion on," I said because it was blistering hot.

She nodded. "Yeah, me too. I always forget and end up having a sunburn."

I went to the bag of supplies I'd put under an umbrella, and after spreading on lotion, I checked my phone to see if my sister wrote anything.

Christine: We got the results. We passed the bar, how about you?

I gasped, biting the inside of my cheek as I stumbled backward. *Way to spring it on me.*

I immediately got jittery. My hands were trembling as I shifted my weight from one foot to the other. I had to check right now. Of course, that's when the internet decided to be extremely slow. Or maybe it was just that everyone was trying to access the results page right now. That was probably more likely.

Finally, the page loaded. I'd passed! I threw my fist in the air, jumping up and down with joy.

"What's happening?" Duncan asked.

I realized the guys had stopped the game. Even Jeremy was looking my way.

"I passed the bar exam. They just posted the results, and I passed!" I hadn't realized that all these months, I had still feared I might have flunked it.

There was a chorus of congratulations. Duncan was looking straight at me with a huge smile, then mouthed, "I'm proud of you."

Then he clapped his hands together. "All right, let's take a break," he said as he got out of the water.

Jeremy was faster than anyone else. He ran straight to me, wrapping his arms around my waist. They were cold from the water, cooling me down.

He looked up at me. "You are the best, Riley."

"Thanks, Jeremy."

Then everyone came over and shook my hand.

"How long is the break for?" I asked.

"Just two minutes, give or take. We need to hydrate," Wyatt said.

"Does alcohol count as hydrating?" Griffin asked.

Wyatt cocked a brow at him. "Unless you want to lose, in which case, yes, please."

I grinned, looking from Wyatt to Griffin. I liked this dynamic between them. How Wyatt seemed to instantly flip into the role of a concerned brother when Griffin was messing around.

"Come on, let's all get drinks," Knox said as they went to the coolers they'd brought.

Duncan was looking straight at the sunscreen I'd started to rub onto my chest before I'd checked the results. There was hunger in his eyes as he cleared his throat.

"Riley, want to help me bring some towels?" he said.

I nodded feverishly.

"Yeah, sure. We need more," I said, glad he'd thought up an

excuse. Whenever he pinned me with that gaze, my thoughts were a useless jumble.

We walked side by side, and once we rounded the corner and were out of sight, he immediately pulled me to him.

"Congratulations," he said.

I smiled, resting my hands on his shoulders. "Thank you. I'm so excited. I think part of me was afraid I was going to fail."

He put two fingers under my jaw and then kissed one corner of my mouth.

"I wasn't. I was sure you'd pass. I'm so fucking happy for you. If I'd known that they'd give the results today..."

"Then what?" I asked apprehensively.

"I don't know, but I sure as hell wouldn't have had all my family here. I'd have taken you somewhere so the two of us could be all alone and we could celebrate properly."

"But this is fun," I said. "I like being with your family."

He captured my mouth, kissing me desperately. How could he need me so much? And how could I need him even more?

I lost myself in the kiss and the feel of his cold skin beneath my fingers. His body got mine wet too. As I pressed myself against him, I realized he was getting semihard. Heat coursed through me at the sensation.

I jumped back and said, "No, no, no." Pointing directly to his swim trunks, I added, "That needs to stay under control."

Duncan threw his head back, laughing. "That ship has sailed when it comes to you, Riley. I have zero control over myself when we're alone."

"Then let's get back to the group before everyone realizes what's going on."

"Yeah, you're right," he said.

We walked back to the pool side by side. Finn was smirking from ear to ear. Knox laughed. I wondered why Griffin was staring at us.

"How about those towels?" he asked lazily.

Holy shit. I'd completely forgotten that we'd used that as an excuse. We wouldn't have been able to go up to the condo even if we'd wanted to, though, because neither of us had taken a key.

"All of them are, uh, in the washing machine or the dryer," I stammered.

"No, they're not," Jeremy said. "I had some in my changing room."

Crap.

"Yeah, buddy. Those are a bit small. I'll go later and bring some after the drying cycle is over," Duncan said.

"All right, everyone," Knox said. "Let's resume the game. We can come back to making things awkward later."

Jeremy blinked. "What's awkward?"

Duncan glared at his brother.

Knox winked. "Oh, this is fun."

———

As Finn had predicted, the pool filled soon after. And what do you know, it was mostly with female neighbors. Hannah and I exchanged a glance and laughed.

"They do like an audience, don't they?" I asked.

The second they noticed they had a gathering, their attitude changed. Before, they were playing to win. Now, they were playing to show off their muscles. Griffin, Knox, and Finn were especially obvious—which was also probably why they lost spectacularly.

"Dad, Uncle Chase, and Uncle Wyatt won," Jeremy declared. His voice was incredulous.

"Buddy, you don't have to sound so disappointed," Duncan said. "That's what your other uncles get for not paying attention." The corners of his mouth twitched as he walked to the edge of the pool.

Wyatt was shaking his head, laughing.

The losing team absolutely didn't seem to give a shit about it.

I liked that they didn't let their egos get in the way of having fun with the family.

As the others got out of the pool, Jeremy yawned. He'd spent a lot of time in the water without any breaks. He was probably exhausted.

"Jeremy," I started tentatively, thinking how to best phrase this. If I suggested that he needed a nap, he'd feel humiliated. "Want to go upstairs with me? I want to get a new bottle of sunscreen."

Once inside, I'd talk him into lying down.

"What a coincidence," Susan said, rising to her feet. "I was going to do just that. You can stay down here, Riley, and I'll bring it back down."

"I'll go up with you, Grandma," Jeremy said excitedly, wrapping a towel around himself.

"I'll come up too," Bruce said. "These old bones have been in the sun for too long."

As the three of them walked toward the entrance, I sat back down again.

"You know, Mom has a sixth sense," Griffin said.

Knox smirked. "I think she knew we couldn't behave for too long. Thought it would be safest to get Jeremy out of the way."

"You read my mind, brother," Finn said.

"I mean, we *were* on our best behavior until now. We do deserve credit," Griffin said.

"My God, Duncan didn't do you justice," I said loudly.

Knox jerked his head back. "What do you mean?"

"He did say you're a handful, but this is far more than I imagined."

"Oh, we're just getting started," Griffin said.

Wyatt laughed and said, "You know, usually I try to back up Duncan and keep everyone in check, but I can't make any promises today."

"Finally, you're joining the dark side," Griffin said. "For a moment there, I was starting to think that you wanted to be part of the older group."

Wyatt jerked his head back. "Low blow, man. Low blow."

I started to laugh, and so did Hannah.

"Oh, Riley, word of warning," she said. "You won't get used to it. I know I haven't, and I've been around a while."

My heart started beating faster. Should I want to get used to it? Duncan and I... well, we didn't really speak about what would happen once I wasn't Jeremy's nanny anymore.

"All right, Riley. We want to know everything about *you*," Griffin said nonchalantly.

Holy shit. The group went silent. I hadn't realized that once Jeremy wasn't here, they were going to come at me like this.

"Sure," I replied. "But first, does anyone want drinks?"

"Got that covered," Knox said.

"It's our designated role for today," Finn added. "We get the drinks. You talk."

CHAPTER TWENTY-SEVEN

Riley

My last weeks with Jeremy passed in the blink of an eye, it seemed. On my very last day working as his nanny, I was feeling very melancholy.

"How did you sleep?" I asked my sister as she was just waking up.

After a heart-to-heart with my roommates, everyone agreed it was best if Paula moved in. She'd sleep in my room, which we'd share while I was still living here. And once I left, she'd simply take over my payments. I'd already started searching for places to live. And, well, I had to say, the future was bright.

I was even tentatively looking at two-bedroom apartments, just in case I could convince Paula to move in with me. But realistically, that would only be a good scenario after she graduated and started working.

"This mattress is surprisingly comfy," she said. It was inflatable but designed as a bed. "How come you're already dressed and showered? I didn't even hear you."

"You sleep very deeply, Paula."

My sister yawned. "You look really nice."

"I do, right?"

I was wearing a white dress with lace straps and a boatneck collar.

"You're dressing up awfully cute. Are you trying to impress that kid you're nannying? Or the dad?" She winked at me, and I blushed.

"You know that I just like to dress nicely."

"Hmm. True. But then again, if my boss looked like Duncan Sterling, I'd put in a lot of effort too. Don't you usually start your day in the afternoon?"

"Yes, but Jeremy had a short school day today. I'm actually picking him up from riding lessons."

"Wow. I didn't even know people did that anymore."

I laughed. "Neither did I until Jeremy."

I'd prepared a whole afternoon of activities for the two of us.

While I applied makeup in the small mirror that I kept in the bedroom, my phone beeped with an incoming message from Duncan.

> Duncan: Good morning, gorgeous. Keep tonight free. I'm taking you and Jeremy out to celebrate your last day on the job.

I squealed.

"Hey, you scared me to death," Paula protested.

I held up the phone with the screen toward her even though she couldn't see it because she was on the other side of the bedroom.

"He's taking us out. See, it's a good thing I dressed nicely."

She smiled sheepishly, then glanced at the huge backpack she'd taken out from under the bed. Maybe she was planning to take a hike today. I didn't want to ask her, though, not wanting her to feel like her big sister was checking in on her.

"I'm sure you'll have fun," she said.

"Wish me luck on my last day, sis."

Forty minutes later, I watched Jeremy as he walked toward me with a toothy grin. This ranch was amazing! It almost made me want to learn how to ride myself. They offered lessons in horseback riding for adults too—I'd already checked.

"I was the first today!" he exclaimed.

"Congratulations."

"I've never been first before."

"Is it a competition?" I asked.

"Not officially. We're just training, but it's always a competition."

I nodded. "Ah, duly noted."

I hadn't realized that Jeremy had a competitive streak, but then again, how could I? I'd never seen him interact with other kids, and he didn't have a brother or sister. But remembering how Duncan and his brothers tried one-upping each other, Jeremy probably picked that up from within the family.

I still had so much to learn about him. But I was running out of time.

"I thought we should start our day together with ice cream."

Jeremy smiled. "This is the best day ever. First, I won our race. And now I get to have ice cream. Where are we going?"

"There's an ice cream parlor near here."

I'd actually been by the house earlier and picked up his favorite toys as well as some puzzles. He liked to talk a lot, but sometimes he needed to keep his hands occupied too. And I enjoyed playing with him. We both liked puzzles.

The ice cream parlor looked exactly like it had in the pictures... and the prices were as exorbitant as they'd been online. Part of me thought that maybe they'd made a mistake and added a 1 in front of each price. Who in their right mind sold a scoop for fourteen bucks? Then again, what could I expect from an ice cream parlor that was close to a riding school?

But I was learning to be more at ease in Duncan's world and, by extension, Jeremy's. No more dragging him to other super-markets because I thought a local grocery store was overpriced. So, Jeremy ordered a Mickey Mouse, which was a stunning $27, and I ordered one scoop of chocolate. That was the most I could get myself to spend in this place. We received the ice cream at the same time, and we both devoured it. Jeremy was so excited that he ate his whole Mickey Mouse in the time it took me to eat my measly portion.

Once he'd finished, he held his belly and said, "I'm so full."

I smiled. "So am I. Want to see what I brought for you from home?"

His eyes lit up. "Sure."

I got out his favorite penguin toy, and he squeezed it to his chest. "You're the best, Riley."

I also took out the puzzle we both loved.

"Want to see how fast we can do it and who puts together the most puzzle pieces?" I asked.

"Yes!"

While we assembled the puzzle, he scrunched his forehead in concentration. I was being deliberately slow; I didn't care a bit about winning.

At some point, Jeremy stopped putting pieces together.

I frowned. "Jeremy, are you okay? Do you feel sick?"

The puzzle wasn't that hard, and he'd done it a million times. No way could he not know what to do next.

He looked at me and abruptly asked, "Riley, would you like to be a mom?"

I jerked my head back, unsure if I'd heard him correctly, and stammered, "Um, well, I mean, yes. But—"

He got the next words out so fast that I was sure I'd misun-derstood him at first.

"Would you like to be *my* mom?"

My heart melted. I smiled, moving closer to him and putting a hand on his back.

"Jeremy, baby," I said, then chastised myself because he

wasn't my baby, "you know this isn't how it works. You have a mom."

"I know. But she's far away, and you do mom stuff with me. You play with me."

I frowned. "I'm sure Ms. Williams did too."

He shook his head. "No. She watched me play, or sometimes she showed me how to do things like a puzzle, but then I had to do it by myself. You're so young and pretty, and I would like you to be my mom."

My chest tightened. "I love spending time with you. You know I do."

"But you're going to have another job, and then you won't play with me anymore. But if you were my mom, you would have to. That's what moms do."

I smiled at him. "I'm sure we can arrange something so that we meet and play," I assured him. I wasn't simply saying this to calm him down. I genuinely wanted to see Jeremy once my job started.

I groaned inwardly, realizing I should probably discuss things like this with Duncan before I made any promises to Jeremy. But the little guy was inconsolable.

"But would you like to be my mom?" he insisted. "Because if you do, I can tell Dad."

That took me by complete surprise. I jerked my head back. "What?"

"I think Dad would like that."

Oh dear God. Duncan and I needed to have a word. I never in a million years would have imagined this. I honestly couldn't reply without causing trouble either way. If I told him yes, he'd get his hopes up. If I said no, I'd break his heart.

Distraction was my best weapon.

"Come on. If you finish your part of the puzzle before me, you can choose what you want for lunch," I said.

The trick worked. Jeremy immediately focused on the table. I didn't even have to pretend he was beating me. The little guy won with flying colors a few minutes later, and we ended up having pizza for lunch.

———

In the afternoon, Duncan picked us up from the zoo. He'd insisted on it, so we'd Ubered to the ranch in the morning even though I could have just used the car he gave me to drive. He had a huge smile on his face when he arrived.

"Dad, today was awesome!" Jeremy exclaimed. "Riley's really the best nanny ever. Do you think you can convince her to stay and not take that new job?"

Jeremy had skills. I was impressed.

Duncan's expression fell a bit. "We've spoken about this, Jeremy."

They did? Maybe that would explain why he came on so strong this morning.

"Ready for the rest of the afternoon?" Duncan asked.

Jeremy nodded.

"Good, because I have a surprise for both of you," Duncan said, looking from Jeremy to me.

"Really?" I asked. "And what's that?"

"I checked the weather, and it's perfect."

"For what?"

Duncan grinned. "Camping."

I gasped. Jeremy was jumping up and down. "Yes, Dad! Thank you so much! I thought you'd never want to do that."

"We're leaving tonight," he informed us.

"But I need to pack and everything," I protested with borderline panic.

Duncan's eyes twinkled. "I've got that covered," he said.

I wanted to jump his bones and kiss him right here, but that was definitely not appropriate.

"What do you mean? I need details before I agree. I mean, I need certain clothes and—"

"Paula already packed your bag. All we need to do is load it in the car. I left the office early and packed Jeremy's."

Huh. Paula the sneak. That backpack under her bed must have been for me.

"I love you, Dad," Jeremy said.

I was stunned—and swooning.

"I love you, too, son. Come on, let's get in the car." He opened the car door for Jeremy, helping him in. Closing the door, he turned to me.

"When did you speak to my sister?" I asked.

"I've been plotting with her for a while."

I could have melted when he waggled his brows. *This man...*

"She didn't tell me anything."

"That's the point of a surprise," Duncan said with an amused expression.

I had so many questions. How were we going to act around Jeremy? Were we going to tell him something? Did it even make sense considering I was starting my new job on Monday? I wanted to bring up the mom issue, but maybe I'd have time later tonight.

We dropped by my house to get my things. There was no one home, but Paula had laid the gray backpack on my bed. Duncan loaded it in the trunk, next to his and Jeremy's bags and the tent.

I had to admit, I was beyond anxious. "Are you going to tell us where we're headed?" I asked once we were in the car again.

"Yeah. To Idyllwild Campground in Mount San Jacinto."

"Yes! We get a mountain experience," I said.

Jeremy was cheering in the back, and I couldn't help but grin. Oh man, this felt so much like we were a family. Was this why Jeremy had asked if I wanted to be his mom? Objectively, there was no need for me to go camping with them—Duncan was perfectly capable of going with his own son.

Just as I opened my mouth, Duncan squeezed my fingers, as if guessing what was on my mind. He gave me one of those devastating smiles, and I relaxed instantly.

We were just going camping. I didn't need to overthink this.

"You've got supplies too?" I asked.

"Yes. I've got some sausage, hamburgers, buns, and bread—stuff we can cook on a campfire."

"Marshmallows too? For s'mores?"

Duncan nodded. "Yep. Couldn't forget those, could I?"

I smiled. He was a great dad.

He was a great man, period.

The drive would take about two hours. I looked up the info on my phone and kept spouting off random facts.

One hour into the drive, Jeremy fell asleep, and Duncan and I stayed silent. Jeremy was a light sleeper, so he'd probably wake up if we started talking. Duncan took my hand again, squeezing my fingers, and I just relaxed into the seat.

An hour later, as we entered the park, Jeremy woke up.

"We're here!" he exclaimed.

I smiled from ear to ear. This was shaping up to be the best weekend ever!

As we got out of the car, Jeremy hugged me. "I know you and Dad both like the nanny starting on Monday, but you're the best."

I smiled, kissing the top of his head, trying not to think that someone else would take my place in a few days.

CHAPTER TWENTY-EIGHT

Duncan

Putting up a tent wasn't as easy as it looked on YouTube.

"This is the largest tent I've ever been in," Riley exclaimed.

I cocked a brow. "Really? I was furious that they didn't have anything bigger."

She laughed. "Duncan, this has separate rooms. That's amazing!"

She'd been a pro, instructing me on where everything went. I'd basically just provided the muscle, and Jeremy hung on to her every word. He was standing in my way more than helping, but I knew how important it was for him to be useful, so I gave him small tasks.

I was happy that we'd managed to put up the tent. For a while there, I'd thought about bailing on this whole thing and returning to San Diego. But these two had been so enthusiastic that I didn't have the heart to suggest it.

Powering through was worth it. The campsite was decent, and the toilets and showers looked fine.

"All right. How about starting on dinner?" Riley asked.

"Good idea." I might have been clueless at putting up the tent, but I was good at starting a fire. I had one going in less than five minutes.

Riley came to me with a package of sausages, and I looked around.

"Where's Jeremy?" I asked.

"He's gathering some twigs. Don't worry, I told him not to go far."

I kept looking around.

"Want me to go get him?" she asked softly.

"No. I mean, he's ten, and you told him to stay close. I have to learn to give him a bit more leeway."

"Thank you for doing this," she said. Her smile was huge. "I've been wanting to come out to camp here for ages."

"I'm glad I could do this for you."

"And for Jeremy," she said.

I winked at her, then, taking advantage that he wasn't here, leaned in and kissed her cheek. She smelled so good that it took all my willpower not to dig my nose in her neck and inhale, then kiss her all over. I'd move even farther down, and that would be slippery slope.

"Duncan," she murmured.

"I just need a few seconds. Fuck, I've wanted to do this since I saw you this afternoon."

I straightened up reluctantly, and she flashed me a shy smile, then looked around for Jeremy.

"Listen, I think we should talk about some things Jeremy said today."

"Sure. What did he say?" I asked.

She opened her mouth, but before she could say anything else, Jeremy ran back to us.

"Look, Dad. I got a whole lot of twigs. Oh. The fire is already going." His smile dropped.

"That's fine. Just put the pile there. We're going to need them to keep the fire going, and to start a new one tomorrow."

"Okay," he said, but his voice lacked enthusiasm.

"Jeremy, do you want to make s'mores?" Riley asked him.

I fucking loved this woman—the way she instinctively knew how to put him at ease. She made him happy. She made both of us happy. I didn't know it was even possible to feel this way. And I was supposed to let her go? No way in hell.

"Oh, I forgot," Jeremy said, shoving a hand in his pocket and pulling out some crumpled flowers. "These are for you."

"You got me poppies!" Riley exclaimed.

"Yes, they're your favorites."

"Thank you, Jeremy." She took the flowers and carefully carried them inside the tent.

Once she returned, she asked, "Who wants to compete and see who cooks the best marshmallows?"

"I do!" Jeremy exclaimed.

"So do I," Riley replied.

I had absolutely zero desire to participate in this. She flashed me a warning look as if to say, "Don't be a grump."

"Yeah, me too," I said, and Riley winked at me.

She was the first one to finish her s'more. I was still assembling the marshmallow between graham crackers by the time she'd started eating it. Jeremy came in second.

"Be careful not to burn yourself," I said as he took it away from the fire.

He nodded, then bit into and said, "Mm, this is good."

I usually had a rule about no sweets before dinner, but who the hell cared? It was Friday evening. Tomorrow was the weekend, and we were camping. The usual rules didn't apply.

The marshmallow was decent enough, but I was more of a meat man, so I ate two of the sausages. Jeremy and Riley each ate one. As the sun set, I could start to see the beauty of camping, with the fire crackling and the silence surrounding us. The nearest tent was quite some distance away. That suited me just fine.

An hour after dinner, Jeremy went out like a light. Riley and I stayed outside in the camping chairs I'd bought. They adjusted into a half-sitting, half-lying position. I'd questioned the function when I bought them, but watching Riley sit back in it, pointing to the sky and saying, "The stars are so easy to see here," everything fell into place.

"What is it?" she murmured when she caught me looking at her.

"I like watching you. You look so happy."

"I *am* happy. This is the best evening ever."

Fucking hell, really? I'd come camping with her every night if it made her this happy.

I sat down next to her, putting my chair in the same position.

"Jeremy's asleep?" she asked. When I nodded, she sighed and said, "Then we should probably talk about today."

"Is something wrong?"

"Not exactly. We had a delicate situation. I wasn't sure why he brought it up or if something triggered it, so I figured it's best to discuss it together."

I took her hand. "Sure. What is it?"

She hesitated. I interlaced our fingers, squeezing them together. "You can tell me anything."

"Earlier today, when Jeremy and I were out for ice cream, he asked me if I'd like to be his mom."

I stilled. "What? He actually said that?"

"I mean, in that cute way of his, you know? He was like 'Yes, because we do so many mom things together.' I just... I don't know. I told him that I love spending time with him. Which is true, of course, and you know that. But obviously I didn't answer his question."

But I wanted to know. Did she want to?

My heart was in my throat. Never in my life did I have a problem expressing what I wanted and needed, but I couldn't just outright ask her. What if she said no? There would be no coming back from that.

"I'm going to talk to him and figure out where that came from," I said. "Don't worry about it."

"That's great."

I leaned in and nudged the tip of my nose against her jaw before descending to her neck. I moved my lips toward her and then stopped.

"Duncan," she chastised, "we can't do this here. What if Jeremy wakes up?"

"I know." Being surrounded by nature made my own natural instincts kick into overdrive. I needed this woman.

"Thank you for bringing us here tonight. It's exactly what I needed before being cooped up in an office all day long."

I felt as if she'd thrown a bucket of ice over me.

That's right. Come Monday, this is all going to change.

"Are you excited about it?" I asked.

"Honestly, yes."

I took her legs, putting them in my lap and running my hands over her calves.

"I love it when you do that," she said. "I've been pursuing this career for so long. I can't believe I'm finally going to be a lawyer, and all my hard work will have paid off. I mean, they're going to work us like dogs. I've already found some of my coworkers on Facebook, and they always post evening shots of themselves at the office, but I'm looking forward to that."

I swallowed hard. Good thing I didn't ask her for her answer to Jeremy's question. It wasn't fair to put her on the spot like that. She was young. She was starting her career. She couldn't commit to my life.

And yet I knew things had to change, one way or another.

I moved my chair, changing the angle. "We need to buy some sort of camping couch."

"Does that mean you want us to come camping again?"

"Of course. It makes you and Jeremy happy."

"So, that means you want to continue... this between us?"

I put my hand on her jaw, turning her head so we made eye contact. "What kind of question is that?"

"I don't know. I figured that maybe this was... a goodbye trip. We never spoke about us and what we're going to do once my employment comes to an end."

"I'm going to tell you how this will go. You tell me if any part of it is wrong. You'll go kick ass as a lawyer and work long hours. I'm going to pick you up, spoil you rotten, and make you rest. How does that sound?"

"I can get on board with that," she murmured.

"Good." I struggled in my chair. "Damn it, I want to be able to sit next to you."

"Oh, I have an idea about that," she said, getting up and straddling me.

I smiled as I brought my mouth to her lips. "This works too."

CHAPTER TWENTY-NINE

Riley

The first day of my new job was even more intense than I'd imagined. I reported at 8:00 a.m., and it was 9:00 p.m. by the time I left. The same thing happened Tuesday and Wednesday.

Even though I loved the job and finally being able to use my degree, there was a dull ache in my chest the entire time. I thought about Jeremy almost constantly. I could almost tell what he'd be doing every single moment of the afternoon. I was jealous of this new nanny. Yep, jealous.

On Thursday afternoon, my heart all but melted when Duncan sent me a picture of the two of them. He'd finished work early and taken Jeremy out for dinner.

There was a physical ache in my chest, like a capsule around my heart. *Crap.* Maybe it would get better with time.

I typed back quickly.

> Riley: I wish I was there with you.

> Duncan: You will be on the weekend. Go kick ass.

And I did.

Duncan kept his promise and picked me up every evening. I knew he couldn't keep it up forever because his mom had to come stay with Jeremy whenever he went out, but I was going to enjoy it while it lasted. Then he brought me home.

On Friday evening, I finally felt like I could breathe again. Duncan was coming to pick me up, and we were spending the evening at his condo. Jeremy was sleeping at his grandmother's tonight, and we'd pick him up tomorrow to go camping again.

Duncan was waiting for me about a block away from the entrance to the office building, mostly because it was the only place where he could park. I was smiling from ear to ear and nearly lost my composure on the walk to him.

Stopping right in front of him, I put my arms around his neck, and he laced his around my waist. I didn't care if anyone saw me. This was my free time.

I groaned. "I can't believe this week is over."

"It is, and I'm going to make sure that you are spoiled rotten the entire weekend."

He'd suggested that I sleep at the condo the past few nights, but we hadn't outright spoken with Jeremy about us. I figured it would be confusing as hell for him to see me there in the morning, so we'd decided to wait and then tell him everything this weekend when we went camping.

"I'm all yours to do whatever you want with," I said before we got in the car. I chatted his ear off on the way. "On Sunday evening, my team wants to meet for drinks."

"That's very smart for the newbies."

I nodded. "Line managers will be there too."

"That's great. It'll be good for networking."

"It just means that we'll have to come back a bit earlier from our trip."

"No problem."

We were only going half an hour away this time, so I figured it wouldn't cut into our weekend too much.

I was so tired that I toed off my shoes. Some of my colleagues were always changing into flat shoes when they sat at their desk. I'd been judging them for about three days, but on the fourth one, I understood why. It was extremely uncomfortable to even sit with high heels on all day. I could see myself adopting the same strategy at some point.

When we arrived at the condo, I felt myself relax from the second I stepped in. It helped that it smelled amazing. I sniffed the air. "What's this?"

"I've got something in the slow cooker," he said. "I figured you'd prefer to have dinner and wine at home."

"You thought right," I said. I was absolutely not in the mood to go out to eat.

I threw my shoes in the corner as we came in, then made a beeline to the kitchen, peering into the slow cooker. He'd made turkey chili. My heart fluttered. His arms came around my belly, and he pulled me back against his chest.

"You spoke to my sister?" I asked.

"No. Actually, I spoke to your mom."

I gasped, turning around. "What? How?"

"I first called Paula to ask her. She admitted that she had no idea what your comfort food was as a kid."

I laughed. "That's not a surprise. She's much younger than me."

"Anyway, then she gave me your mom's number. She's excited that you're visiting her next weekend."

"Oh my God, that's right. I forgot to tell you. Paula and I are going to see her. I promised myself a long time ago that I'd spoil both of them with a spa trip with my first real paycheck, and I'm going to deliver."

"That'll make her happy."

I grinned from ear to ear. "I haven't eaten this in a long, long time."

"It's the first time I've made it, but I did follow her recipe, so let's see if it tastes as good as you remember."

My eyes widened. "You not only asked what my favorite was but you even followed her recipe? I think you might be my favorite person ever."

Laughing, he kissed up and down my neck. "I'd better be."

This felt so amazing. I had my dream job, and this wonderful man had cooked for me and was doing everything in his power to make sure I was happy.

He captured my lips, kissing me slowly. Savoring him, I groaned against his mouth and pressed my pelvis into him, then gasped. He was semihard.

"Riley," he muttered between kisses, "careful."

"Or what? You'll devour me? Spoiler alert: that's what I want."

"We've got time for that after dinner."

Hell, now that he mentioned it, I *was* pretty hungry. I playfully pushed him backward.

He glanced away, drawing in a deep breath. I'd already brought him so close that he was about to lose control. Wow.

"All right. Plate," I said, turning around just in time to hide my smile.

Duncan cupped my ass. "I saw that smile."

"I wasn't trying that hard to hide it."

I served the chili for both of us. It smelled amazing and transported me right back to our small trailer. We'd used the slow cooker a lot because it was easier and cheaper than turning on the stove.

This was delicious. I could tell without even tasting it. The mix of spices seemed just right.

Wait a second...

"You had all the necessary spices already?"

"No, but I went shopping."

I turned around. "I love you," I blurted. I couldn't hide it anymore, and I didn't want to. And if there was ever a time to blurt it out, it was after he'd prepped my favorite dinner. But most of all, Duncan made me feel special, and I loved him for it.

He put down the wineglasses he'd taken from the oversized cabinet and said, "Damn, woman. I'd planned this whole declaration after dinner. I love you so fucking much."

This time, I *did* jump him. There was no one to see and absolutely no reason to hold back.

He kissed me hard as he picked me up and sat me on the counter.

I threaded my fingers through his hair, nipping at his lips, then wrapped my legs around him, putting my ankles above his ass.

"Fuck, woman. See what you do to me?"

"Yes, and I love it."

He'd gone from semihard to hard as a rock almost instantly.

He cleared his throat. "Let's have dinner. I want to bury myself inside you tonight and make you scream this place down. And you're going to need a lot of sustenance for that."

"Ha, well, when you put it like that, I can't argue. It's very good logic."

He moved to open a bottle of white wine. It didn't matter if he was right next to me or at the end of the counter, I felt closer to him than ever before.

He *loved* me.

We sat down at the dining room table. It felt weird to be here without Jeremy.

"What are you thinking?" he asked.

"That I miss Jeremy. He'd like this."

"He'll have some tomorrow. There's plenty left. Tell me if you like it."

"I always eat it with a spoon," I informed him.

"Ah, I was wondering why you put out spoons."

It was still hot, so I blew on it before taking a small mouthful. I closed my eyes, and the trailer appeared in front of me. The mustard couch that was also my bed at night. The small table that was chipped at every corner. Mom's laughter as I took a huge mouthful even though she'd warned me it was hot.

"I take it as a compliment that you're not saying anything."

I opened my eyes.

"That's a very cute smile you have on," Duncan said.

"I swear I just stepped back in time. This is truly perfect."

"Smile again. I want to take a picture of you," he said. "Your mom requested one."

"Wait. I know just what to do." I loaded my spoon with so much chili that I could never fit it into my mouth. I held it next to my face and grinned.

He laughed, snapping a picture. "Okay, I sent it."

We sipped wine while eating—it was a delicious combo. When he gently nudged my leg under the table, I fell in love with him even more.

Could this really be our life? I'd come here from work and spend time with Duncan and Jeremy?

I didn't want to dream too much, but it felt almost impossible not to. I felt as if everything was in my grasp.

After I finished the food and the glass of wine, he asked, "Want to move to the couch?"

"Oh yeah," I said.

He filled our glasses again, and I took those with us as well. As I sat down, I put my feet on the couch. Duncan immediately scooted next to me, taking my legs in his lap. "See, this is why we need a couch on our camping trip too."

I laughed. "Oh, Duncan, we don't have to go camping again. Jeremy and I would be just as happy in a hotel, honestly."

"No, I have photographic evidence from last weekend that you two were having the time of your lives in that cramped little tent."

He tapped his phone, then turned it to me.

There was a picture of Jeremy and me putting the tent together and then another one assembling the camping chairs. And another one where we played with the zipper of the tent. My heart expanded just looking at the time we'd spent together.

"You both had a lot of fun."

I couldn't disagree. Jeremy and I were laughing so hard that I was surprised we didn't pull a muscle. "I miss him so much."

"Fuck, I love you even more when you say that."

He put the phone down, then pulled my leg so that my ass landed in his lap. I latched on to his shoulders for dear life.

"I can't believe you care about him in such a way."

"Of course I do. I love him too," I said. "And this week, it became apparent to me just how much. It physically hurt here to be away from him." I put a hand on my chest. "I can't even imagine how things will be when I have to travel to see clients or something."

He touched my cheek. "You do what you have to do. We'll support you. Both of us. I can't wait to tell him tomorrow."

"Same for me," I confessed.

He kissed one temple, then moved over my forehead to the other one as he trailed one hand up and down my back. I licked my lips, tilting my hips forward and then backward, arching into him.

He groaned.

Oops! I'd done that rolling motion right over his cock. He had a full-on erection beneath me.

I moved back a bit on his thighs, slipping a hand between me and his zipper, and said, "Now, let's free him. Wouldn't want him to get upset that we kept him trapped there."

"Trust me, he's going to be inside you tonight, so he's happy no matter what."

His voice had changed. It was low and so damn throaty, and it was in that moment that I realized I want to spend forever with this man.

He grinned as I undid the button of his jeans. Then he patted my ass, clearly indicating that I should lift it, which I did. He pushed his jeans down as quickly as he could.

"That's better," I murmured. I pulled down the elastic band of his underwear. How was he already so damn turned on? Not that I was doing better.

He squeezed his cock once, and heat gathered between my thighs. I sucked in a breath.

"You're wet, aren't you?" Duncan asked.

I nodded, biting my lower lip. He grinned again, then started pulling at my skirt, to no avail. It was snug around my middle. Finally, he pushed it up around my waist, leaving my ass bare.

"Fuck, you go to the office like this with your ass hanging out?" he said, squeezing my buttocks.

"It's not hanging out, but I have to wear a thong or the lines will show through the skirt."

"The thought of you wearing this all day is going to drive me insane."

"Would it be better if I didn't wear any panties at all?" I teased.

He bit the side of my neck lightly in response, and now my whole body was sensitive. My nipples were painful, pressing against my bra.

I didn't stop kissing him as I awkwardly tried to remove my skirt so I could take off my blouse and then open my bra, but it was impossible. I groaned in protest.

"I'll get you naked, beautiful. Don't you worry. Now, stand up."

I climbed down from his lap, feeling silly with my skirt up around my middle. He pulled it back to its original position, then lowered the zipper and pulled it down my thighs.

I stepped out of it quickly. He sat closer to the edge of the couch and instructed for me to part my legs wide. I sucked in a breath, looking down. He undid the top of my blouse very slowly, opening one button and then kissing my skin. Then he opened another button and paused for yet another kiss. It was pure torture. It set me on fire. I dropped my head back, groaning.

When he finished undoing all the buttons, I shook my shoulders, and the shirt fell off my arms.

"This bra... fuck," he exclaimed. It was one of those that had the clasp between the cups. He undid it quickly. I wanted to tease him that I could also wear no bra at the office, though of course I'd never do it. I just wanted to see his reaction.

But I didn't get the chance before he sucked a nipple into his mouth. He teased the tip by circling it with his tongue and then flicking it, sliding two fingers up and down over my panties in the same rhythm.

I was done for. My thighs shook. I braced both palms on his shoulders, digging my nails in.

"Duncan," I exclaimed.

"Fuck, you're so beautiful. So damn responsive. I love watching you come apart this quickly."

"Yeah, so damn quickly. I needed this all week."

"Tell me, do you go around your office wishing I was there to fuck you?"

"Yes," I confessed. I had no idea where that came from. But now that he'd said it, I couldn't deny that it was true.

He dipped his hand inside my panties. My knees completely gave in when I felt his fingers on my bare skin. I lost my balance, but Duncan steadied me, putting a hand on my hip and guiding me down onto his legs. He'd spread my thighs widely so he had access to my pussy and kept moving his fingers up and down. I became even wetter until I drenched my panties.

His mouth wasn't on my breasts anymore but had moved upward. He kissed my neck, my jaw, and then my mouth. He slid two fingers inside me without any warning, and I nearly came on the spot.

My shoulders hunched before I fell forward. As I pressed my forehead on his shoulder, he started working me in earnest, sliding his fingers in and out, brushing my clit with his palm on every stroke. I gripped his cock, rubbing my hand in the same rhythm.

"Fuck, babe," he growled.

"I want you. I need you."

"Kiss me," he said, tugging at my hair with his free hand so I straightened up. Then he kissed me ferociously, and I lost all sense of myself. I let go of his cock, planting my hands on his biceps instead, hanging on for dear life as he pressed his hand on my clit, driving me completely over the edge. He moved his fingers until I was completely spent, then grabbed my ass, pulling me closer.

When he rocked back and forth, rubbing his cock against my clit, I exploded again. I had no idea if it was a new orgasm or if I was just riding the wave of the last one, but I didn't care. I belonged to this man.

He lifted me into his arms, and I realized he was walking with me through the condo. I figured he might take us to the bedroom, but I was wrong. He brought me to the dining table instead, sitting me down right at the edge.

"Bedroom too far?" I teased.

"I've wanted to fuck you on this table for some time."

"Well, then... no time like the present to make that dream happen."

He smirked. "Sassy, are we?"

"Yes," I admitted.

Now, after two orgasms, or one hell of a long orgasm, or whatever that was, I was *supremely* sassy. He was still teasing me, rubbing the length of his cock against my flesh.

"I like the skin-on-skin contact."

"I love it too," I said.

Then he slid inside me to the hilt. Even though I'd just had an amazing climax, my entire body succumbed to the sensations. How was I so overwhelmed already? He pulled out inch by inch and then pushed back in again even more forcefully than before.

"I'll never tire of this," he said. "Seeing you, kissing you, making you mine."

I was desperate for him. I needed to move, but it wasn't really possible on the table. But he seemed in tune with what I needed. Once again, he lifted me from the table, and we moved back to the couch. He put my ass on the edge of the armrest. I gripped it for dear life.

"Can you hold yourself like this here?" he asked.

"Yes."

I was so desperate that I'd do anything. Besides, the armrest was so wide that it was practically a small seat in itself.

I rolled my hips in the same rhythm with his thrusts. His muscles seemed more pronounced every time we were together. It was as if I forgot how sexy he was and was blindsided every time. Feeling him inside me was so damn exquisite. I might have had an intense orgasm before, but this one was different. It was always better when we were connected. I felt everything more powerfully.

"Fuck, I need to move even more," he said, then stilled.

"No! What are you doing?"

I tried to roll my hips back and forth, but without him thrusting as well, it was fruitless.

"This isn't the best spot."

I really didn't care where we went. We could even lie on the floor and I'd be happy. I just needed him to push inside me again. He shifted me to the center of the couch.

"Lie back," he instructed.

"Gladly."

When he entered me, I reached a new high. The angle was out of this world. I'd never felt him so deep. He thrust fast, his strokes deliberate, filling me up completely. He flicked his thumb over my clit gently, but it was enough to stir me to tremors as he moved quicker and then quicker still. I felt cold all of a sudden, then extremely hot. Duncan grabbed one of my ankles, clasping his fingers around it as though they were a cuff, and put it on his shoulder, changing the angle yet again. I'd never felt so close to him. Our connection was like a physical bond between us.

Then he lifted my other leg, too, and put his thumb on my clit again.

I wasn't aware of anything anymore—not the couch or my surroundings. Nothing except the exquisite pleasure rocking my body. It started in my center but took over completely. I felt him come over the edge with me as well, grunting out my name, kissing my ankles, sliding inside me ferociously. When my aftershocks subsided, he slowed down, looking between us. His thumb was still on my clit.

I swallowed hard when he stilled and smiled at me.

"You're everything, to me, Riley. Everything."

Emotions clogged my throat, and I couldn't reply at all. All I could do was raise my head and kiss him.

CHAPTER THIRTY

Duncan

The next morning, we both woke up early, which was perfect for me because I wanted to enjoy a little more time with Riley before we picked up Jeremy. She was singing in the shower. I promised myself that I wouldn't distract her from it, but I lost my willpower only a few minutes later. I couldn't resist knowing that she was naked under the spray of water.

Jumping out of bed, I headed into the bathroom and opened the door to the shower, stepping inside. She shrieked and then lost her balance. I grabbed her, putting both hands on her rib cage.

"Oh my God, you should announce yourself," she said.

"I did, but you were singing. Very loudly, I might add."

"Oops, I didn't realize."

"It's fine, babe. You were relaxed. But you sounded so irresistible that I couldn't stay in bed by myself any longer."

"Really? My high-pitched tune was irresistible? You're a bad liar."

"No, knowing that you were here naked was very irresistible to me. I thought you might need help washing your back."

"Or my boobs?" she asked as I started soaping up her breasts.

"Every part of you," I said, kissing the tip of her nose.

"All right, then. Allow me to return the favor so you don't feel like I'm using you or something."

I grinned, loving the feeling of her palms on my skin.

After we cleaned up, I intended for us to drink coffee before we left, but then I saw a message from Mom.

> Mom: Jeremy woke up a bit poorly today. He's vomiting and having diarrhea. I think he's got a stomach bug.

"Fuck!" I exclaimed.

"What's wrong?" Riley walked toward me, clutching her hand to her stomach.

"We have to cancel the camping trip."

"What's wrong?"

"Jeremy's not feeling well. Mom thinks he's got a stomach bug."

She frowned. "Oh no, poor thing."

"Come on, let's pick him up and see how the day goes," I suggested.

Riley nodded. "Sure."

I was supposed to pick up donuts for him, but I headed straight to Mom's. If he had a bug, the last thing he needed was donuts.

My mom opened the door, smiling when she saw us.

"Hi," Riley said. "Good to see you again."

"You too."

"How's the little guy feeling?" I asked.

"Not terribly bad, but I don't think he's in any shape for a camping trip. Not the best place to need the toilet."

"No," I agreed.

"He'll try to convince you otherwise, of course."

Riley and I stepped inside. Jeremy was curled up on Mom's couch with his favorite toy in his arms and a pillow between his knees. He looked a bit pale. But I swear to God, the second he noticed Riley, his face completely lit up.

"Riley, how are you doing?" he asked. "I haven't seen you all week."

"I missed you," she said, sitting next to him and hugging him. Jeremy didn't even seem to care that I was here.

"The new nanny's not as nice as you are. No one is as nice as you are. I'm so happy we're going camping."

Riley looked up at me, and I nodded.

"Jeremy, your grandmother says you've been throwing up and going to the toilet a lot," I said.

"Yes, but I'm fine now." But then he turned pale again and said, "Oh no, I need to throw up again." He made a beeline to the toilet.

"I'll go after him," I told Mom and Riley.

Jeremy stepped inside the bathroom and closed the door. "Don't come after me. I'm a big boy."

"Right. I'm going to be out here in case you need me," I said.

He came out a few minutes later. He'd rinsed his face, but he was still pale.

I lowered myself so I was his height. "Buddy, why don't we have a cozy weekend in, okay? And we'll make plans for next week or another time."

He pouted. "No."

"It's going to be very uncomfortable if you're sick. You won't be able to eat any marshmallows."

I could see his resolve weaken. His shoulders slumped, and the corners of his mouth turned downward.

Riley joined us a moment later.

"Riley, help," Jeremy begged. "Dad is trying to convince me not to go camping."

She sat down on the floor with her thighs to one side,

cupping his cheek lightly with one palm. "Jeremy, you don't feel well."

"But I want to spend the weekend with you," he cried before hugging her.

She wrapped her arms around him and held him close.

Now it all made sense. He'd insisted because he thought she was only staying with us if we were going on a camping trip.

I put a hand on his back, making eye contact with Riley. "Riley is spending the weekend with us no matter what. The three of us will stay home, and if you're feeling a bit better later on, we can even go down to the pool."

That was a good compromise. Even if he became sick again, there was a bathroom there.

"Really? Riley's staying with us? Can we do a TV marathon? We can watch all the Disney originals with Dad."

He looked at me with a huge grin. Riley could barely hide her laugh.

"A what?" I asked, because that sounded like hell.

"I've been showing Jeremy the classic Disney movies," she explained. "So many kids these days don't know them anymore."

"They're awesome, Dad. You know them?"

Yes, they were old as fuck. Like me. Of course I knew them. But that didn't mean I wanted a marathon.

"Can we do a marathon, please? Pretty please?"

His eyes were pleading. Riley had a sympathetic expression on her face, so what else could I say except, "Sure, let's go home and watch them."

———

By the time we got back to the condo, I figured they might have forgotten about their plan, but no such luck.

We all headed to the TV room. Riley darkened the blinds, and Jeremy got hold of the remote. Usually, we'd make popcorn when we watched anything in this room, but right now, I just wanted to keep him hydrated.

"All right, what should we start with? *Cinderella?*" Riley suggested.

"No, let's start with *Snow White*," Jeremy replied.

I'm in hell.

"All right, *Snow White* it is," Riley said with a huge smile. Jeremy had an almost identical one.

It made these two happy, so why not? So, for the rest of the day, we watched cartoons back-to-back.

When Jeremy fell asleep, I simply took him to his room, then came back for Riley. She had also fallen asleep. I was the only one who saw the ending of *The Lion King*. Spoiler alert: I'd actually forgotten most of it, and it wasn't too bad. Riley didn't even move as I scooped her up and brought her to bed.

The next day, we started all over again. Jeremy wasn't feeling much better. He could keep water down, but food was trickier. He'd managed to have toast for breakfast, but I'd felt too optimistic at lunch and gave him some of that turkey chili I'd made yesterday. That did *not* go well. Needless to say, he only had water and more toast for the rest of the day.

As the afternoon went by, we went through yet another Disney marathon.

At five o'clock, Riley's phone beeped, but she silenced it. I looked at her over Jeremy's head, which was in her lap.

"What was that?" I asked.

"The reminder that I was supposed to go to that event at work."

"Oh yeah, sorry. I totally forgot," I said. "I'll call you an Uber."

She shook her head. "I'm not going."

I frowned and paused the movie. Jeremy was sleeping, and I gestured with my head for her to step out of the room.

After we tiptoed out, I closed the door and asked, "What do you mean, you're not going?"

"Jeremy's sick. I don't want to leave him."

As much as I fucking loved every word coming out of her mouth, this wasn't right.

"Riley, I'm here with him. There's nothing you can do."

"But he likes having me here."

We both did. I'd been so wrapped up in having these past few hours that I didn't even remember that she had plans this evening. It wasn't just Jeremy who needed her. I needed her, too, but still.

"Listen, we talked about this. It's a great opportunity. I wouldn't want for you to miss your first social get-together."

She waved her hand. "I'm sure there will be more."

"Riley."

She bit her lip.

"I mean it. Go."

"But if he wakes up and he doesn't see me, he might get upset."

"We could wake him up now and explain."

She shook her head. "No way. He seems exhausted."

I stepped closer, kissing her forehead and then one corner of her mouth. "I'll talk to him when he wakes up. If you want, I'll call you and put you on the phone so you explain."

She looked up at me. "Okay, that's a good compromise. But honestly, I would prefer not to go."

"Riley, you can't miss work every time he gets sick. Trust me, if I know anything from the past few years, it's that kids get sick a lot. You actually caught him on a good streak these past few months. But there will be times when you'll be at a client's or whatever and he'll be unwell."

She looked stricken. "Right, okay. But I really hoped to spend as much time with him as possible, especially since I'm visiting Mom next weekend."

"There will be plenty of weekends. I've got this covered," I promised. "You go and focus on your event. Do you still have enough time to go home and change?"

"Yeah, there's plenty of time. I put the reminder two hours before I needed to go. I figured we might need it in case we totally lost track of time on the camping trip."

She was hesitating, but I nodded encouragingly. This event was important. I wanted her to focus on it.

"Okay, then. I'm going to go."

"Before you go..." I pulled her against me, sealing my mouth over hers. I didn't get many chances to kiss her even though we'd been together for the past forty-eight hours. And even though I'd enjoyed this closeness and our time as a family, I wanted her desperately. The more I held Riley, the more I needed her.

I kissed her until she groaned, then took a step back.

"Why did you stop?" she asked.

"Because you've got to go. I don't want to keep you any longer."

"You can always make me late with sexy distractions."

I growled. "No. Go now, before I change my mind and don't let you out that door."

She winked at me, putting her shoes, then taking her bag from the entrance, putting it over her shoulder. "I won't come back here after the event, though," she said.

That felt like a punch to the gut. These two days had felt like we were a family. I didn't like this. Something needed to change.

I nodded. "Sure. I'll call you when Jeremy wakes up."

CHAPTER THIRTY-ONE

Riley

It turned out to be a good idea to join the event because even the equity partners were participating. They seemed to genuinely want to get to know the new hires.

"Look, the hours are still long, but it's very rewarding, and I'm not nearly as stressed as I was when I first started out. Probably because after so much experience, things become routine," Lilly, one of the female partners, said.

I asked her about her day-to-day activities, but I was still on pins and needles, waiting for Duncan's call. Finally, at nine o'clock, my phone buzzed. I was chitchatting with the other new hires and excused myself, going out on the balcony.

"Hey, how's everything going?" I asked. "Is Jeremy awake?"

"No, he only woke up briefly, then fell back asleep. Don't think you'll get to talk to him tonight. But I just wanted to keep you informed so you don't worry."

"Thanks. I'm really glad you called."

"How's the event?"

"It's good that I came. I like mingling with everyone, and even some of the equity partners are here."

"It says a lot about them that they like to personally meet everyone who starts. You're going to kick ass."

Every time he told me that, my heart soared. I had self-confidence, but it was different when *he* believed in me.

"I'll let you get back to it," he said.

"Can you call tomorrow morning and let me know how he feels?" I asked.

"Sure. Now, I want you to focus on mingling and not on Jeremy, okay?"

"I'll try," I said, but I knew I couldn't push him to the back of my mind just like that.

When it came to Jeremy, I couldn't compartmentalize.

———

The next morning, I was hoping to hear from Duncan as soon as I woke up, but I didn't.

I called him right as I left the house. I couldn't start my day without knowing if Jeremy was at least feeling better. Thankfully, he picked up.

"Hey," I said. "Good morning."

"Hi." He sounded absolutely exhausted.

"Oh my God, did I wake you up?"

"No. I didn't sleep much. Jeremy kept waking up during the night and throwing up. I even asked the on-call doctor to come. He's ruled out anything more serious than nasty food poisoning."

"Poor guy."

"Yeah. So, I'm going to spend the day with him at home."

"I can call in sick and stay with him as well," I said. "In fact, I'm going to do that."

"No," Duncan said sternly, almost making me wince.

"I can at least come and see him before I go into the office," I said.

"You'll be late, Riley. It's your first month. What kind of impression will that make?"

"I don't care," I said. I knew I wasn't being rational, but the thought of being away from Jeremy when he was sick was simply painful. I'd never experienced anything like it.

"I do."

"Fine, I won't come now. But I'll skip the briefing they wanted to do after hours this evening—"

"Absolutely not. Listen to me, Riley. You just started a new job that you need to focus on. We can't hold you back."

"What do you mean?" I asked, leaning against the wall. "You're not holding me back."

Duncan huffed out a breath. "Promise me you'll go to work today and give it your best shot. That you will not spend any time worrying about Jeremy."

"But that's unfair," I replied.

"Listen to me, Riley. Law firms are like hawks. Every corporation is. They watch you closely when you first start. They need to see you at your very best. You can't be worrying about your boyfriend's son."

The way he phrased it made my heart hurt. Of course I wasn't Jeremy's mom. I knew that. I just felt like I was.

"You said that this week is going to be brutal and that you'll need to stay at the office every evening," he continued.

"I know," I said quickly. "But I didn't know that Jeremy would get sick."

"He's a kid. They get sick often." Duncan sounded calmer. "But this week I want you to forget about us and give it your best. Don't even think about asking your bosses to let you go earlier in the evening."

"I don't like the sound of that," I said.

"I don't like it, either, but it's necessary. The last thing you need is for us to hold you back."

"You're not," I replied. Why did he keep repeating that? "Send me text updates, okay?"

"I can do that. I promise," Duncan said.

My heart was still heavy as I hung up.

———

Duncan

"Dude, what the fuck? That's a shitty way to tell her not to worry." Griffin had dropped by this morning to discuss business with me after I told my brothers that I couldn't join them at the office.

"Huh?" I asked. I was completely wrecked. I'd slept maybe two hours combined the whole night, probably even less. I woke up often, and then I couldn't fall back asleep.

When Jeremy woke up and threw up again at four in the morning, I called the doctor. I feared he might need an IV or something. It happened so often when he was a baby, and I still had PTSD from it. But the doctor assured me that it wasn't necessary.

"What's with all that talk about keeping her back?"

I shrugged. "It's the truth. What do you think a boss would think if she told them that she's coming late because she needs to check on her boyfriend's son? Or that she has to leave early?"

"That's not the point. Obviously, you're right. It's just, you know, you have no filter when you're exhausted."

"I'm not just exhausted," I said. "I'm demolished."

"Yeah," Griffin said, "I can see that. I shouldn't have dropped by."

"I can't even think about business. I'm going to lie down with Jeremy."

"I can call the family and have us watch him in turns."

I shook my head. "I appreciate that, but it's really not necessary."

He laughed. "Unlike Riley, we own our businesses, so no one can tell us off for taking time away."

I waved my hand.

"Is your nanny coming today?" Griffin asked.

"She was supposed to, but I messaged her this morning and told her that Jeremy's sick. I won't leave him alone with someone new when he's feeling like this. I'll play it by ear."

"Well, whatever that ear says," he said, pointing at me, "make sure you don't scare Riley off. We like her. She's good for both of you."

"I know that," I said. "Stop giving me shit." I had no idea what had gotten into him.

After he left, I fell asleep right away.

———

Jeremy didn't feel better Tuesday either. I told his nanny not to come by. I was going to spend every day with him until he got better.

"Okay, buddy. I think that's it for breakfast." He'd only had toast.

"Dad, can I have a pancake?" he asked.

I looked at him. "If you don't get sick for another few hours, then I'll consider it. How about that?"

"Okay," he said. Then he put his hands under his chin, his elbows on the counter, as he looked up at me. "Dad, do you think I can see Riley today?"

I shook my head. "No, buddy. She's got a lot on her plate this week, but we'll talk to her on the weekend."

"I really, really like Riley."

I smiled. "So do I."

He straightened up. "Really? But then it's perfect. I like her, and you like her, and I know she likes both of us because I asked her, so that means she can be my mom. Don't you think so? My actual mom, not my Dublin mom." He said that as if it was the most natural thing in the world.

Riley and I had planned to talk to him about our relationship when we were together, but the timing felt right now. He'd given me an in.

"Jeremy, let's go sit on the couch and talk a bit."

"Am I in trouble?" he asked me timidly.

I realized that I only used that when I wanted to chastise him. "No, not at all. There are just some things I've been meaning to talk to you about for a while and never found the right moment."

As we sat down on the couch, I looked for signs that he was about to get ill again. But he seemed in top shape so far. He'd even gotten some color back in his cheeks.

"So, as you know, Riley and I have gotten very close. We're dating."

Jeremy stood up on the couch abruptly so he was towering over me. Then he came right up to me, holding my head and laughing. "Yes, yes, Daddy, yes. I told Grandma that I wished you would find a nice lady like Uncle Chase, and you did. Riley is the best."

"I agree."

"Then she can be my mom," he said. "When can she move in with us?"

"One thing at a time!" I patted the spot on the couch next to me.

He sat down, looking at me. "She will move in with us, right?"

"I'll ask her."

"Can I do it?"

I laughed, but an idea was starting to form in my head. Now that I was talking to Jeremy, my neurons lit up out of the coma they'd been in.

Fuck! Griffin was right. I'd been harsh on the phone.

"Did you ask her to be your girlfriend?"

"What?" I opened my mouth and closed it again.

"Dad, you have to do it. That's what they say at school."

"Right," I said, trying to sound like I was on the same page with him. I didn't like for my son to see me discombobulated. He needed to know that I was in control of the situation and could take care of him. "She is my girlfriend," I assured him.

"Since when?"

"Why does it matter?" I asked.

"Because I want to know how long I have to wait to ask her to move in with us. Some of the kids at school were pissed that their dads asked their new girlfriend to move in too fast. But I wouldn't mind."

I raised a brow. "Since when do you say 'pissed'?"

Jeremy grinned. "I always say it when you and Riley aren't around. Uncles Finn and Griffin don't mind."

I was going to have a word with those two.

"We're in no hurry. We need to wait for the time to be right."

"Why do adults always say that?" He sighed dramatically. "It's so boring. Why wait when she can move in now?"

Because she has to want to. She has to be ready.

I didn't say that part out loud, though.

———

Mom dropped by later that afternoon. Unfortunately, Jeremy was asleep.

"Darling," she whispered, "I brought some snacks for Jeremy."

"Mom, he can't keep a lot down."

"No, these are special snacks. I used to make them for you kids when you were sick. They help an upset stomach." She put containers of Tupperware on the kitchen island.

"Thanks." I opened one and peered inside it.

Mom laughed. "You had to double-check, huh? Might I remind you, I raised six boys."

"I know, I know. And you're right. Even the doctor recommended this type of cracker. I just didn't get around to buying them. Want a coffee?" I asked her as we both sat at the dining table.

"No, I'm good. Just a bit worried about the little one."

"Doctor checked him. It's really just food poisoning."

"I keep trying to think what it was that he ate. I think it was that sandwich he asked for when we went to town. It's the only thing I didn't have, too, or else I'd probably be ill."

"It could be a number of things. Maybe even something you had too. Kids are more sensitive."

Her chin wobbled. "I feel so guilty."

I shook my head. "Really, Mom, there's no reason to."

"How are you two coping without Riley?"

"Well, Jeremy keeps asking about her."

"And you?" Mom asked.

"I'd want nothing more than for her to just be here with us. She actually really wanted to come by. I told her not to."

"Why not?" she asked sharply.

I sighed. "Because she's starting a new job. She needs to make a good impression." Even as I said this, I thought the song was getting old, so to speak.

"Oh. You do make a point."

"It's something that's been on my mind lately," I confessed. "She's so young. She needs to focus on her job. I can't help but feel that..."

"The two of you are going to hold her back?" she said when I didn't finish.

I narrowed my eyes. "Griffin talked to you?"

"Yes, he did." Mom looked at me with a kind expression. "Duncan, listen. I know you're used to being in control of everything. Your dad and I fully accept the blame for that. When you kids were young, everything spiraled downward, and I'm sure our unstable marriage impacted you kids. Everything felt out of your control."

"I don't blame you for anything, Mom. You both did your best."

"Well, we tried. I'm grateful that you don't blame us. But regardless, I think there's some impact that probably affects us all. And I think those years really affected you most of all." She looked down at her hands and back up at me. "Because, well, you were older and always trying to look out for the rest. You can't always pave the way and make it smoother for everyone around you, be that for us, or Jeremy, or Riley."

"But I'm going to try damn hard," I said.

"I know you will. But if Riley wants to be here for the two of you in every capacity she can, then it's not really up to you to tell her no. If you love her."

"What?" I asked, though I shouldn't have been surprised that my whole family had apparently figured out how deeply I felt for Riley.

"I know. What a strange concept, right? That woman loves you. And you really care about her."

"I do," I said, still shocked that Mom could read me so well. "But the timing of this..."

"No, don't do that," she said, shaking her head. "The timing is *never* right. I mean, look at me and your dad. We did everything by the book, the way everyone back then used to do things: get married young, start a family, buy a home. And then it all crashed and burned. And now, in the winter of our lives, we... well, I don't want to get ahead of myself, but we're finding our way back to each other."

I groaned. Talking about it was simply awkward. "So, it's a sure thing, then?"

"No, not at all. But, between you and me, I think you inspired him. He's taking me on a weekend away to New York."

"Good for you," I said. "You've always wanted to see New York."

"Yes, I have. But I've always wanted to see it with your dad, too, and what do you know? Thirty-five years later, we're getting the honeymoon we never had." She pressed her lips together. "Don't wait for the right time. Because I can tell you, it's always going to be right now, not some time in the future. Okay?"

I nodded. "You're right."

"All right. Well, since Jeremy's asleep, I'm just going to go. Tell him I stopped by and that I can come whenever he wants me to."

"I will, Mom. Thanks."

She smiled. "Of course. Anything for my grandkid."

————

Over the next few hours, I doted on Jeremy. The plan was consolidating in my mind. I was so focused on it that I forgot that Knox, Finn, and Griffin were stopping by in the evening. They wanted to check on Jeremy. To my surprise, Knox came with a bottle of wine.

"I was in Napa this weekend," he said, "and the team at the winery gave me a bottle of the handcrafted vintage they had in storage."

"Want us to open it?" I asked.

He cocked a brow. "No. It's for you. Rumor has it that you might need it to impress a certain lady."

I stared at him. Finn and Griffin both start laughing.

"Griffin talked to you?" I asked.

"Yeah, obviously," Knox said.

"I'll take it," I said. "Damn, you move fast."

"Yeah, you all give me shit for flying by the seat of my pants, but that's how I get my best ideas," Knox said.

"I won't argue with that," I said.

"Yeah, you do you, brother," Griffin said, patting his shoulder.

Jeremy came running from his bedroom, smiling at the group. He looked much better.

"Buddy, you look good," Knox said. "How about you spend the weekend with us?" He looked from Jeremy to me.

"Yes, Dad, can I? Can I go with my uncles after we make our plan?"

Since Riley was with her mom and Paula on Saturday, we needed to put our plan in motion on Sunday. "You can spend Sunday evening together. After we go to Riley's house."

"Wait, you're both going to Riley's house?" Knox asked.

"Yes. We're going to surprise her," Jeremy said.

"We can pick you up from there," Finn said.

"What do you plan on doing?" I asked my brothers.

"Take him to the movies," Finn replied.

"Sounds good," I assured him.

Knox glanced at the wine. "Good thing I brough this bottle. You need all the help you can get with Riley."

I laughed. "Thanks for the vote of confidence."

Griffin rolled his eyes. "Talking is not your forte. Brother, if you're serious about her, then don't let her doubt it."

"That's unexpected advice coming from you."

"I want the best for you. And you're different around Riley. Doesn't mean it's what I want for myself. Dating is enough."

I raised a brow. "A whole lot of dating."

"Which all of social media knows about, apparently." It was the first time he'd seemed frustrated about it. "But this isn't about me. It's about you. And Riley. Don't mess this up."

"I won't."

CHAPTER THIRTY-TWO

Riley

"My girls, you really do spoil me," Mom exclaimed.

Paula and I smiled at each other. *Oh yeah, mission accomplished.*

Mom had been delighted to see us on the front steps of her home today. The drive to her place took three hours, but it was more than worth it. It had always been a dream of mine to treat her and my sister to a spa day, and it was going even better than I'd imagined.

We didn't go far. I'd booked one of the hotels Mom had always admired, even when we were kids. I'd scheduled a massage for each of us, plus mani-pedis—the whole program.

I couldn't believe it. I could *finally* spoil my family.

My heart was a bit heavy because I didn't like the way things were with Duncan right now, but I was determined to focus on Mom today. I didn't see her nearly often enough, and I wasn't going to waste this day moping around. At the moment, the three of us were alone in the steam room, so we finally had a chance to talk.

"But you girls know you don't have to spend your money on me," Mom continued.

"It's all Riley," Paula said. "She wanted to treat us."

"Thanks for having my back, sis."

"Always," she replied, grinning.

Mom turned to me. "Riley, darling."

"Mom," I cut in. "It's been my dream for a long time. I promised you at my graduation, remember?"

"I do, but I also remember shutting you down and telling you to go buy yourself something nice with that first paycheck."

"I promise I'll buy something with the next one. How about that?"

"Yes, and please send me pictures. Paula, please promise you won't let your sister waste any more money on me."

Paula's eyes went wide. "I will do no such thing. I'll spoil you as soon I get some decent money too."

Mom shook her head. Oh, she had no idea about all the plans I had. I was going to get her out of that trailer and put her in a proper house, but all in due time.

"Now, tell me about that lovely man of yours," Mom said. "I've heard a lot about him from your sister, but you're not very talkative."

I smiled, shrugging. "You know I don't say much."

"Really? With me you do," Paula said. "Mom, everything I relay to you I know from Riley, but for some reason, she's embarrassed to talk to you about him."

Mom looked at me. "Well, be that as it may, I'm very happy that you two are in a good place."

I sighed. "I'm not so sure we *are* in a great place. Jeremy, well, he had some sort of virus or something affect his stomach this week. I wanted to drop by and see him a few times, but Duncan kept insisting that I should focus on work. Like somehow he and Jeremy would stand in my way."

No one said anything for a few seconds. I was almost

wondering if they'd heard me when Mom said, "That sounds like a man who cares about you a lot. I like him even more."

"Really? It doesn't sound like he's trying to push me away?"

"Oh hell no," Paula said. "I think Duncan's ways can be gruff at times, but his heart is in a good place."

I laughed. "Yes, he can be a bit gruff.

"But from what I've heard, he's been so wonderful to you and Paula," Mom added.

"Yes, he has," Paula said. "And I am so grateful."

That's right. Everything Duncan did to help out Paula made me wonder why he didn't understand that I wanted to take care of him and Jeremy. I was going to find out once I was back.

"I don't know about you, Mom, but I can practically hear the lawyer in her putting together an argument," Paula said.

I chuckled. "Yeah, that's exactly what I'm doing."

"Let's get out of here, girls," Mom suggested. "It's like fog in here, and I want to see your faces when I'm talking to you."

"Amen," I said, and we all hurried out of the steam room.

I definitely preferred the sauna. The humid heat was hell on its own.

After showering, we went over to what was called a silence room. It was just us in here, which honestly was amazing.

"I can still feel those neurons moving," Paula said as I closed my eyes.

"Hey, how about we all just enjoy the silence?" I suggested.

"Yep, our neurons do work better in silence. I'll just say one thing before," Mom whispered.

I started to laugh.

"I'm glad that you've softened, sweetheart, and that you're trusting your man with your heart."

I was so surprised that I opened my eyes, looking at her. We were close enough that she could take my hand and put it on her cheek.

"You know what I'm talking about?"

I nodded. I did. Because for so long, I'd kept my heart

guarded. But no more. For Duncan, I was wearing my heart on my sleeve. And I needed him to know that I was 100 percent his.

I took in a deep breath, rubbing Mom's hand with my left one and Paula's with the right.

"Lawyer mode off," I announced. I had a lot of time to think things through during the trip back. Right now, I wanted to soak up the love surrounding me.

———

On Sunday, I arrived home at half past eleven. Paula had gone on the beach with some friends, and I had the house to myself. Christine said they were all out, shopping.

I unlocked the door and stepped inside.

And then I froze because I definitely heard movement from the kitchen. I drew in a deep breath and stumbled backward. *What's happening?* There were vases upon vases with poppies everywhere. I stepped farther into the house and glanced into the living room. Yep. More poppies.

My heart was beating fast as I headed to the kitchen.

Jeremy and Duncan were standing there, side by side. "And when she comes—"

I cleared my throat, and both of them turned around.

Jeremy huffed. "Dad, you were supposed to tell me *before*."

"Damn it," Duncan said. "I miscalculated."

"You brought the f-flowers?" I stuttered.

"Yes, we did," Jeremy exclaimed. "We went to the flower market and asked them for all of their poppies. But they only had a few, so we went to seven more shops."

Oh, be still my beating heart.

Duncan wasn't saying anything, just looking at me with affection.

"But why did you...?" I asked.

"Because they're your favorite," Jeremy explained. "Dad and I thought it would show you how much we both love you."

There were three vases with poppies on the kitchen counter as well. I couldn't look away from Duncan.

He put an arm around his son's shoulders. "Jeremy and I had a terrific conversation, where I told him that you're my girlfriend and that you and I love each other very much."

Jeremy looked at his father. "Dad, can I ask her?"

Duncan nodded, and Jeremy came over and wrapped his arms around my waist. "Dad said I could ask if you want to move in with us."

My heart exploded. I lowered myself to his height and hugged him with all I had. "Of course I want to move in with the two of you. And I want to tuck you into bed every night and hear about your day."

"And Dad said we can take care of you together," Jeremy continued. "We can cook your favorite dinner. And then he said something about spoiling you."

I was fighting tears—the good kind—but I wanted to hold them back because I still hadn't managed to properly explain to Jeremy the difference between good tears and sad tears. And right now wasn't the right moment.

He was my boy. I might not have given birth to him, but I loved him as if he were my own flesh and blood.

When I straightened up, Jeremy asked, "Can we get a group hug?"

"Sure we can, buddy," Duncan said. His voice wasn't working properly. I wondered if that was why he hadn't said much.

He put an arm around my back. I rested my mouth in the crook of his neck. Jeremy was hugging us both. I took in a deep breath to steady my heartbeat. It felt like my heart was finally in its right place.

"Dad, when can she move in with us?" Jeremy asked.

"It's up to Riley," Duncan said, stepping back and caressing my cheek with the back of his fingers. "Whenever she's ready."

I was so ready that I could just leave with both of them right now.

"Will she already be in the condo by the time I'm back?" Jeremy asked eagerly.

I looked down. "Where are you going?"

"Uncle Knox and Finn are picking me up, and we're going to the movies."

I smiled at Duncan. He had a mischievous glint in his eyes.

He'd planned all this, hadn't he? So we could be alone.

"That's not enough time, Jeremy. Besides, we're not pressuring her, Jeremy," Duncan said.

"I definitely can't move in tonight, but I can do it the upcoming week."

"Yes! Then we can finally continue our Disney marathon with Dad."

Duncan's smile fell just a bit. I barely stifled a laugh. "We can negotiate that," I said gently.

"Okay." Jeremy didn't sound disappointed, just surprised.

They had chosen a good moment to ask, though. I was so happy that I would probably agree with most things he asked, which I realized was exactly why he'd done it. The little man had skills.

Duncan kissed my forehead. Then we heard a sound at the front door: a car pulling right in front of the house.

"I think that's my uncles," Jeremy exclaimed, then practically darted at the front door.

"Fuck, there are so many things I want to tell you," Duncan murmured in my ear. "But I need a bit more patience."

"I have none left," I confessed.

"Riley!" He put a hand on my waist and pressed his fingers on my skin. This sexy man was close to losing control. But he was right. Not yet.

The doorbell rang, and I felt as if someone had thrown a bucket of water at us. I stepped back and hurried to the front door, with Duncan hot on my heels.

Knox and Finn were standing on the porch when I opened the door. Knox had a shit-eating grin on his face, looking at Duncan.

Finn just whistled, looking over my shoulder. "What are those? Flowers?"

"Poppies," Jeremy informed them. "Two thousand of them. Dad and I went to eight florist shops to get that many."

Knox jerked his head back. "Man, I've got to give you credit. You've got skills." Then he looked straight at me. "Riley, you've brought out a side of our brother we weren't aware of."

"Yeah, I'd bet all my money that he wasn't aware of it either," Finn continued.

"What do you mean? What side?" Jeremy looked at Duncan, who just laughed.

"They're talking metaphorically, Jeremy."

Knox looked down at my hands and then back up at Duncan. "Jeremy, are you ready to go? Don't want to be late. If we make it there in good time, we can eat before the movie."

"Yes, I'm ready," Jeremy said, then darted toward the car without as much as a goodbye to me or Duncan.

"I'll never get used to it," Duncan said. "Someone from the family comes to pick him up, and he suddenly doesn't give a flying fuck about me."

"About us," I corrected him.

He grinned. "You're right, about us."

"All right, we don't want to be the third and fourth wheels," Finn said, then immediately walked toward the car. He opened the door for Jeremy to climb in.

"Hey, I don't mind being their third wheel for a few seconds longer," Knox said, not moving at all. "Did you like the wine?"

"Knox," Duncan said in a warning tone.

"Oh come on, man. You have to give me some credit—"

"I didn't bring out the wine yet."

Knox's face fell. "Fuck."

"Yeah, exactly."

Knox gave me an apologetic smile. "Forget I just asked that. In fact, forget that I ever mentioned wine."

"Repeating that is surely going to make her forget it," Duncan said, clearly running out of patience.

I was fighting my laughter with all I had, but I wouldn't be able to hold back much longer.

"You know what? I'm just going to go. But wait, did you also not get to the part with—" Knox began, as if he couldn't help himself.

"Knox, car, now," Duncan said.

"Got it. Okay, you two have fun."

"Oh, we will," I said.

Knox turned and headed to the car. We watched them in silence as they drove off. Then we took a step back, and Duncan closed the door. I couldn't hold my laughter in any longer.

Duncan smiled, shaking his head.

"Let me guess. Your brothers had an inkling of what you were planning for today?"

"Yes, they did. And Knox has no clue how to back off." He groaned. "Fuck, I can't believe we're finally alone. It felt like Knox was never going to leave." Duncan put an arm around my waist. I placed both hands on his chest as he brushed his fingers across my cheek, leaning into his touch. I needed it so much.

"How did all of this happen?" I murmured.

"After we spoke on the phone, I opened up to Jeremy. I know we said we'd do it together, but it felt right."

"You're his dad, Duncan. You don't have to explain yourself to me. You know best when the time is right."

"I felt like he had to know about us and how deeply I feel about you. I want you to be part of our life. I love you, Riley, with everything I have and everything I am. You mean so much to me that I don't even know how to express it in words."

"I feel the same about you," I assured him.

"About what Jeremy said... that wasn't exactly what I had in mind. I didn't want him to spring it on you right away about moving."

"But I want to. As long as you want me to," I added quickly.

What if Jeremy had gotten his wires crossed?

"That's exactly what I want, so then I can spend as much time as possible with you. I want to have you in my bed every night, wake up next to you every morning, and be a family."

I nodded, and now I wasn't holding back my tears anymore.

"I've fallen in love with you so damn hard," he said, "and so damn fast. I wouldn't change a thing."

"Really? But you like everything to happen on your own timeline."

He laughed. "True, but as I've learned with you, not everything can happen on my terms, and I'm more than fine with that."

He peppered light kisses from my temple to the corner of my mouth. "Sometimes it's better to just let things take their course and surrender to them."

I never thought Duncan would surrender to anything. And yet he'd surrendered to his feelings for me.

"I fucking love you, Riley." He covered my mouth with his. I gave in to the kiss completely, only pausing to breathe.

Then I felt us move throughout the bungalow. We were heading to my bedroom.

"Wait, my roommates—"

"They're not going to come back for a while."

"You told them about this?"

"Hell yes. Wasn't going to leave anything to chance."

"And what about that wine Knox mentioned?" I teased.

"We'll get into that later. Fucking Knox," he said, kissing me again.

And this time I didn't tease him anymore. In fact, I didn't interrupt him at all.

CHAPTER THIRTY-THREE

Duncan

I was going to devour her. Kissing wasn't enough. Touching wasn't enough. I needed her naked. I wanted to sink inside her. I took off her jacket first, revealing her T-shirt that was tucked into a skirt.

"Why do you have so many things on?" I protested.

"Now you know how I feel when I want to get you naked," she murmured.

She worked on my buttons, while I threw her t-shirt to the side. I found the zipper of her skirt and yanked it down. She yelped, wobbling on her shoes.

"Keep those on," I said as the skirt pooled at her feet and she stepped out of it. "You're so fucking sexy."

Nodding, she opened my belt buckle. My pants and boxers went next while I finished undoing the last buttons of my shirt, throwing that out of the way too. I'd never been more desperate to get us naked.

Riley was my everything. She was my home.

I growled, looking her up and down. I liked that I was the

only one who could see her in sexy lingerie. I was going to be the only one in her life, forever. The lace panties looked fucking exquisite on her. I grabbed my cock and gave it a good squeeze. And then I felt Riley's palm on the crown of my cock.

I let go of my erection, and she pumped her hand up and down. I skimmed my hands over the sides of her body, wanting to touch her everywhere at the same time. I pushed the strap of her bra to one side, kissing the place that it had covered before. She arched her back as soon as my lips made contact with her heated skin. Then I did the same with the other strap, so her bra was hanging loose. Looking down, I could see her nipples brushing against the gaping fabric.

I undid the clasp at the back, and the bra dropped to the floor. I rubbed her nipples with my thumbs while kissing the side of her neck down to her shoulder. I felt her tension build up inside her body, her muscles tensing beneath my touch.

As she squeezed me with more force, I let out a guttural groan. Desire tore through me, and I pulsed in her hand. I moved mine down to her panties, pushing them down on one side. She wiggled her ass, and they fell to her ankles. Carefully, she stepped out of them too. I'd never tire of seeing her get naked for me, trusting me with her body and putting her pleasure in my hands.

With one hand, I was still working her breasts, and with the other, I drew large circles around her pussy. I wasn't touching her clit yet; I only wanted to tease her. The joke was on me, though, because when I felt how wet she was already, I nearly lost my mind.

"You're so damn wet."

"That's what you do to me." She sounded surprised by her own words and her reaction to me.

I drank up everything she had to give me. Because I sure as hell was giving her everything I had. I grabbed my cock, swatting her hand away, then drew circles around her pussy with it, the same way I'd done before with my thumb, coating myself in her wetness. I wanted to make sure she was more than ready.

Looking between us, I nudged her clit with the crown of my cock. She gasped. Then she braced herself, putting her palms on my shoulder.

"I've got you, babe," I said.

I gently pushed her ass against the vanity so she could rest on it, then drew the circles even quicker, pressing harder against her flesh as I zeroed in on her clit. I was focusing on her pleasure and instinctively knew that she was close. But I didn't know if I had enough self-control to wait for her to come before sliding inside her. This was too good.

Her body changed right before my eyes. She hunched her shoulders and gripped one breast. Her other palm was firmly on my shoulder, her nails digging into the skin.

"Let go, beautiful. I need to see you come apart."

She dropped her head back, moaning as her entire body spasmed with her climax.

I was too hungry to even wait for her to ride out her orgasm. I slid inside her, right to the base.

"Duncan," she gasped.

I stilled completely. How could this already feel so surreal? Her inner muscles pulsed, tight and deliciously wet around my cock. I could still feel her coming.

I pulled back and then moved in and out. Fuck, I liked this angle; I could watch her perfectly. But I didn't want to fuck her against the vanity. The wood would keep poking her in the ass, and she wasn't going to be comfortable. But I didn't pull out, not yet. I wanted to draw every drop of pleasure from her before that.

I touched her everywhere, kissing her shoulders and neck before capturing her mouth and pushing my tongue in and out. She kissed me back softly; in fact, her entire body was softening. I knew it was the exact moment when she'd finished riding out her orgasm. And the next one hadn't formed yet.

Yes, there was going to be a next one.

I was always going to give her more than one orgasm. It was nothing less than what she deserved.

I pulled out of her, and she gasped.

"Come on, beautiful. You're not going to be comfortable against that."

She stepped in front of the bed, facing it. I stood behind her, inspecting her ass.

"See, you have marks here," I said, moving my hand over the dent right across her buttocks. My cock was between her thighs. I felt her grab it and rub it across her leg.

"Fuck," I exclaimed, then pushed her forward onto the bed. I slid inside her just as her knees hit the mattress and she dropped forward on all fours. I didn't have it in me anymore to prolong the foreplay. Being inside her was everything I wanted and needed right now.

"Duncan," she whispered.

Pulling out, I bent at the knees, adjusting the angle, then slid inside her once more. She groaned and bent down on the pillow. At first I thought she wanted to hide her screams in it, and I wanted to chastise her, but then I realized she simply wanted to rest her upper body on it.

I moved with precision, pulling back and then sliding in, going deeper every time. Our connection was stronger than ever before. I was part of her, and she was part of me. This woman was mine just as much as I was hers.

I watched my cock move in and out of her. She was pushing backward, too, slamming against me.

She looked over her shoulder and smiled. Her face was red, and her shoulders had hunched forward again. This was a telltale sign that pleasure was crawling through her already, lacing with tension, torturing her.

"Are you close?" I asked her.

"Yes, though I'm not even sure how that's possible." Her

voice shook, her words coming out strangled. "Everything feels so intense."

"It's so damn good and special. Give me your hands and straighten up."

"What?" But even though she didn't understand, she followed my command, straightening and rising onto her knees.

I plastered her body against my chest, which had the added advantage that I could touch her upper body too. Like this, I could reach those gorgeous breasts and her clit, so I did just that. I covered one breast with my palm, flicking her nipple, and then put my other hand over her clit, nudging it in the same way.

Her senses immediately kicked into overdrive. I felt it in the way her entire body tensed. Her groan was guttural and filled the room.

She was so tight that I could barely push in. But I didn't relent. I knew this was going to be out-of-this-world good for both of us. When she called out my name, squeezing me so tight that my vision blurred, I knew I wasn't going to last even a fraction of a second longer. I worked her clit faster and faster, and I exploded seconds before she did.

I buried my head in her neck, but it was no use. Our groans were loud and unrestrained. I was certain the entire street could hear us.

She was shaking and breathing rapidly. Even after my orgasm, I didn't pull out of her; I just held her against me, making sure I was supporting her. Then she dropped her head onto my shoulder, tilting it so her cheek pressed against my clavicle. Her left hand was on my thigh, gripping it tightly.

"Duncan," she murmured.

"Let's lie down, Riley, so we can catch our breath."

We both simply collapsed next to each other on the mattress. She was smiling. Her face was completely flushed, her hair messed up. Had I gripped it before? Probably, though I couldn't remember.

In fact, I couldn't remember anything else, except that this woman and I belonged together.

————

Riley

After cleaning up, I came back to the bedroom, but Duncan wasn't there.

"Duncan?" I asked loudly.

"I'll be right back!"

I lay down on the bed, watching the door. It was so glorious to be here with him all alone.

He walked back to bed, to me, holding a bottle of wine and two glasses. I pouted. "Why did you put on your pants?"

He winked. "I had my reasons."

"But my roommates won't be back for a while, right?" I asked, sitting up on the bed.

"No. Don't worry about that. I bribed them well enough to spend the whole day out of the house."

"You have got to tell me what you did to make them wake up earlier than noon."

"I have to keep *some* secrets," I said with a wink. "Who knows when I'll need them again?"

I stood on my knees on the bed, watching as he uncorked the bottle and then poured wine in the glasses, handing me one. I smelled it and knew already that this was one of the best wines I'd ever had. It smelled exquisite. He twirled his glass slowly.

"And Knox offered the bottle to you?"

"Yeah, but let's not talk about him right now," Duncan said, shaking his head.

"Why not?" I asked.

"Because this is our moment."

I put my glass down, and so did he. Then I pressed both hands on his shoulders, kissing his chest. At least he left that unclothed. *Thank heaven for small mercies.*

"I want you naked again," I said.

He groaned, but before he could say anything else, I undid the button of his jeans and tugged them down. A thumping sound followed and then a metal one, as if a key had hit the floor.

"I think you had something in your pocket."

"Fuck," he exclaimed.

With a groan, he lowered himself to the floor.

"Sorry," I said.

"Don't worry about it."

Since when did he have keys in his back pocket?

He resurfaced a few seconds later. Only he wasn't holding a key. He had a ring. Then he changed positions so he wasn't just kneeling with both knees in front of the bed. He put one in front of him, and my heart nearly stopped, my breath catching in my throat.

"Riley, today was full of surprises. Some went the way I imagined. Then some—" He paused, looking at the ring. "—didn't. But I want to make you some promises. One, that I'll get better at sharing my feelings. And the second one, that I will make you very, very happy as my wife. I love you with a fierceness I didn't know existed inside me. What we have together is incredible. I promise to value and cherish you for the rest of my life. Make sure you're spoiled every day and that you will want for nothing. Will you marry me?"

"Yes, of course. I promise to love you forever, Duncan. To love and support you no matter what. And I promise to love Jeremy, too, and be the best mother figure I can."

"You're amazing, you know that? I love you so damn much for caring about him like you do."

"I want to make his little soul happy even if it means talking you into camping trips," I teased.

He scoffed. "Already siding with him more than me?"

"Nah, just on some things. I just... You and him, it's more than I could ever dream of. Our little family. I'm so immensely happy," I said as he slid on the ring.

Then he rose, putting one knee on the bed and moving toward the center of the mattress.

"And I promise I'll get better at surprises," he said, laughing.

I giggled, pointing at my new gorgeous ring. It was a huge, round diamond with several smaller ones around it. The band was platinum, and I couldn't stop looking at it.

"Oh, you're excellent at it," I assured him.

Then I pulled him toward me, and we both tumbled onto the mattress.

EPILOGUE

Duncan

Each summer, I brought Jeremy to Dublin to spend three weeks with his mother. This year was no different, except that Riley had traveled with us. She and I were going to spend the next three weeks touring Europe while Jeremy spent time with Shona.

"Darling, you grew four inches," Shona said. "And you must be Riley. Nice to meet you in person," she said as the two women shook hands.

Jeremy looked at her excitedly. "When are we going to the zoo?"

Shona laughed. "I bought tickets for later today. I have a surprise for you inside the house."

"Really?"

"Yeah, it's in your room."

Jeremy darted inside the house without even looking back at us.

"Some things don't change about him, huh?" Shona said.

"No, he still loves the zoo," I said. "Still makes me feel like a second-class citizen every time I drop him off with my brothers or with you."

"Thank you, both of you, for bringing him. Riley, thanks for coming to meet me in person. Are you staying in Dublin? Do you want us to meet for dinner or something?"

I shook my head and put an arm around Riley's shoulders, kissing the side of her head. "No, I'm taking her on a tour of Europe. Our plane leaves tomorrow morning. We just want to walk around the city for a bit."

Shona smiled. "I'm so glad that you two are happy together. I mean it. I've never seen Jeremy this ecstatic."

He darted back out the door. "Dad, I have a huge Spider-Man room, like the one back home!"

She winked at us, hugging Jeremy. "I figured it would make your day."

"All right, well, Riley and I will head out now. You can call either of us at any time. We'll be in the same time zone, give or take one or two hours. But you can always reach us," I assured him.

"Have fun. I'm going back to Spider-Man," he said, darting inside the house. We didn't even get to properly hug him, but that was okay.

Afterward, Riley and I strolled toward the city center. She smiled brightly, looking around.

"What is it?" I asked.

"I can't believe that we're here. I can't wait to experience absolutely everything on this trip." Her joy and curiosity were infectious as she looked up at me. "How was it for you, seeing your ex?"

I shrugged. "I used to feel guilty every time I dropped Jeremy off, wondering if we'd tried just a bit harder, if we could have made it work. But now I know that everything happened just the way it was meant to be, so I could meet you and then make both our lives so damn amazing."

"Oh, you sweet talker," she said.

"I mean every word."

Initially, I'd planned to take her to Paris and London. I figured why not try the most romantic cities in Europe? But

Riley had surprised me by saying she would actually love to see Scotland.

"Imagine all those haunted castles," she said. "And besides, I'm a Potterhead, so I'd love to see Edinburgh."

"I'm here to fulfill all your wishes," I assured her.

She narrowed her eyes. "I will never tire of hearing you say that."

"You don't have to because I'm not planning on stopping."

We were spending one night in Dublin before getting on a plane to Edinburgh. Once we'd reached the city center, my phone beeped with a message.

I groaned.

"What is it?"

"Griffin is on the front page of a tabloid." I turned the phone for her to see the headline.

"One of the Most Eligible Bachelors in Town with His Newest Conquest."

"Any publicity is good publicity, right?" she hedged.

"Not really, no. He should be more cautious. This isn't smart."

"How can this possibly harm him?"

I shook my head. "I don't know. But it could come bite him back in the ass."

She hesitated a moment, then said, "Personally, I think you should cut him some slack."

"I am."

"Not everyone can be as serious or have your self-restraint."

I raised a brow. "So, those are positive traits now?"

"I didn't say that."

I laughed, pulling her closer. "You almost had me fooled."

"I did, didn't I? And I'm so proud of it."

"As you should be."

"But you do have a lot of qualities, so that more than makes up for it."

I laughed even harder. "Good to know."

My phone beeped again. Clearly, all my brothers had seen the article. They were already giving Griffin a hard time.

> Knox: Griffin strikes again. At this rate, everyone will think that you're the most popular with the ladies out of all of us.

> Wyatt: That's your problem?

> Finn: Yeah. Mine too!

> Chase: Keeping a low profile would be smarter.

> Griffin: Can everyone get off my back?

I started typing, then decided otherwise and slipped the phone back into my pocket.

Riley smiled from ear to ear. "What, no lecturing him?"

"Nah, you're right. I can cut him some slack. Besides, I have more important things to do... such as making sure that you're having the summer of your dreams."

With that, I stopped her on the sidewalk and kissed her deeply, ignoring the catcalls and whistles.

Life was finally turning out to be everything it could be, and all I'd needed was Riley to complete it.

Dear Reader, This is the end of Duncan's story. The series continues with Griffin's story.

You can order it here (Links coming soon) :
Amazon US
Amazon UK
Amazon CA
Amazon AU

———————

Keep in touch. Please sign up for my NEWSLETTER to receive news about upcoming releases and giveaways.

You can join my READER GROUP on Facebook HERE.

———————

More books by Layla Hagen to binge with Kindle Unlimited (KU)

The LeBlanc Brothers
Amazon US
Amazon UK

The Whitley Brothers
Amazon US
Amazon UK

The Maxwell Brothers
Amazon US
Amazon UK

The Bennett Family series
Amazon US
Amazon UK

The Connor Family series

Amazon US
Amazon UK

The Very Irresistible Bachelors Series
Amazon US
Amazon UK

The Gallaghers Series
Amazon US
Amazon UK

––––––––

You can join my READER GROUP on Facebook HERE. For a list of all books by USA Today Bestselling Author Layla Hagen, please visit laylahagen.com

Printed in Dunstable, United Kingdom

65756387R10157